ALONG THE
FORTUNE TRAIL

ALONG THE FORTUNE TRAIL

HARVEY GOODMAN

JUPITER SKY PUBLISHING
WESTCLIFFE

JUPITERSKY

Jupiter Sky Publishing, LLC
2689 County Road 318
Suite 100
Westcliffe, Colorado, 81252

ISBN - 978-1-617507-47-2
ISBN - 1-617507-47-2
LCCN - XXXXXXXXXX

Cover Design by Alan Pranke

Printed in the United States of America

For Gaby, Matthew, Brian, and Sean.
Thank you, Lord.

Chapter 1

He caught the movement of the bug out of his right eye just as a drop of sweat rolled off his chin and splattered next to it. The bug stopped, as if it suddenly realized that a human predator in a prone position was only inches away. Lonny the Kid looked for a small, thin rock, one that had an edge capable of dissecting the bug rather than just crushing it. He picked up a suitable one and began his operation with a sense of pleasure.

The bug began moving with urgency, but it quickly stopped as the weight of the rock bore down on its right hind leg. At first he applied just enough pressure to halt the bug's progress, but as the bug's other appendages began to flail in panic, the Kid slowly pushed until the leg severed. The bug began moving again, and the Kid waited for a moment, just to let the bug think it might have a chance. To equal things up, the Kid severed the left front leg next, thinking the bug should have an equal handicap on each side.

The bug's movements were quite erratic now. No particular direction or speed could be maintained, and Lonny the Kid, amused by it all, watched for several more seconds before he took off the two remaining legs, allowing adequate time between each to note the effects of his handiwork.

As the Kid fully expected, the bug could no longer move. This assured him of his wisdom, as though his hypothesis had been proven right by his keen intellect. But this result turned the Kid's amusement to boredom, so he slowly applied pressure to the bug's midsection and smiled as the bug's armor-like shell cracked and the mucousy innards found their way out.

"What the hell are you doin', Lonny," Derrick asked, his attention now caught by the sound of rock grating on rock. The Kid was smearing the bug's existence over a six square inch area. It was so emulsified that Derrick had no idea what had created the mess. "Are you playin' with your snot? This is a hell of a time to be playin' with your snot," Derrick quipped.

"I ain't playin' with my snot," Lonny shot back.

"She's comin'! She's comin'!" The yell came from below.

Lonny's heart began to hammer, a slight panic immediately displacing any more thoughts of bugs or snot. He quickly moved to the edge of the overhang and spotted Bones Doublebass twenty feet below with his ear still to the rail.

"Well?" Lonny asked in an almost pleading manner.

Bones pulled his head up. "She'll be here in about five minutes."

"Damn Bones! Get movin', quick!" Lonny yelled down.

Bones wasted no time. He jumped effortlessly to his feet, bounded over the tracks, and ascended the steep bluff in a manner of seconds.

"They don't call that boy Bones for nothin'. He's all arms and legs," Derrick said as he began checking the action of both of his pistols for the third time in the last hour. Bones hustled over to his gun belt and strapped it on.

They could clearly hear the train coming now. The chugging began to slow as the grade became steeper and the turns tighter. Lonny and Derrick each picked up a shotgun, and along with Bones, carefully moved into position at the edge of the overhang. "You know the plan. When we hit that coal car, you boys get a move on," Lonny said. "That vault car should be the first one behind the coal car. If it's not, you got to get to it quick. For sure it won't be more 'n number two back. We oughta get a look at it from here before we jump anyway, so's you'll know where to go," Lonny hammered on.

Derrick looked down and suddenly felt as if he was going to throw up. He thought talking might help and let loose a quick stream of confused and anxious sentences. "Why do we have to kill these boys? Ain't there another way to do it? We'll swing if we get caught." Bones shot a quizzical look at both of them as if he'd just now really considered the plan and the possible consequences.

The talking hadn't helped. Vomit shot straight out of Derrick's mouth with a force that instantly made Bones think of a geyser he'd once seen. Lonny swung the barrel of the shotgun around until it pointed right at Derrick's head. His face was contorted with rage. Derrick stopped vomiting and Bones stopped thinking of geysers. Lonny's voice shook as he spoke. "You were in from the get go. You're doin' this right now the way I planned it or I'll kill you. You think you wanna face down six to eight men? We'll do this my way, get the money, get away, and not get caught. You understand? 'Cause if you don't, you're gonna die right now." Derrick slowly nodded up and down with a pale look of resignation. Lonny turned his attention to Bones. "What about you? You got any problems?"

Bones puffed up a little and almost shouted, "I'm right and ready!" His reply brought to mind the moment's purpose, and so he continued. "Let's get us a pile of money and set on easy livin' . . . nothin' to it."

Chapter 2

At twenty-six years old, Lonny was Derrick and Bones's elder by half a decade and had been the leader right from the start. They'd met two and a half years earlier at a territorial prison in the Oklahoma panhandle where Lonny was serving eighteen months for destruction of property.

Lonny had drifted into Dodge, Kansas, thinking he might try his hand at cow punching for a bit. The notion of hard work didn't really agree with Lonny, but he figured one cattle drive might be adventuresome and he could put a stake together and head farther west, where a man could get rich in all sorts of ways that didn't involve too much physical labor.

He'd heard that big cattle drives came up from Oklahoma and Texas and shipped east from Dodge, Wichita, Abilene, and other rail spurs. A number of the trail hands would collect their wages at the end of the drive and move on. Trail bosses looked for replacements to return south with, so Lonny planned on becoming a replacement. No hard work riding back south and all meals were included. He figured one drive would stake him onto real prosperity, or at least to the next job or scheme, whichever came first.

A week of waiting for one of the drives to show up had left Lonny impatient and bored. After an afternoon of cards and whiskey had reduced his thirteen dollars to three, and turned his mood surly and foul, he burst out of the saloon and strode up the boardwalk, muttering a string of obscenities and not paying attention to where he was going.

Missus Lucy Sinton, the banker's wife, was exiting the general mercantile when she had the displeasure of meeting Lonny. He walked right into her and almost knocked her over. Missus Sinton was a highbred sort who had lived a life of privilege. Raised in the east, she considered herself a woman of status and viewed the west and its inhabitants as mostly uncivilized. She loathed the day her husband, Randolph, had brought her to this godforsaken place, but had come at her father's insistence that it would only be for a year or two. Lucy's father was rich, powerful, and diversified. With his fingers in banking, beef, and oil, he had set his son-in-law up as a bank president in the expanding west. Lucy would live with this circumstance for the present.

When Lonny plowed into Lucy Sinton, his drunkenness and dark mood convinced him that it was her fault, and so his profanity merely shifted from his anger of the recent card game to the inept navigation of the woman now glaring at him. "Get the hell out of the way, you blind heffer!" Lonny yelled.

Lucy absorbed this and gathered herself. "You rude, drunken, filthy, rotten excuse of a man! How dare you assault and insult me!" She continued on in her most cutting tone. She speculated about Lonny's gene pool, his intellectual capacity, the extent of his integrity and bravery, and his future prospects. Initially half-amused by Lucy's verbal onslaught, Lonny's ears began to turn red as he sensed that passers-by on both sides of the street were slowing and looking to see what all the commotion was about. Some people had simply stopped, and everybody around heard Lucy's final declaration, "You're an animal! You should be in jail!"

Lonny, now flustered and very much aware of the number of eyes on him, searched for something to say. The pause was long and self-incriminating. "Go to hell, lady!" he finally blurted out. With tense movement, he abruptly pushed past her, turned the corner, and walked quickly up the alley.

The humiliation of the incident was something Lonny didn't care to stand for. He decided to watch her. When he learned that she was the bank president's wife and lived in the biggest house in town, the idea of some sort of revenge became appealing.

The Sintons had no children, but they did have a big, beautiful Cheshire cat. Lonny spied Lucy Sinton on her front porch several times loving the cat and talking to it in such endearing terms.

The Sinton house sat on the west edge of town. It was a massive two-story Victorian with a porch that wrapped around three sides. To the rear was a small cottage where a maid and young boy lived. Lonny bunked at the livery stable in exchange for some morning work. The stable's position allowed Lonny to note all the comings and goings on the west end of town. He quickly noted the Sinton's routine. The banker rode by each morning at 7 a.m. Lucy, sometimes with the maid and her boy along, and other times alone, came driving into town in her surrey by 9:30. Lonny kept out of sight when he saw her coming.

It was a hot, dusty morning when Lonny spotted the surrey coming up the street with Lucy driving and the maid and the boy with her. Lonny's head was pounding and his shirt was already soaked in sweat, the heat exacting its toll from the previous night's bout with a bottle of cheap whiskey. He decided right then that he was leaving Dodge.

After a month, no drive had showed up, and he was making only enough to eat, stay drunk, and bunk on a cot. He figured he'd drop by the Sinton house and then hit the trail.

Lonny stepped out the livery stable door, pitchfork in hand, and delivered a menacing grin to Lucy. It took her a moment to sense that someone was staring at her. She turned her head and looked at Lonny, who stood confidently and glared at her. Upon recognition, Lucy turned her head back straight, lifted her chin high, and gave the reins a slight whip, causing the big roan to break into a trot. For a moment, Lonny stood and watched them continue up the street. Then he went inside, gathered his things, and minutes later was saddling his horse.

The cat sat on the top of the settee back, its body pressed against the picture window, as Lonny approached the house and tethered his horse out of sight in a stand of nearby trees. Lonny entered through a back door and quickly moved through the house without regard for the possibility of an unintended meeting. He knew no one was home.

The cat looked at Lonny with very wide, but seemingly unconcerned, eyes as he stood at the parlor entry. Its tail moved slowly back and forth. Lonny pulled a tin of sardines from his pocket and knelt down. He broke the opening-key off and cursed his luck, then pulled an eight inch hunting knife out of his belt scabbard, stabbed the tin, and peeled back the thin metal covering. The cat's tail movements picked up a little speed. Lonny put his knife down on the floor and dug out several fish. He held them out on his hand in the most inviting manner and said in a soft, high-pitched voice, "Here kitty. Come and taste what I got for you." The cat kept up its tail swaying and hunched its back slightly, but didn't move. Lonny tenderly implored the cat some more, but with the same result. The cat lied there, watching.

"OK cat, here comes some fish," Lonny said a little more deliberately as he tossed the fish into the air. The cat sprang to a half crouch when the fish plopped on the cushion just below it. "There ya go, cat, try that out," Lonny said sweetly. The cat swung its head low, twitched its nose several times, then extended its body down to the cushion below in one long, fluid motion. It made short work of the fish and licked the cushion where the oil had soaked in. The cat looked up at Lonny, who held his hand out with a new batch of the delectable morsels. Lonny lobbed the fish about half way to the couch, splattering it on the hardwood floor. "There's some more fish for you, kitty," Lonny soothingly announced. The cat leapt gently to the floor, moved to the fish, and sat with its feet together as it devoured the pile. Lonny turned the tin over and bumped it on the floor, emptying the remaining fish into one neat pile. Then he slowly backed up one step, hoping to further gain the cat's confidence. "Come on, kitty. Get the rest now," Lonny almost whispered. The cat cautiously moved to the remaining pile and began to eat. He talked in a soft, loving tone as the cat ate, "That's right, kitty. Eat the fish."

His left hand suddenly swung from his side. The cat attempted to spring away, but it had been drawn in too close. Lonny's big hand closed on the back of its neck as it was in mid air. Lonny scooped the knife off the floor with his right hand. With one quick, brutal slash, he nearly decapitated the cat. Blood sprayed around the room before the spasms subsided.

Lonny held the cat away from his body as he walked with it to the dining room. He threw it on the table and began the quick motions with his knife. When he had peeled away enough hide to be sufficiently pleased with the cat's new appearance, Lonny tied it by its tail to the sterling silver chandelier hanging over the table. Then he found the Sinton's bedroom, sniffed the pillows to determine which ones were Lucy's, and urinated on them. He briefly looked around for any cash in plain view, but came up empty. He proceeded to the kitchen, where he washed up and found some leftover pork chops in the icebox. He had two of them eaten before he was ten minutes down the trail.

Chapter 3

The sheriff and Randolph Sinton caught up with Lonny the next morning. Mister Sinton was not completely gratified holding a Winchester on Lonny as the sheriff kicked Lonny awake. He wanted to shoot him right there and said so. Randolph was most incensed about Lonny pissing on his wife's pillows, rather than what had been perpetrated upon the house cat.

Lonny wasn't buying Randolph Sinton's blustery, tough-guy talk. Sinton looked soft and portly, so Lonny began to taunt him. "Ya know, that cat looked like a dandy hangin' from that fancy chandelier. One thing for sure, he cottoned to them little fish. Too bad he didn't know it'd be his last meal," Lonny chuckled. "Did your wife like the yellow morning scent I left for her? I gave it my best shot."

Randolph Sinton had turned an interesting shade of fuchsia and looked as if he might explode when the sheriff turned to Lonny and said in a voice sounding of gravel and matter-of-fact intent, "Mister, the only time you'd better speak from here on in is if you're answering one of my questions. And then it better be direct and polite or you'll be shot trying to escape."

Lonny took the sheriff at his word and shut up. He spent the rest of the trip back to Dodge wondering how he could have been caught, figuring no lawman would give chase over a cat.

The judge had called Lonny a perverted, deviate misfit, and had openly wondered how such people ever came to exist. The jury convicted Lonny of trespassing and destruction of property. The judge happily gave him the maximum.

Chapter 4

Lonny had been in prison fourteen months when Bones and Derrick showed up. They'd each gotten six months for stealing the proceeds of the collection plate from the Protestant Church office. Both of them had left home in their early teens and had become friends while working at the stockyards in Wichita. Bones and Derrick had a lot in common: independent and predisposed to the recklessness of youth. Taking chances, illegal or otherwise, was part of the thrill of life, and perhaps held the opportunity for getting ahead in a world that demanded self-reliance. Derrick fancied himself the smarter one, but Bones had more nerve and heart. Bones was game and had quickly developed a reputation at the stockyards as the kid who could handle anything thrown at him.

Derrick had hatched the church plan as they viewed the departing congregation one Sunday. "Sure a lot of saved sinners there," Bones remarked as they rode by. "I'll bet from the looks of that crowd they fill those plates all the way up. Wonder what the weekly take is?"

"Let's find out," Derrick had quickly replied.

It turned out to be quite a tidy sum. The church secretary had not made a deposit for the preceding week, bringing Derrick and

11

Bones's take to just over one hundred and forty three dollars, a sum that would have taken them two months each to earn at the stockyards.

If Henrietta Robson hadn't seen them exiting the church office in the last twilight of that Sunday evening, Derrick and Bones might have been one step closer to their dream of starting a saloon. As it was, she couldn't begin to identify them from her front porch, several hundred feet away and obscured by the billowing elm tree in her front yard. Still, there was no mistaking Bones's big paint, which was mostly white and distinctively splashed with brown markings, one of which Henrietta remembered quite clearly as being on the horse's right side and near perfectly shaped like a bell.

One month after Derrick and Bones arrived at the prison, some prisoner shuffling landed Lonny, Derrick, and Bones together as cellmates. It didn't take Derrick and Bones long to recognize that Lonny was quite tilted. Nevertheless, as impressionable young men, they were both taken in by the fictional accounts of his grand exploits, and they paid him the respect of a man they considered to be dangerous. Lonny didn't tell them he was in prison for the cat caper, electing instead to concoct a story about killing two Indians in self-defense but getting time anyway because one of the Indians had been the son of a very important chief.

As the weeks went by, the cell talk increasingly turned toward future plans. Lonny dispensed information about gold and silver strikes in the Colorado Territory as if he were receiving daily reports. "Boys, they're pullin' so much color outta the ground up there, you'd need ya a ten ox cart just to haul it all," Lonny announced regularly. "I'm headin' up La Veta way soon as I clear this hellhole. You gents would be smart to do the same."

The boom activity had been very lucrative for quite a few people. Stories of fortunes made drifted down the trail, keeping drifters and prospectors coming in droves. But the early arrivals staked the best claims, which often played out quickly. As Lonny found out after several months of hard work that he bitterly disliked, making any real money usually involved equal parts of skill, luck, knowledge, and perseverance. Lacking those attributes, Lonny eventually decided to make his own luck by thinking of himself as a ruthless, cunning, dangerous man who would do whatever was necessary and quickest to make himself rich. He decided to steal his fortune.

Lacking anything resembling a really secure facility, the Bank of Stonewall shipped out a significant amount of cash, gold, and silver to its home branch each week on the same train that came in over the pass bringing supplies and people. The town was in the height of its boom, with a population of about three thousand. Lonny knew the outbound train had to be carrying gold and cash.

He initially considered hitting the bank, but soon thought better of it. Too easy to get pinned in, too many people, he concluded. The train seemed a much better risk—one from which he could escape if things went wrong. He managed to get a look at the inside of the vault car as he moseyed around the depot one afternoon. It was not much more than a glimpse, but it revealed what the vault car and its access points looked like. Six to eight armed men served as guards for the trip, and the word was that they were a salty bunch of crack shots.

A plan began to form in Lonny's mind, a plan that would require more than one man. Lonny abandoned lone prospecting, got a job as a laborer for a bigger outfit, and hoped that he'd blown enough hot air at Derrick and Bones about riches to be had that they'd show up. Their last conversation in prison ended with a sort of three amigos pact of linking up and getting rich.

Lonny worked hard enough to stay employed, and he casually speculated to co-workers and comfortable acquaintances about how much money went out on the train each week, hoping to gain information or hear an opinion on the subject. The guesses were mostly stated as fact, running the gamut from a small fortune to a king's ransom. Lonny took the middle of the road on all that he heard, knowing that some of the estimates about wild riches came from men who were half-crazed from events of their migration west. Lonny figured the amount was between eight and twelve thousand dollars. The thought of such a sum made his adrenaline surge and his mind race with thoughts of what he could buy. He knew he could sell the plan to Derrick and Bones.

In his spare time, Lonny scouted the terrain of the pass. How he and a crew could board the train was something he hadn't figured out. There was no stretch in the canyon's terrain that allowed them to simply ride up alongside the train and board. Even if there was, the chances of being spotted boarding seemed more likely. But then one day he came upon it. Five miles out of town along the path of the train tracks, he came across an overhanging ledge. Only ten feet in length, it extended out far enough that you could look almost directly down at the tracks some twenty-five feet below. Lonny figured it would be less than a ten-foot jump to the top of the train. He reconciled it would be perfect. Derrick and Bones showed up six weeks later and the partnership was formed.

Chapter 5

"Get that cigar lit, Bones!" Lonny commanded. The smoke of the train drifted above the closest horizon, drawing a sooty line against a brilliant blue sky. One more bend, and the train would be in sight.

Bones cupped his hands, holding the match to the cigar, and puffed hard. The bright, red glow spread like a fast moving prairie fire, encircling the entire circumference of the cigar tip as he sucked deep and hard. Bones blew out a great cloud of smoke and coughed violently, causing his whole body to spasm and fold over at the waist. He straightened up a moment later with tears streaming down his face and hoarsely proclaimed, "She's a-goin' good now!"

"Well, keep it goin'! You won't have time to be lightin' matches," Lonny fired back. That thought prompted Bones to take some more pulls at it, being careful not to inhale the smoke.

With the cigar clamped between his teeth, Bones knelt down and pulled a bundle of dynamite from his saddlebags. He stood up, hoisted the saddlebags over his shoulder, and then carefully stuffed the bundled four sticks of dynamite halfway down the front of his pants.

Derrick, who had said nothing since he had vomited and had

had his life threatened, watched intently as Bones performed this procedure. "Here we go, Bones. Let's give 'em hell," Derrick weakly said, his voice almost quavering. Derrick was scared now and Bones knew it. They'd been friends long enough that Bones knew Derrick had now lost any stomach for what they were about to do.

"Don't worry, partner. We'll get through this fine," Bones said with a wink and a grin. "Just stick close."

The train rounded the bend and came into full view, shooting puffs of thick, black smoke from the stack as if being fired from a cannon. The noise level instantly tripled. Lonny, Derrick, and Bones could feel the ledge rumble beneath their feet with an ever increasing force as the train approached. Lonny momentarily feared that the ledge might collapse. He clenched his teeth and squeezed his toes inside his boots, trying to gain some extra sense of feel. The number fifty emblazoned the front of the engine, looking like a giant eye coming at them. "It's right behind the coal car boys," Lonny shouted to ensure he was heard above the roar of the engine.

Derrick suddenly became aware of the speed of the train, as it was now almost underneath them. "Jesus! We better time this right!" he shouted.

"That's for sure," Bones yelled back, as they all inched to the very edge.

"Let's go, boys!" Lonny yelled.

"Hang on to your hats!" Bones yelled. Then they jumped.

Derrick felt as if he were floating. The brief descent seemed like minutes instead of an instant, time enough to have recollections and see a picture of his life without even thinking about it. He wondered if the rush of images meant he was about to die.

The train was going slowly because of the steep grade and sharp turns, but it had enough speed to send Bones rolling upon impact. He caught himself at the edge of the car, an instant before he continued on over the side. The cigar was still in his mouth, hanging limply because he had nearly bitten through it. He bit it off at the break and gave it some quick pulls to reinvigorate it. Collecting the saddlebags, he looked up track and saw Lonny slowly mountain crawling over the jagged coal on his hands and feet toward the engine. Derrick was sitting ten feet away clutching his right ankle, pain etched on his face. "I snapped it clean in two!" Derrick wailed above the roar of the engine.

A downdraft suddenly diverted smoke from the engine's smokestack in to a swirling cloud that hovered right on top of the coal car where Derrick and Bones were located. The instant burning in Bones's eyes was only outdone by the sharp constriction in his chest as there became nothing left to breath but smoke. He spat the cigar out and hacked, tasting the hot coal soot searing his lungs. He couldn't see and tried to avoid breathing, but the need for oxygen became too great and he instinctively inhaled, taking more smoke into his lungs. His head spun as consciousness began to wane.

The lethal cloud blew out as suddenly as it had blown in, and Bones was bathed in blue sky and fresh air. For the next several moments, he alternated between gasping for air and coughing out chunks of black phlegm, as his eyes watered and his nose oozed snot.

Derrick was on his belly, his head hanging over the edge of the car. He coughed uncontrollably, each spasm shooting bolts of pain to his broken lower leg. The dampness he felt in his boot was his blood, flowing freely from the compound fracture just above his ankle.

Bones suddenly remembered the cigar and quickly began scanning the cracks and crevices of the coal around him. Finding it, he began dragging on the shredded cigar, as it occurred to him that he'd had about enough smoke for one day. Still, he worked to bring the cigar back to life.

In a low crouch, Bones moved over the uneven surface to Derrick's side. "I'm done for!" Derrick yelled, the pain and worry obvious in his voice. "My leg's broke bad. The only way I'm movin' from here is crawlin' or hoppin', and ain't either one of those prospects lookin' too good on this mountain a shit."

Bones took a soft pull on the cigar as he looked at Derrick's right leg. It took a grotesque forty-five degree turn just below the outline of the top of the boot, the pants bulging where the tibia and fibula bones pressed against the inside of the boot. "I'll tell you what, partner," Bones said hoarsely. "You just sit tight and I'll take care of business. Matter of fact, I think I can pull this off without killin' anyone, and then I'll get you outta here."

"Okay, Bones. I'll be right here waitin'," Derrick said, in awe of his friend's confidence and composure.

"Get that bandana up in case there's any more smoke storms. I'll be right back," Bones said. Like a lizard moving over sand, Bones moved along the coal on his hands and feet and disappeared over the end of the car.

From a crouch at the front of the coal car, Lonny looked down at the engineer's platform. The coal mover was a black man dressed in sooty bib overalls and a soaked white undershirt. He leaned on the handle of his shovel and wiped the sweat off his face with a well-used rag. Lonny sized him up as being six feet, 230 pounds or better, and powerfully built. The furnace door was open, and the fire was hot and well built. The engineer stood at the controls peering out the front of the train, his silvery hair flapping slightly from the warm breeze blowing through the front of the engine.

"You!" Lonny yelled at no one in particular. They looked around and up at Lonny, both their expressions instantly registering anxiety upon seeing the shotgun trained in their direction. "Blackie! You lay that shovel over nice 'n' easy, then close that furnace door, and don't think of nothin' foolish. And you, engineer man! You just hold steady and don't move an inch!"

The shoveler laid it down easily and moved sideways to the furnace door, keeping a compliant expression on his face, but never removing his eyes from Lonny. "Get it closed!" Lonny barked. The man used the rag to swing the door shut and latch it. Then he slowly put his hands halfway up and shuffled several steps away from the furnace. "That's real nice," Lonny mockingly said, motioning his shotgun directionally as he spoke. "Now you move on over to the edge there and jump or I'll kill you where you stand," Lonny announced. The black man spoke with his eyes, as if to implore Lonny to some other alternative. The terrain out the left side of the engine was steep, falling away dangerously from the tracks, and strewn with trees and rocks except for an occasional patch of bare, open hill. "Get movin', Blackie! This train ain't goin' too fast. You'll be all right unless you stand there for a few more seconds. You do that and you'll be dead."

The man turned his head to the engineer, "So long, Mistah Henry," he said in a forlorn voice, and moved to the edge of the platform. He watched a moment till he spotted an opening, and was suddenly gone.

"Now there, Mister Henry," Lonny shouted. "You just turn around and keep your eyes out the front and I'll be with you directly." The engineer turned slowly to the front and stood stiffly while Lonny descended the ladder sideways, using one hand to grasp the side rail and the other to keep his shotgun trained on the engineer's back. Seconds later, Lonny pushed the business end of the shotgun against the engineer's side. "I seen that 30-30 in that scabbard there all along, but figured you were too fat and slow to make a move for it. Right, Mister Henry?"

"Mister," the engineer began, "you sure are right. My name is Henry Salmon, and I'm too fat, slow, and old to think about anything other than cooperatin' with you. I've got a wife, six kids, nineteen grandchildren, and less than half a year left on this job. I'm sure not going to give you any trouble. No, sir. What is it you want me to do?"

Lonny looked the man in the eye, not completely convinced of the sincerity of all that he'd just heard, and now slightly more on guard. "You can start showin' me how this train works. How do you stop this thing or make it go faster? Which one of these levers is the brake? How far's it take to get this thing stopped?" Lonny asked rapid fire, not allowing time between each question for an answer.

When he finally paused, the engineer said, "There's not that much to it," and he began showing Lonny the basics.

Inside of two minutes, Lonny figured he knew enough about the operation. Then he asked, "Is that fire good enough to get us a few more miles?"

"Oh yes, sir," the engineer replied. "We don't pour much steam to her with these turns, and even this grade don't eat it up much only pulling five cars. But we'll be at the top soon, and then it gets tricky going down because you need to work some of these pressure valves and controls at the same time," the engineer said, sensing that he might be the next one forced to jump if he wasn't needed. "I can sure run this train for you however you like, son."

Lonny didn't answer. Instead he began looking around the cab, intently curious about all the controls. "What's that thing up there for?" He motioned with his shotgun to the inside corner of the roof of the cab. The engineer looked up, trying to determine what it was Lonny was asking about.

Henry Salmon felt the deep pain in his stomach as Lonny's knife went in to the hilt. The engineer's sudden shock and disbelief was quickly followed by panic and an instinct to fight for his life. He grabbed Lonny, who was leaning hard into him, in a desperate attempt to throw him off. Henry had been a strong man in his younger days, and he started to push with all he had. But Lonny had begun violently pulling upward with the knife, gutting Henry, whose strength quickly faded as Lonny jerked the knife up farther and farther. Henry Salmon stopped pushing and thought of his wife, his family, and all that had been in his life that he'd loved. He prayed to God to watch over his loved ones, and then he died.

"No, I don't think I'll be needin' your services anymore, Henry." Lonny backed away, causing the limp body to collapse to the deck. He pushed it out of the way and returned to the controls, looking out the front of the engine, trying to determine where he was.

Chapter 6

Bones had worked his way down between the coal car and the vault car and stood on the small platform at the front of the vault car, next to the heavy wooden door leading into it. The door had a portal opening at upper chest level that measured eight inches high by a foot and a half wide, making it nearly identical to the six other openings on each side of the car, proportionately spaced running the length. Other than these openings that served as rifle portals for defense, and the walk-in doors on each end of the car, the vault car looked very much like a freight car, with a large sliding door at mid-car where a ramp could be attached for loading big objects. The portals had slide coverings that were all presently open and created enough of a cross breeze to make the inside of the car almost tolerable on this hot, June day.

Bones felt the speed of the train slightly increase, and then came two short blasts from the train's whistle, signaling that Lonny was at the helm and the next phase was to begin. He took a few quick pulls on the cigar and lit the long fuse on one stick of dynamite that he'd separated from the bundle. Bones wheeled around facing the slat opening with his finger on the butt end of the stick and flipped it through the opening, propelling it ten feet inside the car, where it landed on the floor with a thwack. Two men inside were laid out napping on the floor at the back of the car next to four others who sat on boxes playing cards on a crate. The man who was seated facing the front of the car gave a startled "Hey!" when he saw the stick of dynamite hit the floor twenty feet in front of him.

In an instant, the stick of dynamite had the full attention of the others who were playing cards, and the two who slept awakened quickly when Bones's voice boomed through the opening. "You boys best throw that side door open and get the hell off this train—or your insides is gonna be outside your bodies real soon! And don't think about goin' out that rear door. There's dynamite burnin' right outside it, and one a my partners has a shotgun aimed at that door." Bones had his pistol in the opening and popped off two shots as a man made a move, crawling for the stick of dynamite. The shots hit the floor right in front of him, splintering wood into his face. "I won't miss next time! Now get!"

The man backed up quickly while the others stood dumbfounded, unsure of what to do. Bones knew they wouldn't have time to consider the truth of his story, and it would be a lot tougher for them to hit him through the small opening than for him to hit them. Time was running out as the fuse sparkled away.

"Get that door open, Rusty!" one of them yelled to the man sitting closest to the slider. Rusty wasted no time. He threw the latch and pulled hard on the door, causing it to slide open. The hillside falling away from the door was not as steep as when the shoveler had jumped, but the train was going faster now that Lonny was at the controls.

"You boys can take your gear if you want, but you better move quick 'cause there ain't no more 'n ten seconds left on that fuse," Bones yelled into the car, knowing that there was probably twice that amount of time left, but wanting to get this crowd moving fast.

Young Rusty grabbed his saddle and his gun belt, and was first out the door. The others were close behind. The next two moved quickly to the door and went one at a time, but the final three figured time was up and all jumped together.

Chapter 7

E thel Mckeever sat in the passenger car, daydreaming and gazing out the window at God's beautiful creation serenely rolling by, when she saw young Rusty hit the ground. He began rolling and kicking up a dust cloud as he and his gear naturally made the best of life's new course. As she realized what she was seeing, she uncontrollably exclaimed, "Oh my!" The other sixteen passengers in the car noted the direction of her attention in time to see an avalanche of men and gear tumbling down the mountain.

"What the hell is that?" a man yelled in a high-pitched tone. The rest of the passengers broke into nervous conversation, wondering why men two cars in front of them were abandoning the train.

"Maybe someone should go forward and see what's happening!" a woman said.

"That's a freight car right in front of us. There ain't no way to go forward save to climb over the top of it," an older man replied.

"Well, me and my partner can sure do that," said a young man nodding to his friend who looked equally fit. The explosion interrupted the conversation.

Bones had just cleared the top of the coal car and was lying spread eagle, face down, when the stick blew. He felt a sensation

24

of being pressed into the coal and then separated from it, as if some spasm had coughed him up in the air. The momentary levitation had Bones wondering if the car was derailing. He slammed back onto the coal again and lay dazed. When his head cleared, Bones realized the car was still on the tracks, and in fact the whole train was still rolling smoothly courseward. He looked forward toward Derrick and yelled in a voice ringing with confusion and amazement, "If I'd thrown that bundle a four in there like Lonny had planned, we'd a-killed them boys all right, and we'd all be somewhere other 'n on these tracks! We almost skipped 'em on one stick!" He'd gotten all the words out before he realized that Derrick was no longer there.

Bones thought his eyes were playing tricks on him. His mind raced backward. He'd climbed up over the edge of the coal car just before the dynamite blew, and he'd seen Derrick face down near the side, his head slightly beyond the edge of the car. He'd seen him, hadn't he? The thought that Derrick had maybe gone over the side accelerated Bones's instincts. He figured the best hope for helping his friend now was to carry out the rest of the plan and get the train stopped fast.

Bones leapt to his feet, turned toward the vault car taking two fast, powerful steps and took flight, easily clearing the expanse between the two cars and landing on his feet. He moved down the length of the vault car, avoiding the ragged surface of the roof where the force of the explosion had done the most damage. The car swayed side to side under his feet as he maneuvered his way. He reached the end of the car and descended to the platform, then yanked hard several times on coupling ring before it broke loose. Bones took a deep breath and slowly exhaled, letting his muscles relax as the rear half of the train began to fall away, the separation growing greater with each second.

Bones's brief respite halted instinctively. He turned and ascended the ladder with long, easy movements, then ran forward along the top of the car to its end and leapt over the chasm and into the coal car.

Moments later, Bones looked down at the engineer's platform where Lonny stood with his hands resting on the throttle and his eyes searching the hillside for familiar landmarks.

"How much farther?" Bones yelled down at Lonny. Lonny wheeled around, startled by the break in his concentration. But he was now more interested in getting his own questions answered.

"Are we loose of 'em?" Lonny shouted back.

"Yeah, we're loose," Bones yelled, "But I think Derrick fell over the side when that dynamite blew . . . and he's got a busted leg . . . bad."

"Well, what about them dudes in the vault car?" Lonny asked, as if he hadn't heard what Bones had just said about Derrick.

"They're all breathin' and long since clear of this train. I wrangled 'em off with a stick a persuasion. Where's the engineer?" Bones asked, not sure if he wanted to hear because of all the blood he could see on the platform.

"They all got off," Lonny replied. After a brief pause of silence, Lonny continued, "I figure we got about two miles to go, so get on back and get that safe wired, you hear! We don't wanna be wastin' time once we're stopped."

"Which one you wanna blow first?" Bones asked.

Lonny froze, not sure if he'd heard Bones right or if Bones simply wasn't making sense. "There's more 'n one?" Lonny blurted out in a disbelieving tone, his eyes large with anticipation as his mind processed the possibility of additional loot. Before Bones could answer, Lonny was already calculating, and fired the question at Bones loudly and directly, "How much dynamite we got?"

"Nine sticks left. I only used one stick gettin' them boys off. Good thing too, 'cause if I'd thrown that bundle a four in there we'd a-derailed for sure."

Lonny let that go by, even though it had been his plan for Bones to throw a short-fused bundle of four sticks in and simply kill the guards. He knew they were out-gunned, so killing them seemed the least risky. "Hell," Lonny said, "get movin' and wire 'em both.

Bones disappeared and Lonny returned his attention to the landscape, knowing that it wouldn't be long before they were at the rendezvous point.

Chapter 8

C ody Royals had rolled and smoked a dozen cigarettes over the several hours he had waited, most of which he spent sitting in the shade of a stand of cedars. It was getting on toward noon, and Cody was becoming impatient to hear the sound of the train coming. He'd told the horses all his best stories and conversed with them about all manner of things, pausing briefly after he'd ask the group a question about horse life, then continuing on as if one of them had filled him in. Tethered to different trees that naturally formed a sort of semi-circle to the tree Cody sat leaning against, the horses occasionally stamped and snorted, giving him the impression of an audience that stood mesmerized with all he had to say. But he had run out of conversation, and his tobacco pouch was beginning to dwindle, prompting Cody to think about rationing his smokes and turning his thoughts to how much longer he'd have to wait.

Cody had met Lonny a month and a half earlier at the Red Beaver Saloon. The nineteen-year-old had recognized Lonny as a co-worker at the mine and offered to buy him a drink, which Lonny gladly accepted at the price of listening to the lad ramble on. Lonny came to know the boy was just smart enough to be of some use in his plan, and so he befriended him.

Within a few weeks, a deal was cut. Cody would hold the horses at the rendezvous point for seventy-five dollars per man. Lonny knew it was a bargain, and Cody thought he'd hit the mother lode.

Cody decided he'd have one more cigarette and had just put the match to another perfectly-rolled smoke when he heard the train. "Well partners, guess it's time to burn some oats," Cody proclaimed to the horses, who looked at him with blank expressions. "You just wait here a few minutes and enjoy the shade. You'll sure nuff be lathered up soon." Cody carefully snubbed his smoke, put it in his shirt pocket, and began working his way down the hill toward the tracks.

Lonny pulled back hard on the handbrake with both arms, ratcheting all the clicks he could before he could move it no farther. He looked up the hill at the patch of boulders he had used as a landmark, feeling proud that he'd managed to stop the train right where he had wanted to. As he jumped off the train, he saw Cody coming down out of the trees. "Where's the horses?" Lonny yelled up at him in an impatient tone.

Cody stopped and stood dumbstruck a moment. "Well, damn yes, I guess I oughta bring 'em now," he finally blurted out and began marching back up the hill.

"When you get 'em down here, stay with 'em at the front of the train and keep 'em tied good. I don't want that dynamite spookin' 'em loose, you hear?" Lonny yelled. Cody didn't look back, but nodded just before he disappeared into the trees.

Bones jumped off the front platform of the vault car as Lonny approached. "I got one wired and ready to go. Best to blow 'em one at a time so's one don't foul up the other," Bones proclaimed.

"Light it up," Lonny commanded. Lonny turned facing up the hill and yelled with all the force he could, "Cody! Keep them horses tied up there until after it blows, you hear?"

"Yep," Cody yelled back in a sharp report.

Lonny and Bones had just gotten to a safe distance when the dynamite blew. The concussion shook the ground and sent shards of lumber flying from the side of the car, causing Lonny and Bones to instinctively throw their arms up in front of their heads and fall back against the hill. "That shoulda got somethin' open," Bones said after a moment on the ground.

Lonny was on his feet and moving to the car, now pouring smoke from a ragged, new hole in the side. They wasted no time getting in and immediately had to use their hats to fan the thick smoke.

As the air cleared, they could see one of the vaults had toppled over and was pressed against the sidewall of the car. The one that Bones wired lay face-up near the back wall, its door bulging upward along the hinge seam. A sliver of an elliptical opening, several inches at the widest point, had been created by the blast. "That sure as hell ain't gonna be enough. Did you wire two at each hinge?" Lonny asked in an accusing tone laced with rising anger.

Bones shot Lonny a piercing gaze and spoke in a steady, even tone. "I sure wired it the way you said it should be wired—the way you planned it—a two bundle on each hinge with the same length fuse for each bundle. Looks like the top one went but the bottom didn't. You said even if they weren't timed right, one would set off the other. You were the dynamite expert here, as I recall."

Lonny's temper held check. He knew Bones was worn thin and ready for a fight if Lonny wanted one. Lonny turned his attention back to the safe. The top hinge was gone, but the door and frame were warped together at the point where the hinge had been. "Get a breaker bar. Maybe we can pry this thing open. That's the only way we can save the rest of the dynamite for the second safe," Lonny said with obvious disgust. Bones said nothing and was instantly gone.

Chapter 9

L onny removed his bandana, wrapped his hand, and knelt by the safe. The steel was warm but didn't burn Lonny's hand as he slid it into the opening several inches before his forearm stopped the progress. He rotated his hand in an effort to feel anything that might be within reach. He came up empty. Then he put his face to the opening and peered in, hoping to see some sort of riches waiting for him. In the dark interior, he could only detect several shapes. He fished in his shirt pocket and retrieved a stick match, struck it, and held it carefully while slowly slipping his hand into the opening. Lonny anxiously jammed his face to the slit and nearly burned his right eyeball.

Four medium-size heavy leather satchels were in the main chamber. Lonny felt a rush of excitement, sure that the satchels held the big loot he dreamed of. "Oh yeah, we're gettin these out where they need to be," he whispered out loud to himself.

Bones reappeared with the breaker bar and promptly wedged the end into the opening near the hinge. He began to push down on the end of the bar with all he was worth. The steel began creaking and visibly moving, giving immediate hope that fueled Bones's effort even more. Lonny saw an open spot on the bar and joined the battle. They yelled and pushed and shouted and quivered, but soon became aware that there was no more creaking or movement.

"That son of a bitch ain't goin' no more. We'll have to wire that second hinge again!" Lonny yelled.

Bones pulled out a blue and red-wrapped nugget of chewing gum and barely got the wrapping off before he popped it in his mouth and worked his jaws hard and fast to prepare the gum. Seconds later, he pulled the gum from his mouth and molded it into the trough at the nape of the hinge. Pulling two pieces of dynamite from his saddlebags, he twisted the fuses together and stuck the sticks together with another piece of quickly-chewed gum. Bones pushed the bundle against the trough of the hinge where it affixed to the gum. "It's ready to go," he announced and pulled a couple of stick matches from his front pocket. "Looks like about a twenty second fuse."

He lit the fuse and they skedaddled. The explosion rumbled the ground and shocked the air with thunder that reverberated up the canyon walls for several moments after the blast, lingering for a length of time. The duration of it made Lonny suddenly anxious, reminding him that time was not something he had much of.

Lonny shot into motion, walking briskly toward the vault car and yelling back over his shoulder as he walked. "You get that second one wired and fired right now! I'll get the haul outta this one!"

Bones instantly yelled back, "There's three sticks left! How do you wanna wire it?" Bones had already figured that wiring one hinge with the rest was the best shot. He was curious what Lonny would recommend.

Lonny stopped and turned to face Bones, looking him in the eye, but managing only a confused look for several seconds. Finally, in a slightly sedate but stern tone, Lonny said, "Strap the whole wad to the lower hinge. If we get that one, we can pry it open." He turned and was on the move.

Bones was gratified to hear Lonny repeat the same strategy.

Chances would be excellent of getting into the second safe if they could get a clean blow on one hinge. He popped more gum in his mouth.

The door on the first vault had been blown off and now rested in the front corner. Lonny's eyes grew big as he surveyed the open vault. Four large brown satchels were smoking, but intact, waiting to be retrieved by Lonny the Kid.

Bones set the dynamite as Lonny wrapped his hand and began pulling the satchels out with cowboy speed. "Grab those other two bags on your way out," Lonny said as he hustled out the door with a satchel in each hand.

Moments later, Bones arrived at the front of the train to find Lonny throwing papers out of one of the open satchels while Cody stood wide-eyed, watching and instinctively knowing that the papers being thrown to the wind were not what this whole operation was about. "God damn! This ain't nothin' but a bunch a bullshit files . . . paperwork and such," Lonny said, the disbelief causing his voice to quaver and fluctuate as if something were caught in his throat.

Bones immediately dropped the two satchels he was holding, fell to his knees, and ripped each open. A sinking feeling washed over him as he realized the contents looked to be the same as that which Lonny continued to throw into the air with fury and disgust. "This ain't lookin' no better here," Bones said in a dejected tone.

Lonny had just thrown his first satchel aside and was pulling the second one wide open when the blast ripped the air. What Lonny saw inside the bag shut the explosion out of his mind. He was oblivious to everything except what his eyes were now feasting. The tight bundles of cash were piled several rows deep and rested next to triple-fist-sized leather pouches, each of which were neatly stenciled "Bank of Denver." Lonny knew they contained some kind of loot, and there looked to be about ten of them.

The yell burst from Lonny's throat with uncontrolled jubilation, "Yeeeeeeehaaawwwww! I reckon I got the right bag here!"

Bones and Cody crowded in close, peering down into the bag with open mouths as they took in the vision. "Will ya look at that," Bones said, the wonder and marvel in his voice making it almost a monotone whisper.

Cody shook his head around as if he were trying to right his brain, then nervously said, "You could buy a heap a tobacco and boots with that!"

The comment brought Lonny out of the hypnotic haze he was in, returning his thoughts to the task at hand. "Damn, Cody," Lonny said as he looked around and up at the boy with an expression that reeked with what an idiot he thought the lad was. "You're really lookin' for the high life. Get them horses settled down before we all end up afoot. And Bones, you go look at that safe and see what we got. We can't be sittin' here all day. I'll count the loot."

Bones disappeared around the corner of the train and Cody moved over to the horses, petting each one and talking in a low voice, making clicking noises every few words. Whatever mental deficiencies Cody had, he sure knew how to handle horses. Within a minute he had them standing easy again.

Chapter 10

L onny pulled out the banded bundles of bills. He counted forty-three bundles, each of which had twenty-five bills. He separated the bundles into three piles when Bones reappeared. "I don't know, Lonny. She must a-misfired again. That hinge didn't go. We got a little warp on the seam, but nothin' I could get the bar into. I gave it a go, but there ain't no way."

The pile of money in front of him quickly displaced Lonny's disappointment over the news. "We got us a payday right here."

In all, there were twenty-four bundles of ones, thirteen bundles of fives, six bundles of tens, six bags of silver dollars, one pouch of gold dust, two pouches of twenty-dollar gold pieces, and one pouch of gold nuggets. After figuring out that much, it became apparent that nobody present had the time, or math skills, to figure what that all amounted to. If Bones hadn't taken a last look in the bag and pulled out the file giving a full accounting of the contents, it might have been quite a while longer before they knew that they now had 6,765 dollars. When they read the total at the bottom of the ledger sheet, there was a long, uninterrupted minute of whooping and hollering.

As the celebration began to dwindle, Bones sensed what was coming next. He tensed his muscles several times in preparation for action. "Let's get this loaded up 'n' ride," Lonny ordered. "We'll be at Sandy Springs by sundown . . . then we'll split 'er up proper."

Bones paused a moment. "I'm goin' after Derrick. I'll only take half the money for me and him, and you can have the other half yourself . . . but I'm not leavin' him behind. And I reckon you ain't payin' him no more thought, so we'll be partin' company now."

"Like hell!" Lonny shouted back. "If you leave now, you're leavin' empty. That soft lilly ain't nothin' but dead or caught now, and you sure as hell ain't ridin' outta here with a cut for him!"

Lonny's hand flashed for his gun, but Bones had known it was coming. He had his pistol drawn and aimed at Lonny's chest before Lonny had cleared his holster. Lonny froze in mid draw. "You just drop that iron so's I won't half to kill you," Bones said. The hate in Lonny's eyes didn't matter to Bones, who stood with deadly ease. Lonny dropped his gun. "Move over there and take a seat," Bones said, motioning with his pistol.

Lonny stood his ground, glaring at Bones, then spoke slowly in a rage-filled voice, "I'll see you dead, mister."

Bones fired a shot that landed inches from Lonny's left foot. "Move, Lonny!" Lonny walked over and sat down, his face red and his upper lip curling.

Bones backed up a few steps and turned his attention to Cody, who looked as confused and unsure of what to do as a man could. "Cody, you unstrap that gun belt and bring it here. I got no trouble with you." Cody looked nervously at Lonny, unsure of what to do. "Now, boy!" Bones yelled. He didn't want Cody looking to Lonny for anything at this particular moment. Cody jumped slightly, startled by the ferocity of Bones's command. He stumbled forward, undoing his buckle as he moved toward Bones. "Go take a seat next to Lonny and relax. I'll be on my way in a minute."

Bones flung their gun belts and Lonny's shotgun fifty feet up the hill and quickly retrieved his saddlebags, keeping his eyes and attention on Lonny, who sat muttering. He knelt by the loot and used one hand to methodically put half of each pile into the saddlebags, making sure that he took only half of each denomination of the bills and four of the ten pouches, three of which were silver dollars and one with twenty dollar gold pieces. "I left you a little more 'n half here," Bones said as he stood and backed toward his horse, keeping the gun on Lonny while he untied his big dun and hoisted the saddlebags over its neck. "I'm goin' after Derrick and I'm takin' his horse. If you follow me, we'll be tradin' lead, so's it's best if you just get on down your own trail. So long."

In an instant, Bones had mounted and was gone around the downhill side of the train. Lonny jumped to his feet and hurried up the hill to retrieve his gun belt and shotgun. Moving to the front of the train, Lonny looked around the corner where Bones had disappeared. He saw that Bones had already put on some distance, both horses loping at a good rate for the terrain.

Bones was out of range and into some trees, but Lonny popped off a couple of pistol shots at him anyway. The rhythm of the rider and horses continued on, uninterrupted by anything behind them.

Lonny cursed to himself for a moment and turned back toward Cody, who was strapping on his gun belt with a sort of helpless expression on his face. "Get it packed up and let's get the hell outta here," Lonny said. Minutes later, Lonny the Kid and Cody Royals were riding up the hill, heading south.

Chapter 11

S ammy Winds was seven years old when Comanches attacked the small wagon train his family was traveling with
in New Mexico Territory. The men of the party had circled
the wagons, unhitched the teams, and pushed the wagons over, attempting to fix a better defensive barricade. Sammy's father had
ordered him into a small hole-like depression in the ground that
the Winds wagon had rolled over on. He gave the boy a pistol and
ordered him to keep quiet and stay put, no matter what happened.

From his little hiding place, young Sammy listened to the attack for the next hour, but it seemed like eternity. He could hear
men shouting directions and information back and forth. Close
movement outside occasionally interrupted the rays of light penetrating the tiny opening he had wiggled into, while the sound
of gunfire and rumble of running horses took his thoughts away
from the cramped heat of his surroundings. The screams and an-
guished sounds of the final desperate struggle slowly faded. All
that remained was the yipping and howling of swarming Indians, who seemed to be everywhere. Overwhelming numbers had
wiped out the entire wagon train, including his mother, and father, and older brother.

Sammy could hear them rummaging through wagons, pulling things out and throwing much of it aside. Suddenly, the wagon covering him began shifting and creaking as Indians climbed on and ripped apart all that had been carefully packed two months earlier. His eyes stayed fixed, wide open, as he held the big pistol with both hands. Tensed in a balled-up position, he waited to shoot the first Indian he saw. But, the wagon was never rolled back upright, and within an hour, all that could be heard was the wind of the prairie singing a lonely song. Still too frightened to move, he stayed in the safety of the hole until his unrelenting thirst and the fading daylight overcame his fear and drove him out.

It was the better part of a week before three riders came across the site of the attack and found the young boy who had survived alone. Sammy told how he had found a full canteen and some smoked meat amongst the ransacked wagons. The men were amazed to discover that the boy had also managed to bury his parents and brother by digging a shallow grave next to where each had fallen and using the shovel to leverage the bodies into the holes.

The men spent the next day and a half burying the other nineteen members of the wagon train, then gathered what they could find of the boy's belongings and mounted up. Lundy Flower took the boy on his mount, and the men rode hard for home.

Lundy was the ranch foreman at the famed Twin T. Ranch of northern New Mexico Territory. It was the biggest cattle operation in all of New Mexico. Owners Homer and Reuben Taylor, had welcomed Sammy and given him a home. Sammy had been naturally attached to Lundy, who fixed up his own special quarters in the bunkhouse and looked after the lad like a doting grandparent, making sure that the ranch hands held their cuss words and acted right around the boy.

At forty, Lundy was a blend of stamina, wisdom, humor, and know-how. He'd worked for the Taylor brothers for two decades and oversaw much of the operation. Lundy had never been married and was happy to take on the upbringing of Sammy, keeping the boy with him through all the jobs and activities of each day.

He taught him about cattle and horses and land and people, and told him Bible stories and tales of the west, and talked to the boy about all manner of things under God's endless sky.

As Sammy got older, he began taking on more and more work. He worked the roundups and cattle drives, fixed fence, branded cattle, shoed horses, birthed calves, hunted predators and game, busted broncs, doing all manner of jobs associated with running an operation. He could do a man's work at twelve years old, and he had the respect of all the hands on the Twin T.

When Sammy bit off his first plug of chewing tobacco, he turned a sort of pale green and laughed with the boys as they got a kick out of his new coloring. Three months later, Sammy had perfected an ability to hit anything within fifteen feet with a stream of tobacco juice. The plugs he bit off were so big that there was usually a little dribble out of the corner of his mouth, so the boys began calling him "Leaky." Sammy's talents with tobacco juice became a source of entertainment for the boys as they enjoyed the sunsets from the bunkhouse porch. Leaky was the "Champeen" against all challengers in every manner of spitting contests, ranging from distance and accuracy to pure showmanship, such as hitting a moving June bug while lying on his back atop the hitching post. The boys figured someone might beat Leaky if they made balancing or some other requirement part of the show.

When J.P. Stover came up with the idea of hitting a silver dollar in the dirt from ten feet while performing a headstand, the boys laughed and whooped it up, thinking it would certainly even up the odds. But man after man either toppled over before getting the shot off, or ended up with half of their shot pushing out just far enough to run directly up their noses or into their eyes, causing stinging pain to the contestant and uncontrollable laughter from the gallery. Leaky managed the headstand and a shot that was within inches of the silver dollar, proving he could spit from any contorted position, and furthering his legendary exploits with tobacco juice.

The years went by and Sammy Winds grew up straight and

true. His easy manner and intelligence was equaled by his sense of humor, kindness, and humility, and Sammy was flat tough. He was the hardest working, most talented hand on the Twin T., and he never complained. Instead, he always pointed to the positive side of any situation, lifting the spirits of all who knew and worked with him.

The sun broke through the pines as shafts of piercing light that instantly brought a measure of warmth to the frosty, fall morning. Sammy Winds squatted in front of his fire rubbing his hands together, his breath forming little clouds of vanishing vapor each time he exhaled. The coffee was almost ready, the scent of it mixing with evergreen and the crisp air. Sammy took a deep breath, drinking in the morning aromas and feeling keenly alive as the fingers of sunlight massaged his back with increasing heat.

He saddled his horse, packed his bedroll, and ate the biscuits and jerky that Jacqueline had packed, stopping between bites to sip the hot, black coffee that was strong enough to take rust off a plow. The high country brought out his appetite and enhanced the flavor of the food. Sammy ate two grapefruit-sized biscuits and a half-pound of jerky before he mounted up and headed for town, twelve miles away. An hour later, he hit the stage trail and turned onto it for the remaining miles, then dozed in the saddle as his horse, Dobe, ambled along, knowing to follow the road.

The work of the week left Sammy tired. He'd had to pick up additional chores after one of the other ranch hands broke a collarbone trying to break a spirited young bronc named Pepper. Pepper had bucked high and hard, then galloped a few paces forward and stopped suddenly, bucking up his rear end and launching his rider straight over the front, where he landed hard in the dirt on his right shoulder.

Sammy had worked sixteen-hour days to pick up the slack for the injured ranch hand. At twenty years old, Sammy Winds stood six feet tall and carried 180 pounds of muscle on a thin, broad frame, giving him a slim appearance that concealed his true power. Thick, sandy colored hair and a straight angular jaw line framed his hazel eyes. The thirteen years he'd spent growing up on the Twin T. Ranch had honed Sammy into an expert with a horse, a rope, and a gun, and the boy was now a man.

Chapter 12

Dobe whinnied at the rabbit that flushed out of the brush, waking Sammy from his ten-minute saddle siesta. He reached up with both hands over his head and stretched hard, letting out a long groan that sounded like a bear coming out of hibernation. The morning sun was well up now and the icy chill was gone, replaced by a seasonally-perfect temperature of early October.

Sammy pulled out a stick of tobacco and bit off a hunk, chewing it for a moment, then letting go with a shot of juice. "Well Dobe, this looks like one fine day to be visitin' town and pickin' up my new boots. What say we stretch out a bit?" Sammy flicked the reins and gave a light squeeze with his legs, which was all the encouragement Dobe needed. The muscular appaloosa leapt to a full gallop, pounding the trail and putting a wind in Sammy's face that caused him to whoop and feel overcome by the beauty of the morning and the joy of the moment. The last half-mile went quickly.

At the edge of town, Sammy brought Dobe back to a trot and turned up the main street. The morning activities at Agapito's general store were in full swing with folks loading wagon's in front. Sammy heard the ring of the hammer on the anvil over at the livery stable and picked up the scent of apple pies baking at Watson's boarding house, the delicious aroma wafting on the light breeze.

The trip up Main Street offered the chance to tip his hat and bid good morning to folks he knew, which was nearly everyone. If Sammy didn't recognize someone, it was because they weren't local. He'd been to town twice a month for the last fourteen years, making a point to get to know everyone. Some people had moved on and new folks came, and Sammy got to know most all of them. Still, he was shy talking about himself, but he always wanted to say hello and listen to what other folks had to say.

Sammy pulled up in front of King Leather Works and dismounted. He reached into his saddlebags for the treat, then tied the reins to the hitching post and fed the piece of hard candy to Dobe, who bobbed his head up and down in approval as he chomped. "That's a pretty good deal, eh boy? Don't run off with some filly . . . I'll be right back."

A small bell attached to the door jingled when Sammy entered, alerting Jake's dog, Pinto, an old, white haired chihuahua, who began barking a sort of lazy alert. The small shop held the rich aroma of leather and pipe tobacco. It was an arranged clutter of saddles, saddlebags, boots, rifle scabbards, belts, purses, hats, wallets, and most every leather good known. If Jake King didn't have it, he could make it.

"Come on back," came the yell from beyond the counter. Sammy edged down the thin aisle and worked his way past the counter, pausing for a second to let loose with a shot that found the hole of a spittoon a few feet away. As Sammy entered the workshop in back, Jake looked up from a holster he was working on and smiled through his long, gray beard. "Hello Sammy. Thought you might be in today."

Sammy smiled broadly. "Yes, sir, Mister King. I've been thinking about those boots the better part of a month." Sammy's eyes scanned the room, settling on the beautiful, hand-tooled boots with the letters SW smartly engraved near the top of both. He spoke as he walked to the shelf where the boots stood amongst other recently completed work. "How've you been, Mister King? Busy as ever looks like."

"Well, I ain't hardly got no time with flintnappin' lately. I've gotten right popular with special orders and such, saddles mostly. But I enjoyed makin' yer boots. Those rat killers you got on look pretty well done in. I think you'll like them new ones just fine when you get 'em a little wore in."

Sammy was inspecting the workmanship with a look of awe. "These are plum beautiful. Prettier 'n a sunrise at Poncha Lake . . . or chimney smoke at the east-end line shack in February."

Jake laughed. "Well, didn't know boots could be so excitin', but I'm glad they strike yer fancy. Set 'n' try 'em on."

Sammy sat down and wasted no time getting off his old boots and pulling on the new ones. The fit was perfect. Sammy stood up and shuffled a little jig. "Well, sir, I don't know how these could feel any better. Nice and snug, but no bind." He walked around the shop, then stopped and pressed his toes up against the inside of the boots. "I believe another masterpiece has been created," Sammy declared with a theatrical ring as he cocked his head and gave a hard stare at Jake, who in turn gave the same hard look back.

"Well, keep 'em oiled up good while yer breakin' 'em in, and them'll be masterpieces for a long time," Jake said. He stroked his beard and looked at Sammy with a glint in his eye. "I'll bet you could turn a fancy step wearin' 'em with Jenny Simpson. I got a notion that girl's got 'er cap set fer you. I reckon she'll be at the big shindig tomorrow night at the Buckskin. The Miller boys 'll be fiddlin'. You comin'?"

Sammy smiled and shot him a wry look. "Now, Mister King . . . you fixin' up one of cupid's arrows with your flintnappin'? I'll admit, she turns my head. But I get tongue-tied around her, and dancin' ain't my strong suit."

Jake gave a mock look of disgust. "Get Jacqueline to show you a few steps! That woman could turn a two-step like nobody's business in her day."

Sammy looked surprised. "Jacqueline? No kiddin'?"

"Oh yeah," Jake said with knowing authority. "I took some spins 'round the floor with her some years back. Well, 'bout a score now that I ponder it. She showed all them ladies up with her style. I reckon I should of married her," Jake mused whimsically. "I'd sure be eatin' better 'n my own cookin'."

"That's a fact," Sammy said. "She's sure the queen of the ball at the Twin T. Half the boys would pack up and move on if she ever left."

The bell jingled in the front of the store, sending Pinto into another round of intermittent barking that sounded raspily unnatural and prompted a vision in Sammy's mind of what a big rat might sound like if it barked. "Ole Pinto says you have another customer. Thirteen dollars, right Jake? Or did the price spike a little cause they turned out so fine?" Sammy said as he smiled and fished in his pocket for the money.

"In the back," Jake hollered toward the front of the store. Jake turned and looked at Sammy. "Tell you what. Come on back to town tomorrow night . . . or better yet, just stay over. Take a few spins around the floor with Jenny and you can have 'em for twelve. I know I told you thirteen, but it'd be worth a dollar to see you two spark."

"She's a fine woman," Sammy said. "But I'm not sure I can get back so soon with J.P. on the mend from his broken collarbone. I had to strike out part way last night so I could spend a little time in town this mornin' and be back on the T. this evenin'."

"Well, yer just one big heartbreak story," Jake said. "I'm glad you like the boots. Twelve dollars."

Sammy slapped his silver down on the workbench and the two men shook hands.

"See you down the trail, Jake. Thanks for these fine boots. They're sure worth every penny."

Chapter 13

Sammy stepped out onto the boardwalk and Dobe raised his head in anticipation of moving on, or maybe another treat. "Not just yet," Sammy said, as he gave the horse a pat on the neck. "I've been hankerin' for a sarsaparilla all month." He stuffed his old boots in the saddlebags and walked across the street toward the Frontier Saloon, still admiring the feel of his new boots and wondering if they could improve his dancing enough to give him a chance with Jenny Simpson. Sammy laughed to himself and said out loud, "Ole Jake sure can get ya thinkin' a whole new direction."

Sammy pushed the batwing doors open and turned his head to the right, letting go with a shot at the spittoon that always sat next to a near life-size carving of a downed buffalo being stood over by a frontiersman with a raccoon cap and a Hawken fifty caliber rifle. As always, the shot of juice found its mark perfectly. Sammy paused to admire the statue. It was a favorite attraction of all who wandered in, routinely serving as a conversation piece that began all manner of stories.

The rays of morning sun pushed through the two front windows to the back of the narrow room where the card games took place. Two men sat at one of the rear tables with a half-full bottle of whiskey. They were the only other people in the saloon besides Sammy and the bartender, Bernie, who looked up from under the mountain lion head hanging above the bar. "Hello, Leaky! Been a while since you made town!" Bernie joyfully boomed.

Sammy had just arrived at the bar with a smile and an out-stretched hand to shake Bernie's when the loud, sarcastic voice came from the rear table. "Leaky! Did yer mama name you that? Watch out, Cody. There's a flood coming . . . I don't believe he's diapered up!" Lonny the Kid laughed hard at his own wit and slapped his thigh several times.

"Looks like you've got a couple of live ones, Bernie," Sammy said as he shook the bartender's hand, his disposition calm and unaffected.

The bartender leaned in close and spoke in a low tone. "They were here when I pulled in this mornin'. Randy said that one fell-er lost a pile last night and then flipped him a sawbuck to keep the place open. That's their second bottle."

Sammy gave Bernie a knowing look and came to the point. "I've gone a long time without a sarsaparilla. You have any?"

Lonny jumped right in. "Did you hear that? Leaky wants a sarsaparilla. He might get leakier!" Lonny gave himself anoth-er deep belly laugh and Cody looked a little curious about what might come next.

"Mister Winds here is a respected customer who don't need no smart lip," Bernie fired back, clearly agitated. "If you can't mind your own business, you'll have to leave."

"It's all right, Bernie," Sammy said. "I'll handle it if it keeps goin'."

Lonny paused, and then said in a comical tone of disbelief, "Did you just say Mister Winds? You mean to tell me this sarsapa-rilla swizzler's name is Leaky Winds?" Lonny put on a horrified expression, slapped Cody Royals on the back, and yelled in a tone of panic, "Watch out Cody! He might let loose with a stink cloud!" Lonny erupted in laughter, stomping his foot on the floor and banging the table with his fist hard enough to tip the whiskey bottle over and make the shot glasses dance from spot to spot. Cody quickly grabbed the bottle and managed a nervous chuckle.

Sammy laughed and casually took a drink of the sarsaparilla that Bernie had put in front of him, not offering up any retort or even seeming bothered. The lack of response really bothered Lonny, though, and emboldened him. He'd lost several hundred dollars hours earlier to a salty bunch who knew each other. Lonny had been just drunk enough to bet stupidly, but not drunk enough to call anybody out. Now his mood was dark and he was itching for a fight. The months since the train robbery had been a succession of towns and nights of losing big money in card games, mostly because of being arrogant and too drunk. It hadn't mattered to him at first, but now his take from the train had been whittled down to well under a thousand. He had paid Cody's way to keep him company and remain a big shot in somebody's eyes. Now all the waste settled into the single moment at hand.

"I believe your mama must a-popped out a leaky, stinky worm 'cause your daddy had nothin better in 'm," Lonny said with deadly contempt.

It took Sammy a moment to realize what had been said about his dead parents. The bright, beautiful morning went black as anger descended. He looked at Bernie with an expression that let the bartender know to stay put. Sammy turned and walked straight to the table where Lonny was rising and Cody was worrying. Sammy looked at the twin pistols Lonny was wearing and remembered packing his own tie-down in his saddlebags when he'd broken camp that morning. He didn't see the knife Lonny wore on his right back hip.

Sammy stopped two feet in front of Lonny, who now stood to the side of the table and was opening his mouth again. "I guess I'll have to—agghh!" The stream of tobacco juice hit Lonny in the right eye and was followed by a crushing right fist that splattered Lonny's nose and sent blood spewing. Lonny slammed back against the wall and slid to the floor. He sat stunned for several seconds, blood pumping from his disfigured nose that flattened out grossly to one side.

Suddenly, Lonny's eyes bulged. He began screaming something incoherent, but there was no mistaking his right hand flashing for his gun. Sammy swung his foot at Lonny's hand as his pistol cleared the holster, but Lonny was already pulling the trigger. Sammy's boot hit Lonny's gun hand from the side just as the muzzle flashed and a thunderous bang deafened the room. The hot lead hit Sammy in the upper chest and knocked him back two steps, but his kick had found its mark and sent Lonny's pistol flying. It landed on the wood floor and slid a few feet, inviting Sammy to contemplate making a move for it. But Lonny was already reaching with his left hand for his other Mahogany-handled pistol. Sammy knew there was no time. He dove at Lonny as the pistol was coming level.

His shoulder hit Lonny in the chest, and his hands clamped on to Lonny's gun wrist. Lonny grunted at the impact and squeezed the trigger rapidly, sending two shots errantly into the woodwork of the bar. Sammy slammed Lonny's gun hand on the floor several times, causing Lonny to lose his grip. The pistol bounced a few feet away and Sammy instinctively reached out for it, almost grasping it, when he felt the knife pierce his back and hit shallow bone, causing it to turn and skid along a rib.

Frantically, Sammy grabbed Lonny by the chest and pulled as he rolled to his right, flipping Lonny over him, where he landed hard on the floor. Sammy grabbed the wrist of Lonny's knife hand and held it tight while he found his target, clamping his teeth around the top joint of Lonny's thumb and biting down like a wolf. The joint began to sever as Lonny screamed and was no longer able to grip the knife. Sammy ripped the knife from his hand, then bulldogged his way on top of Lonny with an adrenaline-driven instinct to end it. Lonny was stretching with his left arm to retrieve his pistol, while attempting to fend off the attack with his right, when Sammy plunged the knife deep into Lonny's chest. Lonny exhaled hard with a look of shock on his face, which worsened as Sammy withdrew the knife and plunged it several more times into Lonny's chest until his eyes fixed in a lifeless stare and his breathing stopped. Lonny the Kid was dead.

Cody stood off to the side, frozen with an expression of disbelief at what he had just witnessed. Sammy attempted to get up, but wavered, then stumbled and fell, the deep red stain on the front of his shirt spreading wider with each second.

"Get the doctor, kid!" Bernie yelled at Cody as he hurried to Sammy's side. "One street down on the right, next to Agapito's store! Hurry up!"

Cody broke loose of his trance and ran to the front doors, where he bumped his way through a small crowd now gathering outside. He yelled as he ran, "I gotta get the doctor! I gotta get the doctor!"

Chapter 14

I t fell thick and dry, drifting to the earth on a light breeze as so many leaf-sized flakes of shaved frost. The Chintah range had grown cold, soaking up the white of an early winter snow that fell unending for a week. Sammy awoke in a slow advancement of senses, the room coming into focus as if lifting away a haze of hibernation. He felt the comfort of the bed and stared at the potbelly stove against the adjacent wall, aware of the warmth of the room and the aroma of charcoaled pine. The painting on the wall depicted a woods cabin in a winter setting with chimney smoke and a goodly store of stacked firewood against the wall. Sammy imagined he was warm on the inside of the cabin in the picture, and instinctively turned to the near window at the right of the bed to see if the outside matched the terrain of the painting. The window was mostly fogged with condensation, but he could see the eaves of another building through the very top, which offered a slim view.

The events of the bar suddenly flooded his mind as he recognized the pale-blue color of Watson's Boarding House through the window and realized he was in town. He remembered that he'd killed a man and began to search his body for wounds as the recollection of being both shot and stabbed came back. The padding of the bandage was thick, covering much of his chest and giving no indication of the exact location of the bullet wound. He could certainly feel it, though, as he pressed easily around the expanse of the bandage and located a severe soreness at the area of his right pectoral. He lifted his head slightly off the pillow to look, the small stretching motion making him aware of the dull throbbing in his back and causing him to wonder if it was a bullet exit wound, or where the knife had entered, or both. But those thoughts were quickly overcome by an onset of thirst that made finding a drink feel more immediate than the need to breathe.

Sammy could smell the water in the pitcher sitting on the small bedside table. He rolled to his left and reached for it, the motion sending agonizing pain through his upper body, but not slowing his retrieval of what he absolutely craved. Sammy didn't bother with the glass next to it. He pulled the pitcher to his face, steadied it with both hands, and began to drink like a man who'd been without for days. He gulped the water with a quenching satisfaction, draining half the pitcher before he quit for need of air. Sammy fell back on the pillow, exhausted and heaving. He coughed violently several times, the spasms shooting bolts of pain from his chest to his head, which instantly pounded. It took a minute before he was breathing normally again. Then he was out, his last conscious sense being disbelief at his weakened condition.

The pitcher rested next to Sammy's side for half an hour before he shifted and sent it rolling off the bed, crashing on the floor. He heard it as part of his dream and kept sleeping.

Doc Payton sat reading a month-old edition of the *Chicago Herald*, noting the increased price of beef, when he heard the commotion upstairs. He called out to the adjacent room, "Ruth, you better go next door and see if Missus Watson can fix up a plate. I believe our patient is stirring."

"Yes, Doctor," came the reply. "I think that was the water pitcher we just heard," she added. A moment later she closed the door and left.

Doc Payton carefully folded the paper for later reading, then climbed the creaking stairs and entered the second door on the left. Sammy lay sleeping, his head turned to the side with his mouth wide open. The small lake on the floor next to him contained mostly large pieces of the pitcher. Doc Payton began picking it up. He said conversationally as he deposited chunks of the pitcher in a waste can under the table, "Sammy, can you hear me?" Doc Payton continued on as if Sammy might be listening. "Missus Watson is fixing up a plate of her good cooking for you right now. Looks like you've already been working at getting a drink," he said, looking at the wet bed sheet where some of the water had spilled. "Sammy," he said more deliberately. He shook Sammy lightly on the shoulder. "Would you like to have a bite to eat?"

Sammy opened his eyes, closed his mouth, and blinked several times as if trying to establish focus. "Doctor Payton," Sammy said in weak, raspy voice. "How are you, sir?"

"I'm a sight better than you at the moment," Doc said with a half smile. "But I believe we can change all that if we get some food and water into you and give you a lot of rest."

"How long have I been here?" Sammy asked, now looking a little more alert and scanning the room.

"We brought you in last Friday, and this is Wednesday morning. Most of that time you've been unconscious, except for some brief periods of rambling delirium. You lost a lot of blood, son. Enough so we weren't sure whether or not you'd be with us."

Doc Payton began loosening up the bandage to inspect the bullet wound. "There's certainly no question about the Lord making you strong, because you sure tested your constitution," Doc said as he examined the wound. "This one looks good. Lucky, too, 'cause it couldn't have missed your lung by more than an inch or so. Broke a couple of ribs on the way out, though. Let me roll you up on your side and take a look at your back. You've got almost fifty stitches back there from a stab wound."

Doc assisted as Sammy slowly rolled to his right side. "I sure am sore," Sammy said weakly. "Feel like a bull stomped me for a week."

"It will be a while before you get a chance to be stomped by anything else," Doc said as he inspected the back wound. "Looks to be healing up nicely, though. Now you need to eat, drink, rest, and let nature work her magic. Ruth will be here in a moment with some food, and then we'll clean you up some and change out these bandages. Some visitors been by to see how you're doing . . . the Taylors, Jacqueline, a few of the boys from the T., the sheriff, and some townsfolk. I can't even remember them all now. My office has been like a stage stop. And Lundy's been here every day. Been staying in town since Saturday. He's been a downright pain in the neck," Doc said, smiling.

Sammy smiled weakly for a moment, and then relaxed into a serious and distant gaze. "I believe I killed that man . . . but damn if he wasn't tryin' to kill me."

"The way everyone's heard it, you didn't have much of a choice. Bernie gave the whole story. A man acting like that in this country more than likely meets a bad end. Nobody knows who he was. His partner skedaddled after he yelled in my door about the fight. Folks said he hot-footed it over to Parker's, collected his rig, and lit out. Sheriff Ritter's got that new deputy, Jason, traveling to Stratford to check the territorial wanted list and see if they can shed some light on who that dead feller was. No sort of identification on him, but a whole lot of money, which has most folks speculating that he didn't come by it honestly. His horse and saddle are at Parker's. No brand on the horse, just the initials L. B. on his saddle. If he had any saddlebags, that other feller's made off with them."

"Where's my horse?" Sammy asked, concern in his voice.

"I believe he's still down at Parker's." Doc retrieved a bedpan from under the bed and placed it by Sammy's hip. "Use this when you need to go. Tap on the floor with this cane if you need some help," Doc said, rattling a cane that hung from the headboard post.

The stairs groaned as the doctor's assistant, Ruth, made a careful ascent with a tray of food. A moment later, she entered the room and walked to the bed where she waited until Doc helped to prop up Sammy. She put the tray carefully on his lap. Ham, eggs, and fried potatoes overflowed the plate and gave off a wonderful aroma that made Sammy salivate.

Doc Payton's eyes widened as he looked at the enormity of the portions. "Well, give 'er a go," he said with some skepticism. "Looks like Missus Watson was pretty ambitious about how much your stomach could handle. I imagine it's shrunk up some after five days, so take it easy. Don't make yourself sick."

"I sure appreciate your concern, Doc, but I believe I could eat the Irish into another potato famine and swallow the roast out of all the beef on the Chisholm Trail. And I'd sure be obliged for some more water. I'm drier 'n a tumbleweed in a dust storm." He looked to the table and saw only the glass. "There was a water pitcher here a minute ago."

Ruth shot Sammy a wry look. "It had an accident," she said flatly. "Seems as if your senses are in good working order now. You just do as the doctor says and all will be fine."

"Oh yes, ma'am. I will," Sammy politely said, understanding that he must have caused the pitcher's end, and feeling that he may have offended her with his witticisms. "I'll make that pitcher up, Missus Jenkins . . . soon as I'm able. Please thank Missus Watson for her cookin' . . . and thank you too for bringin' it and lookin' after me."

His sincerity melted Ruth back to a smile. "You just rest up and get well," she said with warmth. "I'll pass on your thanks to Jenny Simpson. She made your breakfast. Better eat it while it's still warm."

"Jenny made this?" Sammy looked down at his plate with a whole new appreciation for what was before him. He picked up his fork and dug in. Halfway through the plate, he knew he couldn't eat another bite, and soon after that he was asleep.

Chapter 15

The days went by and Sammy improved steadily, at least at staying awake while visitors came to call. He was grateful for the company, though, and he quickly accumulated enough reading material and pieces of pie or cake to keep him eating and occupied. And naturally, the better he felt, the more stir crazy he became. It came to a head when Lundy showed up one morning.

Sammy started right in on him, not even giving him a chance to say hello. "It's time to go, Lundy. I've gotta get outta here today! Doc says another week, but I'm not doin' it. I'm just layin' here gettin' soft and bustin' with cabin fever. Parker's got an extra horse. Go check would you, Lundy? I'm good to ride right now." Sammy was already swinging his legs to the floor and preparing to stand up.

"Whooaaa down there, Leaky. I don't know if that's such an all-fire bright idea."

"I'll tell you, Lundy," Sammy quickly injected with straight seriousness, "I don't believe I care to be called Leaky anymore. It's caused me too much trouble. You just get me back to the T. and I'll be all right. Come on, Lundy, I'm askin' for your help now."

"Well I do have the buckboard here," Lundy mischievously

said. "You think we oughta pull the big caper and spring you out-ta here, huh?"

"Now you've got the right idea, partner," Sammy said with a grin of relief.

"Let me run that one by the doc for the sake of courtesy. I'm sure he won't put up too much of a fuss. I don't reckon he'd mind seeing you go unless he really figured it'd be dangerous for you."

"You go have your conversation and I'll be dressed and ready in five minutes," Sammy said with a tone of resolve and determination that let Lundy know that he was leaving the premises, one way or another.

Lundy shook his head with a look of mock disgust. "You sound like a man who's ready for work, but somehow I don't think you're up to it yet. But then again, you've been a surprise since day one."

Lundy left the room and Sammy slowly got dressed. He was stiff, and each movement brought pain, but pulling on his new boots again and putting on fresh duds took his mind off it. Moments later, he stood at the top of the stairs and knew it would take some concentration to get down them in some other way than a tumble. He steadied himself and began the descent, his legs feeling rubbery and his ribs aching with each downward step. But his determination delivered him to the bottom without incident.

He walked through the parlor to Doc Payton's office where Doc sat at his desk, his attention on some paperwork that he had a pen to. Doc continued writing and spoke without looking up. "Lundy says you're leaving. I don't recommend it, but I don't reckon it'll kill you. Just lay up and stay off a horse for a good while. You sure don't want to re-injure those ribs anytime soon. They're another two months from being fully healed."

Sammy knew the doc was right on that score. "I'm much obliged to you and Missus Jenkins for all your care. I'll follow your advice 'cause I know from that trip down the stairs that my ambition is presently a whole lot stronger than the rest of me. What do I owe you, Doc?"

"You can settle up later. Just take it easy and stop back in next time you get to town. We'll get another look at you."

"Here's ten dollars against what I owe," Sammy said, pulling the money from his pocket and putting it the on the desk.

"Then five more will settle it . . . but no hurry. Pay me when you can. Lundy said he'd be back in a few minutes. Why don't you sit down?"

"Thanks, Doc, but I'm goin' outside just to be there. It's been too long."

Chapter 16

The frozen wagon ruts on Main Street were lined with crystals of ice that shone brilliantly in the morning sun, giving the appearance of jeweled rails. Sammy surveyed them, knowing that they would soon thaw and give way to an avenue of mud, eventually to be recast by the day's activities and the evening's freezing temperatures. He stood on the boardwalk, happy to be outside absorbing the crisp air. The need to stretch overcame him, and he slowly raised his hands over his head as if reaching for the sky. The motion was painfully needed. He continued with it as he pushed up on the balls of his feet and held an elongated position for several more seconds before relaxing back down and feeling better, his circulation now in working order.

He sat down on the bench, prepared to watch the activities of Main Street while waiting for Lundy, when he heard a door close. Sammy's heart sped up and the sensation of cold gave way to excitement as he looked at Jenny Simpson walking toward him. Her movement was graceful and elegant. The simple blue gingham dress she wore might as well have been a royal gown, for her beauty was striking. Her long dark hair was presently pinned up in a bun and contrasted with her deep blue eyes that were soft of expression and hypnotically alluring. She smiled as she approached, a smile that melted Sammy's soul and left a puddle of confused emotion and anxiety. When she stopped in front of him, Sammy quickly stood and removed his hat.

"Hello, Sam," she said, the tone and quality of her voice as appealing as the rest of her. "What are you doing out here? Are you well enough to be leaving?"

Sammy joyfully noted the concern in her voice. "Yes ma'am, Miss Jenny. I'm feeling much better, and I couldn't lie in that bed anymore. I'll be much happier resting up at the T. and doing what I can to help out."

She looked at him with warm eyes and invitingly said, "I'd like it if you'd just call me Jenny."

"All right . . . Jenny. I just didn't want to be disrespectful, ma'am . . . I mean Jenny."

They smiled at each other as their eyes locked and held for long, lingering seconds. Without conversation, there was a powerful communication of feelings between them.

"I sure appreciate the meals you made, Jenny," Sammy said, breaking the trance they had both fallen into. "Your cookin' is what's got me better in such a hurry," he said with a laugh.

"I was happy to cook for you, Sam, and I'm so glad to see you're feeling better. I came by to visit several times, but you were asleep, and I didn't want to wake you."

Sammy's heart leapt at the news of her attempted visits. He could hardly believe it. "You should have woken me, Jenny," he said with a deep sincerity, causing her to search his eyes again.

"I wish I had . . . if that's what you would have wanted," she said, in a softer, revealing tone.

The wagon rounded the corner and rolled up the street with Lundy at the reins, his hat pulled low. Jenny and Sammy looked at the approaching wagon and then at each other, sensing the end of their short visit. "It sure is good to see you, Jenny," Sammy said almost sadly. "I'm sorry I didn't get to dance with you at that fandango. I would have really liked that."

Jenny gave a look of disappointment mixed with another

warm smile. "After I heard what happened to you at the Frontier, I wasn't in the mood to dance. I didn't go. They said you might die. I prayed for you, Sam."

Jenny suddenly gave Sammy a hug, her hair brushing against his face for a brief second, but long enough for him to drink in her clean, wonderful scent. She stepped back quickly and looked at Sammy, who stood as if hit by a bolt of lightning. "I'm so glad God didn't take you now."

"Me too," Sammy replied in a sort of dreamy daze. "Thank you for your prayers, Jenny," he said, still dumbfounded.

Lundy pulled the wagon up and stopped, but sat quietly, not wanting to interrupt the conversation that he knew Sammy was more than happy to be having.

"I'd be pleased if you came by for a visit when you're feeling better, Sam." She turned and began to walk away, then looked back after two steps and said with the slightest intonation of sweet hope, "Goodbye for now, Samuel Winds."

Sammy watched her walk down the boardwalk as if nothing else existed in the world, fixated until she disappeared into the general store a block away. He finally looked at Lundy, who was looking back at him with a knowing smile. "I think you oughta do as that girl says and pay her a visit when you're feelin' better," Lundy casually said.

"I believe I will."

Chapter 17

The wagon rumbled along over the gently undulating upper plains, the land colored by the mid-autumn hues of yellow, gold, green, purple, and red, and rolling out in an easy ascent that eventually vanished into a forest several miles ahead. Sammy was laid out in the back amongst the supplies, his head resting on a sack of beans. His ribs ached, but the pain had let up some since he'd taken up residence on the wagon bed, having been forced there early on by the pain brought from sitting up front at the beginning of the trip. He and Lundy had talked for an hour about the goings on at the ranch, the current herd, and Sammy's ordeal. Lundy understood that Sammy had deep regret over having to kill a man, his first, but knew that the west was a volatile place where a man did what a situation demanded of him to survive. For his part, Sammy was simply mad that he'd been forced to kill the unknown stranger. "That loud-mouthed son of a bitch won't be causin' anybody else trouble," Sammy had said before the conversation fell silent.

Several miles went by with each man riding in his own thoughts. Sammy gazed at the deep blue sky, choked with billowing, puffy clouds, his senses keen with the outdoor movement and his unexpected encounter with Jenny. Lundy kept the team at a good pace and sat easily with loose reins in hand, happily singing a medley of trail songs.

It was early afternoon. They had just passed the canteen between them and were preparing to indulge in some fried chicken and biscuits when Sammy spotted the rider moving up their path several miles behind them. "Rider comin' up behind us, Lundy."

Lundy turned around and looked for several seconds, noting the rider's speed and direction. "Looks like he's tryin' to catch us . . . movin' fast . . . sod's flyin' . . . and lookin' right at us . . . must be." He pulled back easily on the reins. "Whoaa, boys. Let's stop this travelin' palace and pay this meal the attention it deserves while we let this feller get here." Lundy got the wagon stopped and moments later tore into a fat chicken breast, chewing with dedicated purpose and quickly replacing what he'd swallowed with other large bites as if there were a time limit involved.

Sammy was making short work of a thigh and biscuit and intently watching the rider. He stopped chewing as recognition began to form. "I think that's Sheriff Ritter. Looks like his horse, and he wears a gray bowler like that . . . don't he?"

Lundy peered hard for a moment while he chewed away. "I think you're right," he said through a mouth full of chicken, causing a morsel to be ejected that landed on Sammy's nose. "Sure looks like that blue roan of his," Lundy continued, not noticing as another piece flew out and landed on Sammy's chest.

"You keep talking, Lundy, and I'll have a whole nuther piece of chicken down here soon," Sammy mused, brushing the pieces off of his face and chest.

"Well, you couldn't go wrong 'cause that's about as good as fried chicken ever gets," Lundy replied without hesitation.

Both men continued eating and watching as the rider slowly grew closer. Minutes later, the rider pulled up alongside the wagon, his horse breathing hard. Lundy smiled at the tall, burly man whose hat was pulled low over bushy eyebrows and a weather-beaten face. His thick, brown and gray handlebar mustache curled up slightly as he smiled back, looking Lundy in the eye with the familiarity of their twenty-year friendship. "Hello, Greg," Lundy began. "I hope you didn't bust your horse into that kind of lather tryin' to get here for some chicken 'cause the invalid in the back just ate the last piece. Couple of biscuits left, though."

Sammy looked up toward Lundy with an amused expression, then he looked at the sheriff. "Good to see you, Sheriff Ritter . . . or maybe not. Usually if a lawman's pursuing you, it's not a good thing."

"That's true enough," Sheriff Ritter said, as he swung down from the saddle. He tied his horse to the back of the wagon and stretched as he walked. "Glad to get down from there. I been humpin' it trying to catch you boys."

"No doubt your horse is glad, too," Lundy chuckled. "You look to be gettin' an early start on a winter coat."

"I reckon I'd be fatter 'n this if I was eatin' Jacqueline's cookin' on a regular basis." The sheriff turned his attention squarely to Sammy. "Yes, sir, Sammy. I'm most often callin' on folks to make 'em answer to the law or give 'em news they'd rather not hear. But I know this is going to be a memorable moment."

Lundy and Sammy looked at each other for an instant, then back at the sheriff, who was happy to let the statement hang for seconds with no follow up. "What the hell are you talkin' about, Greg?" Lundy finally said, half irritated.

Sammy cut in right behind with a tone of curiosity. "You found something out about the dead man?"

"I sure did," Sheriff Ritter said in a tone that signaled he was winding up for a big delivery. "Seems that hombre headed up an outfit that robbed a train in the Colorado Territory. His name was Lonny Ballantine and he killed the engineer . . . ole boy who'd worked for the railroad's owner, Mister Barclay Westerfeld, since the beginning. The word is, this engineer was about to retire. Mister Westerfeld wanted Ballantine's hide stretched over hell. He put out a ten thousand dollar reward for him, dead or alive."

The last sentence hung in the air, momentarily unrealized by Sammy as if he'd misheard something. But Lundy had sure enough heard it. "Did you say ten thousand dollars?" The slow delivery and wonderment in Lundy's voice indicated a sudden need to hear it said at least one more time.

"That's right," Sheriff Ritter replied, delighted to see the reaction by Lundy and the trance-like expression on Sammy's face. "You'll have to go to Denver to claim it, though. That's where this railroad owner lives, and he wants to personally give out the reward . . . get some publicity out of it, I imagine. I got all the information right here," the sheriff said as he pulled an envelope out of his coat pocket.

Lundy reached out and took it, then handed it down to Sammy, who immediately pulled out the papers within and began reading. "How'd you land on all this, Greg?" Lundy asked.

Sheriff Ritter stepped back to his horse and began to tell the story as he unstrung his canteen. "It's quite a show. Had Jason over to Stratford a couple weeks back to see if he could find out anything pertaining to Sammy's unlucky acquaintance at the Frontier. They didn't know anything then, but got a wanted poster on this Ballantine feller a few days ago. The poster had his name on it and a good description. Story goes, one of his partners fell off the train during the robbery and busted his leg. They caught him directly, and he was happy to sing like a bird about Ballantine. Said he was leadin' the deal. Must not of liked him 'cause he told 'em all they wanted about Ballantine, but wouldn't say nothin' about another man that was said to be in on it. Nobody's caught up with him yet. As it turns out, there was a fourth man too . . . a shavetail kid really. He's sittin' in the Stratford jail now . . . and he's the one that was with Ballantine at the Frontier."

The sheriff paused and took a long pull off his canteen then capped it, hung it on the side of the wagon, and started rooting in the wicker basket on the floorboard. "I'll take you up on one of those biscuits."

Sammy kept reading the information papers while Lundy was content to sit quiet for a moment, sure that the sheriff would resume the story any second. Sheriff Ritter pulled out a biscuit and stood still, looking at the biscuit, which he was shaking slightly as if it contained the rest of the story.

He took a bite and continued as he chewed. "This kid . . . Royals . . . Cody Royals, I believe it was. Well, he got put afoot by some Navajos over near Flathead Butte after he left town. Not real sure what happened there, but he lost his horse and he's still breathin' . . . so he got lucky somehow. Two young hands off the Handy J. happened by this Royals fella . . . good thing too. He'd been wanderin' around for a couple days. Those boys saved his bacon. Got him fed and watered and to town . . . but not before they drank some whiskey together. Royals was so happy he thought he'd brag about who he'd been keepin' company with and how big a life he'd been livin' . . . from the train robbery right down to Sammy's killin' of this Lonny Ballantine. Those boys off the J. were even younger than Royals. Guess he figured they wouldn't say nothin' to nobody. He figured wrong. Sheriff Hardy ended up getting all the pieces . . . first my deputy's inquiries, then the wanted poster on Ballantine, then this Royals idiot shootin' off his mouth. Sheriff Hardy showed up in my office this mornin' about an hour after you boys left town. Knew you'd be anxious to know the whole story on that curly wolf . . . not to mention the reward."

Sammy looked up from the papers he'd been intently studying and smiled at the sheriff like a man who'd had a heavy burden lifted off his shoulders. "I don't know how this day could get any better. Much obliged, Sheriff, for bringing this news."

Sammy's expression turned thoughtful. "This letter says I've got six months to claim the money, and that I'll need some sort of identification or letters from the proper authorities to prove I'm the man that killed Lonny Ballantine. Do they already know who I am?"

"They know that Ballantine is dead and that a man named Sammy Winds killed him," Sheriff Ritter replied. "Sheriff Hardy will get word off as soon as he gets back to Stratford lettin' 'em know of your current condition and that you'll get word out when you can figure your plans a little better. I'll fix up some sort of official letter for you. By the time you get there, they'll have had a heap of advance notice about Sammy Winds," he said with a chuckle.

Lundy pulled his hat brim up. "It's gonna be a spell before you'll be ready for a trip like that. It's near five hundred miles to Denver, and by the time you'll be ready to travel, it'll be winter. I'm guessin' you'd have to travel most of it by horse just to get to where a train or stage was part of a Denver route."

Sheriff Ritter began speculating out loud about where one would have to travel to catch a train or stage bound for Denver or the possible connection points. But Sammy didn't catch much of it. His mind had slipped back to the ten thousand dollars and was paralyzed with rapture as he considered the possibilities of what he could do with such a sum. He lay there in the back of the wagon, leaning against the bean sacks, his mind clicking through all the enterprises that he knew, or had heard of, and had been interested by. The possibilities seemed endless. Sammy knew his life had been transformed at that moment, much like when he'd been rescued from the plains and brought to the Twin T. thirteen years earlier.

Lundy and the Sheriff jawboned about the travel options, unaware of Sammy's mental absence, but coming to agreement over the certainty of several routes and the probable conditions. They finally turned their attention back to Sammy to note his reaction to their collective wisdom. "I don't think he's listenin' to us, Greg," Lundy said, appreciating the kind of impact the news was having on his young friend.

The Sheriff smiled. "With that kind of money, he won't have to listen. He'll be givin' the orders."

Having heard the last two sentences, and game to join in on the amusement, Sammy said with authority, "Well since I'm giving the orders here, maybe we oughta think about headin' to the T. 'cause I believe that front hangin' over Hammer Pass is gonna dispense a storm all over us if we sit here talkin' all afternoon. And somebody of my apparent influence and station shouldn't be gettin' wet."

Both men shot him a hard look. "The boy's a natural all right," Sheriff Ritter said. "He'll be settin' the world on fire in no time."

"Well hell then," Lundy shot back, "We better do what he says so he don't forget us when he's fat 'n' rich. Why don't you ride on with us, Greg? It's four hours back and two to the T. It'll be dark in three. Jacqueline always has more than enough fixed up, and we have plenty of bunks."

"That's a good idea, Sheriff," Sammy agreed. "Come on with us."

Sheriff Ritter looked to the north toward Hammer Pass and didn't particularly like what he saw, the dark clouds rolling closer as the breeze began to increase slightly. "That's surely an inviting offer, but I'm gonna put in at Ward Sones'. Saw him in town before I left and told him I might have need. That'll put me close in and I can make his place before sundown."

The sheriff untied his horse and mounted up. "I'll wait to hear from you, Sammy. If I get any word that you should know about, I'll find a way to get it to you."

"Truly obliged, Sheriff," Sammy replied.

"One of the boys will be to town within a week. I'll have 'em check with you for any news," Lundy said. Then he reached into the basket on the floorboard and flipped a biscuit to the sheriff, who caught it one handed. "See you down the trail, Greg."

"Yep," the sheriff replied. "Get well, Sammy."

"Just about as fast as I can. So long, Sheriff."

Moments later, the wagon was rumbling along to the southwest, and Sheriff Ritter rode at a canter to the northeast with stiffening wind in his face.

Chapter 18

Homer and Reuben Taylor led the spontaneous welcoming yard party at the ranch, which included everyone currently on the premises. They all poured out of the house as supper was about to be served. Sammy felt slightly embarrassed that such a fuss was being made over him, but nevertheless enjoyed the attention and was glad to see all the crew at once. After five minutes of hellos and well wishes, the boys all drifted back in, mindful that they were starving after a long afternoon of work. Homer, Reuben, and Jacqueline remained with Sammy, while Lundy put the team up.

Sammy politely, but adamantly, refused the Taylor brothers' suggestion that he finish his convalescence in the main house, a sprawling log structure that had separate wings for Homer and Reuben, and also had a number of other guestrooms that went mostly unused. "I appreciate the offer, but I'm healin' up in the bunkhouse . . . otherwise the boys will think I'm a royal loafer."

"Suit yourself," Homer answered in his relaxed, lazy drawl.

Reuben added his final thought on the matter. "You'd probably be more comfortable in the house . . . if you change your mind. Supper's on, let's eat." The two brothers headed for the house as a fiery sunset hung along the ridge of the bluffs.

Jacqueline took more offense at the refusal than either of the Taylor brothers, and she looked at Sammy with a mixture of concern and anger. "I can look after you much easier if you're in the house . . . not to mention keep you fed up till you're good and healthy."

Keeping the crew fed and healthy had been Jacqueline's stock and trade for the better part of two decades. Her hair was salt and pepper now, held regularly in a bun with a silver hairpin her mother had given her when she was a girl. Married at sixteen, she had three children by the age of twenty, and was widowed at twenty-six when her husband was killed by lightning. Her youngest child, a girl, had died of cholera a year later, leaving Jacqueline with her twin sons and an uncertain future. She had seen the poster in town advertising for a cook/house manager and went to work for the Taylor brothers, who welcomed her and her boys into their young operation, employing the boys as helpers in a variety of jobs. Ten years later, the young men told their mother they would write regularly, and struck out for California hoping to make their fortune in one of the many opportunities they had heard about word-of-mouth. True to their promise, they wrote often, but had yet made little more than a small living as laborers in a freighting company. They were, however, happy and optimistic that they would eventually be in business for themselves and be able to set their mother up in a life of ease.

Sammy looked into Jacqueline's brown eyes and said reassuringly, "I'll be just fine. I'm more at home in the bunkhouse, and I don't want to be any extra work for you. Fact, I'll be doin' whatever I can to help out, since I'm not supposed to be on a horse for a while."

Jacqueline raised her eyebrows. "I know you're a hard worker, Sammy. With you, I'm worried you'll be trying to do too much too soon. Don't you let those boys goad you into doing something before you're ready. Now come and eat." Her stern tone indicated her seriousness on the matter. She suddenly turned and headed off in the direction of the kitchen, as if she remembered something unattended on the stove.

71

Sammy looked after her, realizing again that in many ways she had been like a mother to him, and he loved her for it. "Yes, ma'am. I'll take it slow till I'm good and healthy," he called out to her just before she disappeared into the house. He stood alone for a minute looking around the ranch yard, taking it all in and understanding that his life there might come to an end. Ten thousand dollars would change things. He imagined a spread of his own in a picturesque setting and thought about life's possibilities. He thought about Jenny.

Sammy gazed at the remaining sunset as a cold breeze blew several snowflakes around the yard, one of them landing on his face and prompting him to remember that winter was beginning. He knew he had a lot of thinking and planning and recovering to do. His life was getting ready to go a new direction, all because of a chance encounter with someone who tried to kill him. He suddenly prayed for forgiveness and wisdom, knowing that he'd had to kill Lonny Ballantine, but hoping that in the future he'd have enough wisdom to avoid having to repeat such an action. Sammy also knew that some circumstances were beyond wisdom, so he also prayed for strength and luck.

"What are you doin' standin' out here by yourself?" Lundy asked, having emerged from the barn and walking at a brisk pace as he brushed hay and trail dust off himself. He stopped in front of Sammy, who had a mildly thoughtful look on his face. "You all right, son? You need a hand in?"

Sammy regained a glint of alertness in his eyes. "No . . . I can sure enough get to *that* table."

"Well, let's get to it before the rest of them boys clean out the fixins'," Lundy declared as he headed for the door.

Chapter 19

S upper was always an event at the Twin T., mostly because Jacqueline became a legendary cook, and there was always enough to bloat half the country. Multiple platters, serving bowls, gravy boats, biscuit baskets, and pitchers circulated up and down a twenty-foot table with the speed and precision of team roping. While each man loaded his plate and kept the supply chain racing, the conversation was alive and peppery about the day's events. The talking tapered off as feasting became the priority, but picked up again during the brief intermission between supper and dessert. Homer would press the head of the brass wind-up turtle that sat on the table at his place. It emitted a ring that signaled Jacqueline and her helpers, Lucilla and Raquel, that phase two was ready to begin. The women would emerge from the kitchen like an army, quickly clearing the table and replacing it with the night's dessert, which usually included pie or cake and plenty of strong, fresh coffee.

On this night, the conversation had been steady. There was a lot to catch up on and the men were curious about Sammy's whole ordeal. J.P. Stover asked the question that brought the news right to the front. "You hear anymore news 'bout them two?" The question seemed innocent enough, but drew a couple of looks to J.P.

before all eyes turned to Sammy.

Sammy glanced at Lundy and took a slow, deep breath. His tone was measured as his eyes drifted around the table, making momentary contact with each man's face. "As a matter of fact, Sheriff Ritter caught us on the trail today. He said the man I killed robbed a train up in Colorado last June. His name was Lonny Ballantine." Sammy took a sip of coffee, then finished with the words that landed like an anvil in the middle of the table. "Ballantine murdered the train engineer, so the railroad owner put up a ten thousand dollar reward for him . . . dead or alive."

The room stopped for a moment. Homer Taylor held his pie fork up as if he were holding the bible. "Greg Ritter told you that?"

"That's what he said," Sammy replied.

Seeing the subject was open, Lundy jumped in. "The instructions say Sammy has to collect it in Denver . . . personally, from the railroad head. I believe he wants to thank young Mister Winds in person for doing away with the man that murdered his engineer. Greg said the engineer was a short timer . . . getting ready to retire."

"Well that's a hell of a thing," Reuben Taylor opined. "You did the world a favor, son. Seems you're a man who's got a mountain of thinking to do."

"That's pretty much all I've been doin' since I found out. It sort of feels like finding the mother lode on the edge of a cliff. Gettin' at it might be treacherous. Hope you don't mind if I ask you all advice from time to time . . . while I'm working on this." Sammy paused and scooped a last bite of pie on to his fork, then delivered it to his mouth.

The other ranch hands, who had been respectfully silent while Homer, Reuben, Lundy, and Sammy led the conversation, now all chimed in their willingness to dispense advice, if asked. "You bet." "Sure." "Hope I know somethin' of use." The replies flew from around the table.

Sammy looked around the room, feeling at ease with the familiarness of the Twin T. The faces around the table had changed over the years, some men staying only long enough to build a stake toward the next grand adventure, and others lasting for years. Aside from the Taylor brothers and Jacqueline, only Lundy, J.P. Stover, and Franklin Edward had been at the T. all of Sammy's years. They were the senior men of the outfit and ran the show, but commanded no more respect than Sammy, who earned everyone's with his hard work, cowboy skills, wisdom, and knowledge. Sammy was special, and folks knew it.

"It's good to be back. I was gettin' cabin fever at Doc's."

"Good to see you, amigo." "Welcome back." "Great to have you back," rang out from around the table. Sammy suddenly felt the effects of the day's travel, his eyelids heavy and his body yearning to stretch out in sleep.

Chapter 20

The next morning Sammy felt as if he'd been dragged the twenty-five miles from town back to the T. Appalled at how weak and stiff the wagon trip had left him, he spent the early morning in the bunkhouse, reading old western catalogues, his mind consumed with anger about his condition as he mindlessly turned the pages. The boys were long gone for the day's work, and his greatest desire was simply to be part of the action.

Jacqueline knocked and entered the bunkhouse for the second time that morning. "Have you got an appetite yet?"

Sammy had declined two hours earlier, but knew his recovery would be a lot faster if he were eating. "I'm gonna put this body to work just as fast as I can, so I guess I better be feedin' it on a regular basis. I just can't eat very much yet."

"That will come to an end soon. I'll bring you out a plate." She turned for the door.

"No, no," Sammy said, rising gingerly from the chair. "I'll come on in."

His incapacity with food did end soon. Sammy forced his eating for the next several days and stretched his stomach so much that he could eat like a starved man inside of a week. After one of his belly-expanding conquests of beef stew, biscuits, and two pieces of chocolate cake, he felt like some tobacco and a rocking chair in front of the bunkhouse might set the world perfectly right.

He hadn't had a chew of tobacco since the episode at the Frontier, thinking he'd quit for a while since it had been his nickname that started the whole thing. As usual, he was very ambitious about how much he could stuff in his cheek. So he bit off a sizable hunk of the tobacco stick and slowly rocked while contemplating the beauty of it all. A few moments later, he let loose with a stream of juice that landed directly on a hoof print he was aiming at and felt momentary pride at the resumption of a skill.

Then quite suddenly, the sky began to spin and his neck and ears felt flush with the onset of what he knew was coming next. He stood up and took two quick steps to the hitching post, grabbing it with both hands and leaning over it as the first violent spasm hit. The tobacco shot out and was immediately followed by the beef stew, biscuits, and chocolate cake in several more heaves. It seemed to come out in three courses, although it looked nothing like when he had eaten it, except for a couple of distinct bits of carrots and a few visible peas. "Son of a bitch!" He exclaimed to himself as he worked to steady his breathing. He wiped the sweat from his forehead and weakly sat back down in the rocker. His ribs were on fire from the convulsions.

Sammy was mad all over again, the pain reminding him of his condition and fixing his resolve to get healed up. After several minutes, his ribs eased up and his head cleared of the tobacco induced dizziness. He collected his gun belt and headed slowly down the path that led along the outer corrals and fed into a lane of cottonwoods. Their golden leaves had mostly fallen, covering the ground like a mosaic of time and color.

Sammy's stride lengthened, as his muscles warmed and his sense of mission increased. He turned on to Old Angus Trail, named by him for a dog he'd been given shortly after he'd arrived at the T. those years ago. The trail led across open meadow, flanked by cedar and pine along the well-worn path, visible in the short grass of autumn. After leading through a brook that flowed seasonally at the base of the bluffs, the trail climbed as a series of switchbacks up the side of the bluffs behind the T. and came out on top to a wondrous, sweeping view of the ranch in the valley below.

He and his dog, Angus, had made the trip countless times during their six years together, always getting to the top and running until they reached the ancient tree that stood at the uppermost point like a sentry to the sky. Now he sweated from fatigue in the coolness of the fall day, as he hiked the trail and remembered the dog he had so cared for.

Angus had been a short-haired daschund, who'd eventually come to resemble a small, black hog more than a dog, primarily because the boys delighted in feeding him scraps on a regular basis. His short legs limited his speed and prevented him from working the cattle with any regularity. But he showed a fierce determination in the first several years, chasing the strays out of ditches and the brush, barking incessantly all the while. Mostly, he roamed around the ranch yard and barked at anything he thought might be moving anywhere in the New Mexico Territory.

The regular trips up the bluffs had kept Angus in some sort of shape, although that battle seemed to be going badly during his last year. In the end, it was a snakebite that took him, an ordeal that Sammy thought his dog might survive. Angus had held on for two days. The memories seemed distant now, which Sammy was strangely grateful for. It had been a crushing blow to him when Angus died.

Sammy reached the top of the bluffs, his thighs burning and his lungs pulling for air. Each rapid breath renewed the steady ache in his ribs. He walked the final quarter mile to the ancient tree at a steady pace, his breathing coming more under control and his legs recovering a bit. A sense of happiness filled him from just making it to the spot where he and his dog had so effortlessly arrived many times before.

Sammy looked with reverence at the century-old tree. It stood fixed like an immovable object of defiance with twisted, gnarled branches that had yielded any sign of life decades before. The carving in the trunk looked as clear as when he had made it seven years earlier. He said it out loud as he read it: Angus. Then he looked down at the large piece of flagstone that served as a marker for where he had buried his dog. His eyes glistened with the vivid recollection of his dog, who once more flooded his mind. "Run through my heart, Angus, run through my heart," he said, softly, then turned and began heading back.

Chapter 21

The next day, Sammy threw a lead rope on Dobe and made the three-mile round trip again, walking and leading his horse. He wondered if his horse was confused about being walked the whole way. "I'll be saddled up soon enough . . . but we'll do it this way for now. Truth is, Dobe, my legs need the work a whole lot more 'n yours. I'd let you take a shot at ridin' me, but I see you didn't bring a saddle." He sensed how much the horse was enjoying the outing, so they made the trip every day for the next two weeks, during which Sammy's strength and wind improved daily.

He finally saddled the horse and mounted up one afternoon, wanting to find out how his ribs would react to an easy ride. But he had trouble restraining Dobe, who wanted to run. He turned him loose, feeling confident that it couldn't be too bad. The horse ran as if speed were a magical tonic. Across the open plain of the high valley floor, Dobe ran at breakneck speed, his mane flapping and nostrils flaring, with his eyes fixed on the horizon as though he were running to catch it. Sammy hunkered down and hung on, relieved that his ribs were noticeable, but not causing him any real pain. "Yeeeehawww!" he belted out with wild exuberance, as the cold wind burned his face and filled his lungs like pure adrenaline.

About a half-mile into the gallop, they approached the Needles, a series of small drain ravines from a large arroyo out of the bluffs. Dobe took them as jumps. "Here we go!" Sammy shouted as Dobe's heavily muscled shoulders and haunches propelled horse and rider airborne to clear the first of the four needles.

The landing sent a mild shock through Sammy's ribcage that became more severe with the next three landings, leaving him unable to draw breath for a moment. He let Dobe run out for another half-mile across good ground before reining him to a walk. The deep throb in his ribs let Sammy know that he wasn't yet ready for any real time in the saddle. He turned his horse toward the Twin T. at a trot. "We'll be doin' that again real soon . . . runnin' and working. Yes sir, it won't be long now."

For weeks, Sammy had done every conceivable chore around the Twin T. that his recuperation would allow. He hauled wood and water for the ranch and bunkhouse, fed out the ranch livestock, cleaned and serviced the horse tack, and brushed out half a dozen horses each day. He cleaned all of the Taylor brothers' rifles and pistols, plained and refitted some of the ranch house doors, and oiled all the mechanical household appliances.

Now, his health had improved enough to take on something he was itching to do: chop wood. The muscles in Sammy's upper body had not yet fully recovered from the atrophy. He knew that swinging an axe for a while would help.

Before he started, he spent ten minutes just slowly stretching out his upper body. Then he swung the axe easily into the chopping block for another five prior to putting up the first piece of wood and ramping up his speed and power. Splitting the dry-cord pine was therapeutic physically and mentally. He paced himself and proceeded to chop wood for most of the afternoon.

The fatigue in his arms and shoulders felt good, reminding him that simple work was good for the soul. Sammy continued chopping for much of the next week, working through the soreness with unrelenting determination, and feeling pride at tripling the stacked woodpile, which had already been plentiful. The rotation schedule, that included most of the crew taking turns in splitting wood, could be abandoned for a while because of Sammy's newfound obsession.

As bunkhouses typically went, the Twin T.'s by comparison was like a five star hotel. There were small, but separate, quarters for the top eight men in seniority. The rest slept in the large open bunkroom at the end of the hallway. A coffee pot sat atop the stove, while oil lamps illuminated hardwood floors and log walls that had bear, elk, and deer heads mounted in several spots. An area of counter and cabinets held every manner of things, including a cupboard where pie, cake, biscuits, and jerked beef routinely resided.

Six of the boys played cards at the center table, while four others occupied a few of the big cowhide chairs that ringed the room. The black, potbelly stove blazed from the other front corner opposite Sammy and produced enough heat to radiate down the long hall. Franklin Edward looked up over his cards at Sammy and asked with curiosity, "You chop all that wood, Leaky? Jeez, the whole south wall of the ranch house is piled high!" Lundy shot Franklin a look, who instantly understood his mistake and made a face that implored some understanding. "Yeah . . . stepped in it. No 'Leaky.' Call the man 'Sammy!' It's tough fer an old cowhand like me to remember that someone all of a sudden has a new name," Franklin said with mock disgust.

"Well it ain't new, nimrod. It's his preferred name," Lundy casually remarked. "In fact, once he gets his money, you better be callin' him 'Mister Winds.'"

Sammy looked up from the book he was reading in the front corner of the bunkhouse, considering the question put to him and the brief exchange that had taken place between Lundy and Franklin. "Call me whatever you want, Franklin. As long as I understand you're talkin' to me, I'll be fine. Yep, I chopped it all. So if you'd like to address me in a manner that recognizes my superior feats, I'm sure I'll know you're talkin' to me." Sammy flashed a broad, toothy grin.

Franklin's level gaze held onto Sammy's for a moment. Then, he looked at Lundy and said placidly, "The little pecker head just shanghaied me." The rest of the men laughed.

Chapter 22

The Taylor brothers had come west three decades earlier with nearly eighteen thousand dollars in U.S. government bank notes, earned as employees in their family's liquor production and distribution business in New York City. They had another thirty thousand each of reserve deposited in various New York City banks.

Taylor Liquor Sales specialized in Irish potato whiskey and stout beer, which was served by virtually all of New York's saloons and refined restaurants, as well as many establishments throughout New England. The business employed seventy-three people, and it had facility space of an entire city block in an eastside area of Manhattan known as "Little Dublin." Their mother kept the books and order, while their father and his two younger brothers provided the recipes and production know-how, learned through generations of well-known whiskey distilling in Ireland.

But like their grandfather, who had left the thriving family concern in Ireland to pursue the adventure and opportunity of America, the twin grandsons, Homer and Reuben, had an insatiable desire to chase their own challenge. They dreamt of becoming cattlemen in the American west.

As young boys in New York, they had awakened a grand canyon full of adventure reading western dime novels, whose stories and articles portrayed a vastness and call of the big country that drew each of them from the core of their beings. They made their plans as boys and carried them forward into manhood like a blood oath of mission and honor. After a dozen years of sales careers steeped in legendary achievement, they left the family business and headed west with a pledge from their parents that they could return to the business at any time. They never did.

It had been a risky proposition, traveling west with such an amount of money and no pre-determined destination other than the Colorado/New Mexico area. They accepted that challenge as part of the adventure and necessity of it all. In early 1845, six months after they arrived and thoroughly scouted an area they believed to be perfect for their endeavor, they bought sixty thousand acres of northern New Mexico Territory from a vicar of the Spanish government for twelve thousand dollars. They used the remainder of in-hand cash to build, stock, and outfit the ranch, which they immediately named the Twin T. The land had multiple tributary water sources and was a mixture of foothills, forest, and high-plains grasslands marked by elevation changes that included buttes and valleys with good vegetation and retreat. With the help of a small army of hired hands during construction, Homer and Reuben spent a year building the main ranch house, bunkhouse, corrals, barns, pens, line shacks, and wells.

The first few years had been sketchy, mostly because of the lack of practical experience associated with running a cattle operation. But Homer and Reuben had never been short of perseverance and natural talent. They were self-educated and brimming with confidence and a can-do spirit that was aided by gathering every bit of information available on cattle and cattle ranching. Early losses were minimal and buried by the joy of living their dream and having the means to sustain it. They started with small herds and operated the ranch mostly by themselves.

At the conclusion of the Spanish/American war in 1848, the treaty of Guadalupe-Hidalgo ceded vast Spanish territories, including New Mexico Territory, to the United States. The Taylors thought they might lose their land. But as good fortune had it, the U.S. government recognized their Spanish-issued deed as legitimate, and the worth of their land tripled shortly thereafter. In 1850, Homer and Reuben negotiated a beef contract to supply western U.S Army forts, and their cattle ranch quickly evolved into a big operation. The ensuing decades had fulfilled all that as boys they imagined could be.

Homer was three hours older than Reuben, whom he occasionally referred to as "little brother," even though Reuben was almost two inches taller and twenty pounds heavier. Both men were tough, proud, and all business in ranch matters, though Reuben had become more flamboyant in personality and action after nearly being killed by a grizzly in the Twin T.'s sixth autumn. Reuben credited the bear attack with delivering him to a new plane of existence that spawned episodes of ravenous appetite for whores, whiskey, and gambling, concluded by periods of introspective retreat in which he wrote poetry.

Homer indulged Reuben's eccentricities as God's handiwork and took no issue, mostly due to Reuben's fierce work ethic and steadfast business skills. Homer, for his part, had occasionally engaged in some of the same activities, but was considerably more private and discreet in his affairs. He knew of the whispered speculation over the years connecting him with Jacqueline, but neither of them wanted marriage and were never public enough to confirm anything.

When seven-year-old Sammy Winds had arrived at the ranch in the summer of 1857, both brothers had thought it providential that Sammy, as the sole survivor of a murderous Indian attack, had come to land on their doorstep. They took it as a mission to do right by the boy.

Reuben instructed him in hunting and fishing and trapping, and the workings of guns and gear. Sammy took to all of it, quickly learning timeless techniques of utilizing the earth's bounty and demonstrating intuition that marooned of a born breed, as the essence of man personified in purpose.

Homer concentrated on giving the boy classical education, and read Grimm's, Aesop, and Andersen to young Sammy. Initially, Homer explained the morals, ethics, and lessons of the stories. Gradually, he sought the boy's opinion and judgment in the aftermath of each tale, asking deep questions in the simplest of ways and stringing together questions that lit a stepping path of logic and reason. Homer was a natural teacher, and Sammy was a natural student.

As the years went on, he taught Sammy history, philosophy, science, and math, and he further kindled the fire of his intellect with Aristotle and Plato and Plutarch and Virgil and Dante, and The Bible.

With the mentoring of Homer, Reuben, and Lundy, and all that everyone else on the Twin T. had dispensed and offered to Sammy as their advice or wisdom, or the one or two things they knew to be truly invaluable in living, it had been quite an education.

Frigid wind whistled through the treetops with the song of winter's lullaby, and a full moon hung low in the sky, glowing dully through a lone opening in the clouds like the night's soul. Sammy dismounted and walked Dobe into the barn, then lit a lamp and pulled his saddle. It was caked with snow, as was Sammy's hat and coat, and icicles hung in his beard. Both man and horse were grateful to be out of the storm they had endured for the last hour of the ride back from town.

Sammy rubbed the horse down with hay for the next ten minutes, then quit and looked at Dobe. "You're on your own, pard. I'd like to have a cup with you, but I don't figure you'd drink it . . . and right now I need it. Rest up." Dobe snorted and stamped, and Sammy was gone toward the ranch house in earnest pursuit of hot coffee.

Jacqueline was whipping cream, while Lucilla and Raquel worked on potato pies and biscuits. The smell of roasting beef wafted by Sammy as he entered the kitchen. "Happy to see I made it back in time to be on the front end of this deal," he said, grabbing a coffee cup and heading to the stove, where two oversized coffee pots always faithfully stood.

"What deal is that?" Jacqueline asked.

"That deal of a meal that's permeatin' my olfactory sense and creatin' an anticipation of beautiful satiation."

"What you say, Mister Sammy?" Lucilla asked.

"He said he's hungry," Jacqueline answered. "Supper's at 6:30, like always. So if you look yonder to the cuckoo, you'll 'cipher about forty more minutes. Homer was here a minute ago asking if you were back yet. He'd like to visit with you. I believe he's back in his den."

"Yeah? You know what it's about?"

"No. Mister Taylor keeps his own counsel. But you can tell me what he wanted when you're done and then I'll know," Jacqueline said with a mischievous smile.

"What if he wants to consult with me about whether or not we need a new head cook?"

Jacqueline quickly retrieved a dishtowel off the counter and snapped it like a whip, hitting Sammy mid-thigh and causing him to spill a little coffee as he flinched back and yelled "Ow!"

"Tell him he'd be doing me a favor," she said. "Yes, maybe I'll just take Lucilla and Raquel and we'll open our own fancy dining in town. Then this whole outfit would be a bunch of starvin' pilgrims!" Lucilla and Raquel laughed hysterically with a few whoops and snorts mixed in.

"Now you better not keep the man waitin'," Jacqueline declared. "That cuckoo will sure enough be punctual come 6:30 . . . and so will supper."

"Okay, I see we're done laughin' for now." He refilled his cup and headed for Homer's den.

The door was slightly ajar, and Sammy knocked lightly several times. "Come in," Homer called. Sammy walked into the den, a cavernous room with a massive stone fireplace that reached through the highest vault of the ceiling and was flanked on both sides by bookcases containing the western classics along with books of all sorts. To his right was an ornate, wooden hand-painted globe of the earth, suspended at axis by a wrought iron frame. It sat next to a grouping of four leather chairs facing each other with a low oak table between them that featured a two-foot tall bronze of a running buffalo pursued by an Indian on horseback with his spear at the ready. Along the log walls were maps and various paintings, mostly western, but with two depicting New York and San Francisco skylines that belied the rest of the room and revealed a small measure of the owner's depth. Log cabinetry on the far wall displayed a gun case with an extensive collection of antique muskets and pistols and knives, and adjacent shelving held a maze of artifacts and keepsakes collected from travels that included five continents. Wall-mounted oil lamps ringed the room, throwing a pale ghostly light upon the colossal eight point bull elk head looming high on the wall behind Homer's desk. A bank of four windows on the far wall faced east. The glass was frosted at the corners and presented a picture of large white flakes blowing by horizontally that contrasted quite visibly against the dark bluish background of night.

"Looks like you got back just in time," Homer said, motioning for Sammy to sit down. "It's flat gettin' with it. Another hour and you'd have been hunting cover before you made it back."

"Yes, sir. I'm glad I pulled in when I did. A night in Pico Caves or Scrub Hollow would have been a miserable prospect." Sammy sat down opposite Homer, who was repacking a pipe. "Who knows what manner of varmint or beast I'd have been sharin' either one of those with?"

"Might have been a good deal compared to hunkerin' down under a tree in the open," Homer offered as he struck a match and lit his pipe. He took a strong pull and blew out a billowing cloud that mixed with the scent of the burning pine. The aroma was pleasant and reminiscent to Sammy of the many evenings he had spent in the room, studying with Homer.

"It's mid January, and you've said you'll likely make the trip to

Denver in late March or early April—just a few months from now."

"Yes, sir," Sammy replied.

"Well, Reuben and I have had a number of discussions about this whole circumstance of yours and we're in complete agreement about an offer we'd like to make you . . . and we feel like the time's right to tell you about it. Give you some time to think about it before you make your journey. Reuben's up in Truchas right now, but he wanted me to go ahead and have this conversation without him. The fact is, Sammy, we both think of you as a son. I know Lundy does, too, for that matter. You're family. You've more than pulled your weight here ever since you were a boy . . . and we're damn proud of the man you've become."

Sammy straightened up a little in his chair, feeling his throat constrict slightly and his eyes glisten just a hint.

"We're not young men anymore," Homer continued. "We've lived the way we wanted to and made a fortune doing it. Lord willing, we'll keep at it for some good time yet. But now were at a point where cutting back the size of our operation makes sense for us. We don't need sixty thousand acres anymore. Sammy, we'd be happy to sell you the Escalante corner for what we paid. The Escalante area is about twenty thousand acres . . . water and grassland as good as anywhere else on this ranch. Of course, you know that. It cost us twenty cents an acre, four thousand dollars. If you decide you want to do this, you can pay us when you're up and running and profitable—or, more to the point, whenever it suits you. There's some selfish motivation here. We'd like to see you stay in this country. Hell, we'd give you the land, but it's important a man pays his way. Understand this though, Sammy . . . you don't owe us a damn thing. If you decide you're movin on,' or you want to keep things the way they are now, you'll always have our respect. The truth is, a man like you can do or be anything he chooses. It's a big ole world out there, and you could rope it a lot of different ways."

Sammy sat forward a little. "Mister Taylor, I owe you everything. And with all respect, sir, that land's worth at least ten times what you just quoted me. That ain't exactly payin' my own way.

It's more like being given a gold mine and payin' a filing fee."

Homer took another pull off his pipe and shook his head. "Well, there's just no getting past you. I see you're exploring as usual. You've paid your way since the day you arrived in '57. If it preys on your thinking, you should know that we have individual arrangements with Lundy, J.P., and Franklin that benefits each of them. And Jacqueline is provided for also. They've all been with us a long time. These are all confidential matters, Sammy."

"I would imagine, sir. I'll say no more."

Sammy looked out the window a moment. It was snowing harder, but it didn't register as he absorbed the weight of the conversation. He swung his eyes back to Homer. "Growing up here has been . . . well, I can't imagine the Lord could have provided any better. I am in debt to you and Reuben and Lundy for my life. I hope you know that I would honor any request of yours to my last breath.

"Then honor this, son. This is not an implied request. Neither Reuben nor I extend any obligation to you. You can climb any mountain you choose with nothing but our best wishes."

"I appreciate that, sir. Ranchin' is in my blood. I love horses and cattle and everything there is to life here. Until this whole fracas at the Frontier and the reward money, I never really imagined anything else. But I'd be false if I didn't state that the possibilities been rattlin' around in my head."

"I'd be amazed if they weren't. Now you've got another possibility to throw on the pile. So take your time. . . . No rush on anything. This ain't an offer with a time limit."

"I'm much obliged, Mister Taylor. But I don't need time to figure this out. I'd be honored and grateful to accept your offer."

"Good, son . . . good. In case that high-city excitement of Denver sways your thinking, we'll wait till you return. If you're still of a mind to it then, we'll have Buck Thornton do the legal work and prepare a deed. Now tell me about your trip to La Jara. What's new in town?"

"There was mail from Mister Westerfeld confirming that he

received word of my plans to be there in April. And he received the affidavit from Sheriff Ritter and Judge Stanley about me being the man that killed Lonny Ballantine. He also sent me two hundred dollars for travelin' expenses."

"Two hundred, eh? That'd see you through to New York, much less Denver."

"Yes, sir. I thought it was generous, myself. I also found out there's no stage runnin' between Stratford and Cimarron or Kinglow and Raton . . . not countin' the other holes in the route that might be. Word is, there's been Apache attacks against some of the Butterfield stages. I never gave much serious thought to anything save ridin' up there, anyway. That'll be high adventure."

Homer raised an eyebrow as he exhaled a pull from the pipe. "Riding alone through some of that Apache territory might turn up more adventure than you want. The Apaches are generally good and honorable people, but there are renegade bands that are murdering thieves."

"Yes, sir. I've heard about them. But I believe ridin' east through Cisco flats and the La Planta country then turning north would dampen the chances of meetin' up with hostiles . . . 'least that's what Sheriff Ritter thinks."

"Sheriff Ritter usually gets good word on Apache movements. Only make sure you're finding out all you can just before you leave. Your thinking holds right now. They usually winter more northwest . . . up in the Valle de Sol country. But come spring, they'll be on the move, and predictability on where they're at can be a real sketchy thing—especially with the renegades."

"I'll find out all I can before I leave," Sammy replied.

"It may have occurred to you, but let me tell you anyway. You'll need to keep your wits about you in every respect. If it's not certain, then it's likely that word of your purpose and arrival will end up known by more unsavory types before you get there. If so, schemers and charlatans of every con game will be looking to fleece you. And they'll bring sophistication to their purpose with which you're not acquainted. So be on guard . . . always."

92

Chapter 23

"C'mon, Dobe!"

His dream was frightful with Indians bearing down on him. Then Dobe pulled up lame just as he rode off the open plains and into some trees where he knew he had a chance to get out of their direct line of sight, and perhaps he could find a defensible position.

"C'mon boy! You can't fold now!" he yelled. But the rock of reliability could move no farther and stood with quivering forelegs and raspy, heaving breath that Sammy mystically understood as Dobe's cries for him to get away and leave him behind.

He grabbed his rifle from the scabbard and two boxes of cartridges from his saddlebags, then he slung his canteen over his shoulder. "I'll be back for you, boy! I'm comin' back!" He ran a jagged course through the trees up a mild slope, his eyes searching for a natural redoubt, something somewhere where he had cover and could make a fight. He saw the rock outcropping fifty yards ahead and scrambled to it with the sound of pounding hooves and yipping Indians close behind.

Jenny's voice floated from all around him like an echo of last hope. "Hide Sammy! Don't let them get you!"

He reached the outcropping and jumped into a hollow that offered a perfect hiding space with a rifle portal between the rocks, giving him good visibility of both flanks. Sammy jacked a shell into the chamber of his rifle and sighted in on the Indians. They had reached the trees and were fanning out as they cantered up the slope. There were about a dozen to his left, their course veering away from his position. He trained his rifle toward them as they gradually disappeared from sight. When he could see them no more, he listened to the retreat of sound as it faded like a rising wish. Minutes passed, and the silence came as a beautiful comforting blanket, a void from all sound that enveloped like the warmth and safety of a womb.

Sammy looked back down the slope. Through the trees a hundred yards away, he could see the lone Indian examining Dobe, running his hands over the right shoulder and foreleg. He knew the Indian had deduced the horse was lame. He trained his rifle on the Indian, knowing what would come next as the Indian pulled the long knife from its sheath. The Indian was about to cut Dobe's throat. As Sammy took final aim, the sudden sensation of nothingness in his hands turned to disbelief and horror as his rifle vanished like the treachery of unstoppable fate. The Indian moved smoothly into position, holding his blade low at his side.

"Nooooooo!" Sammy yelled as he leapt from the rocks and sprinted down the slope, pulling his own knife in a desperate rush to save his horse.

He hit the wall with a force that broke the doorjamb and awoke everyone in the bunkhouse. A moment later, Lundy appeared at the open doorway to Sammy's room with a lit oil lamp in one hand and a pistol in the other. J.P., Franklin, and several other men were right behind Lundy and all had either pistols or rifles.

"Light a couple of them wall lamps so we can see what the hell's going on here!" Lundy said to no one in particular. Sammy was on his hands and knees just inside his room, his head hanging and blood dripping to the floor from a cut on his head. He was dazed and just becoming aware that he was in the bunkhouse.

Lundy could see the increasing puddle of blood on the hardwood. He knelt down close to Sammy as the stunned cowboy rolled over on his hams and looked past Lundy at the men huddled in the doorway, cast in the eerie half-light of Lundy's lamp.

"What happened here, Sammy? Are you all right? I heard yellin', and then there was a giant crash like a bull had stampeded into the wall," Lundy said.

Sammy's heart still pounded from the adrenaline rush of the dream, a nightmare he now realized as the cause of his current position on the floor. He took a deep breath and exhaled slowly. "Teach that son of a bitch Indian not to mess with a man's horse."

"What the hell's he talking about?" Franklin said as he stepped around Lundy and Sammy who were blocking the doorway. "Were you havin' a dream? Some kinda nightmare or something?" Franklin asked.

Having regained all of his senses, Sammy felt slightly embarrassed. He got up and looked blankly ahead as he spoke. "That was the realest damn dream I ever had. Crazy savage was gonna kill my horse. I had to go for him."

"Well, did ya get that red varmint? 'Cause ya sure got that wall," J.P. teased. Laughter erupted down the hallway.

"You know, I think I head-butted that ole boy up to Wyoming Territory," Sammy replied with a goofy grin and blood running down his face. The men laughed again.

"I reckon you might a-taken too big a pull on that cough syrup," Blaine Corker speculated. "Doc warned me that too much would stone ya crazy. Said it has some opium in it."

"Yeah? You drink some of his loco tonic, did you?" Lundy asked.

"Sure did. Had a cough this evenin' and Blaine said it would help."

"That's right . . . I remember," J.P. said. "Come to think of it, you did swig on that pretty good."

"Well, I ain't coughin' no more," Sammy replied.

"No, you ain't. Now you're bleedin'," Lundy said.

Chapter 24

Ten days had passed since he'd run his head into the wall because of the Indian spook dream. Jacqueline had surveyed the gash the following morning and proceeded to sew six stitches into his head as if she were working on a torn shirt. She quickly and methodically poked the needle through the folds of skin she'd pinched together, all the while oblivious to Sammy's wincing and squirming as she pulled the thread through and dispensed proclamations. "Contrary to some thinking, there are better ways to gain sense than trying to knock it into yourself," she said. "These stitches will need to stay put for awhile . . . and maybe you should too. Dreaming about Indians and such may be a sign that traipsing after money could have a bad ending."

"Traipsing?" Sammy asked with a tone of disappointment. "I won't ever traipse after anything in this world . . . least of all money. Let's just say I'm seizing an opportunity to expand my means and horizons—and any such venture comes with some risk."

"I didn't mean it like that," Jacqueline said. "It's just that we all care for you so . . . and Denver is a long way to go . . . especially alone. Can't that railroad man just send the money to you? Or to the bank in Santa Fe in your name? Or some arrangement like that?"

"I don't know, and I ain't really in a position to find out. If he wants me to collect it personally, then that's what I aim to do."

From deep within the den, the luminescent eyes peered toward the gray dot of daybreak perched at the opening. A labyrinth of small tunnels and entrances made up much of the thirty-yard long granite butte that was part of a south-facing slope. It was home to a pack of coyotes. They had pulled down several Twin T. beeves over the last month and showed no inclination of slowing down.

Sammy and Blaine Corker had shot six of them when the pack had come back for a second day of feeding on one of its kills. The cowboys had staked out the carcass with Blaine on one flank and Sammy on the other, their positions downwind from where they suspected the den, hence the approach, would be. The coyotes had arrived cautiously, continuing to scan as they fed. When Blaine took the first shot, Sammy instantly answered, and the hot led gallery commenced with the coyotes running and each man jacking shells, sighting and shooting in delirious speed and accuracy.

Only two had escaped. Now, a day later and three miles from where they had shot the others, Sammy and Blaine were staked out in a flanking and elevated position to the rock butte where they believed the coyote den was.

Sammy scanned the granite below as he chewed on the last piece of beef jerky. The rest of the food cache of biscuits and more jerky resided with the horses that were tied to trees a quarter mile upslope. Both men were ready to finish this business and return to the T. after three cold nights at one of the line shacks. They were out of coffee and low on tobacco, and a hot meal would be particularly welcome.

Sammy took a swig from his canteen and looked across the slope to where Blaine's position revealed nothing more distinguishable than rock and creosote brush. His eyes returned to the target area, as he reached up to his hairline and felt the knot of thread at the end of the stitches. Sammy looked skyward at the gray that seemed to be thinning, showing slivers of blue sky as the morning sun slowly pushed against its veil. A hawk glided overhead in lazy circles, its eyes piercing the landscape in the endless pursuit of prey and survival. Sammy turned his eyes back to the den and began picking at the knot of thread at the end of his stitches. Working it loose, he pulled out just enough to get his knife under it and cut off the head. Then he dug out each stitch with the point of his knife, pulling the thread back through its original path as if unlacing a shoe. A minute later, the operation was complete. He was surprised that the poking and prodding had not drawn so much as one drop of blood.

The overcast slowly relented until the sun cracked the sky with a searing light, rolling back the gray from its edges and unfurling a blue wave that chased all. Sammy could see the glint from Blaine's barrel. He wondered if they'd get lucky and see the coyotes before afternoon. It was a fair ride back to the Twin T., and he was hoping to make it before dusk.

His mind wandered to Jenny. He wanted to see her again, to talk to her and look at her and be close to her and tell her of his dreams, and hear of hers, and hold her in his arms and love her. The unexpected wave of feelings for her surprised him. So far, they had never advanced beyond chance meetings and a few conversations together. He hadn't even kissed her. Not yet.

He was snapped back to the moment by the sudden bawling of distress that cried out and reverberated with a slight echo. Sammy immediately knew what it was, but he couldn't believe he was hearing it. "Well I'll be," he said under his breath.

"W-a-a-a-a-a-a-a-h-h! Wa-a-a-a-a-a-a-ah!" came the cries. One after another that sounded perfectly and precisely like a bawling baby calf in distress. It was coming right from Blaine's position. Sammy knew men who could imitate calls of animals. Reuben could do every varmint in the area, but was best with his elk call. Lundy's specialty was a distressed rabbit. But Sammy had never heard anything as spot-on as what was presently coming out of Blaine. If he hadn't known Blaine was there, he'd have bet his boots that it was the genuine article.

Sammy stretched forward and retrieved his rifle. He planted his elbow and sighted in on the butte, slowly pulling from right to left to reestablish the probable exit points for the coyotes.

Blaine bawled loudly on and on and then whimpered for a bit before bawling hard again, followed by more whimpering. On and on he went with intermittent rest, then resuming with a trace of weakening in his call, as if the fight to escape some entanglement or circumstance was exacting its toll.

The coyotes did not appear, and the minutes turned long as the morning unhurriedly warmed. Blaine continued to work his distress calls with cajoling deliverance and dogged perseverance. He was determined not to stop until he had imposed his will, compelling the coyotes to pursue what they most wanted: fresh meat.

In an instant the two coyotes appeared, trotting along the front of the butte, their heads hung low with ears up and purpose in their movement. Both men now had their sights trained on them. They instinctively waited for the pair to clear the butte and hopefully stop. The coyotes were moving in the general direction of Blaine, who was artfully hidden. Blaine fell silent. The coyotes paused for a moment, as if wary. The crisp report of Sammy's rifle cut the air and was followed straight away by Blaine's shot. Both men found the mark.

Sammy walked up on Blaine who was already skinning one of the coyotes. "Good shootin'."

"You too."

"Where'd you ever learn to make a calf call like that? I've known you about two years, and I never heard you do that before."

"Guess I never had reason to when you was around. This is the first time we worked together on a huntin' job."

"That's the best calf call I ever heard. Thing like that could come in handy. You got others you can do?"

"Yep, I got a few others. Learned wild turkeys back growin' up in Missoura. Them's my best. I reckon I got a few that's a close second. Calves is in that bunch. I was beginnin' to wonder if them coyotes was havin' any of it. I thought my voice was gonna give out 'fore they showed, but I didn't feel like waitin' all day for a shot. Figured you rather a-seen 'em sooner than later too . . . so kept at it."

"Hell, if I'd known you could call like that, I'd a made you start from the get-go."

"Yep, guess so. Sorry for the deeeelay."

"You use the hides?" Sammy asked, pulling his knife and dropping down in front of the other coyote to skin it.

"Yep. I generally collect 'em when I shoot 'em. Sell 'em or fashion somethin' out of 'em. Done a few blankets . . . maybe make a coat. You don't want that other hide?"

"Nope, she's all yours."

The men quickly finished the skinning, then washed the blood and hair off their hands with some canteen water and went to collect their horses. They rode at a good pace for the first hour until they came to woods and slowed to a trot.

Blaine pulled the makings from his shirt pocket and began to roll a smoke, holding the paper in one hand while tapping the tobacco out with the other. His saddle bounce was causing him to miss badly, as most of the tobacco went elsewhere than to the paper. "Whoa! Hold up, Seesaw. I'm losin' all my tabackee," he said to his horse, who felt the constriction of the cowboy's legs and immediately came to a stop. "Take me just a flash." He had it rolled up in seconds, then fished out a stick match and sparked it off his belt buckle. He took a long drag and casually looked about, noting the occasional patches of drifted snow against the mostly bare ground. "You ridin' to Denver or takin' stage coaches? Or is there trains runnin' anywheres about in these parts?"

Sammy was taking a pull off his canteen. He raised his left forearm and wiped his shirt cuff across his mouth, then screwed the cap back on. "Word is, they finished that transcontinental railroad last year. Runs clear across the United States from the east coast to the west coast. But no spur lines in this territory that I know of. The main route don't even run through Denver.

Runs north of there, somewhere in Wyoming Territory. I imagine they'll run somethin' through Albuquerque one of these years with all the beef gettin' trailed there. No stage routes that hook up all the way neither. But even if there were, I wouldn't do it. Sit in a coach all that way? Stop or go only on their schedule? No, sir. I'd rather see the country my own way—on my horse."

"How long you reckon it'll take?" Blaine asked, taking another drag.

"A week or two. Depends on a lot of things . . . mostly on how fast I want to get there. But I'm in no hurry yet."

"Yeah, me and my compadre ended up takin' a couple a months when we come out from Missoura a few years back," Blaine said. "We was bound for Californy . . . or some such promise land. Didn't really have no set destination. I guess we figured we'd know it when we seen it. High ole time it was . . . but almost got kilt by some injuns in Kansas. Fast horses saved our hides. They just come ridin' out on us. Open country it was, save for a little stand a cottonwoods where they was hid—'bout eight of 'em. The way they broke outta them trees was sure sign they was lookin' to take our horses and our lives. Ended up just a pure horserace. We had the faster horses and 'bout a quarter mile head start. We threw the spurs to 'em and kept 'em runnin' a good long time. They was shootin'—few zingin' by too close—so we kept 'em a-blowin' and goin', and then finally they weren't there no more. Then my amigo got hisself throwed in jail for cutting a rascal who cheated him at cards . . . town called Sharon Springs. Sixty days he got. It weren't exactly hospitable there for me after that, since the man he sliced was a local with friends. So I told him to meet me in Santa Fe. Got a job there haulin' water, and waited. Finally got a letter sayin' he was goin' back home . . . wished me luck. I guess the whole deal turned his adventure blood to wee wee. I heard about the T. and it bein' the biggest ranch in the whole territory. So I rode up here and Mister Taylor—Reuben—hired me on. Them two been awful good to me." Blaine took a last drag and flicked the cigarette to the ground.

101

"They've been awful good to anybody who does a good job—and they'll send you packin' quick if you don't," Sammy replied.

"I know it. They ran that last hombre, Antonio, down the road in three days flat."

"Yeah, well aside from provin' lazy, he didn't strike anybody as a trustworthy sort. Lundy's run a lot of 'em out over the years that he didn't figure were honorable men. He figures it out pretty quick, too."

"Well, this here's beautiful country," Blaine wistfully said. "I don't know that it gets any better 'n this anywheres. It's been a good couple of years, but the itch has done set on me again. Come spring, I'll be movin' on. Already told Lundy and the Taylors. I saved me some money and been thinkin' 'bout seein' more of the Colorado and Wyoming Territories. Might try some trappin' or buffalo huntin' . . . or who knows. But I'm movin' on to find out. If you want some company, I'd ride with ya to Denver."

Sammy was biting a plug of tobacco and looking west at the gathering clouds over the Chintah range when Blaine made the offer. Surprise clicked in his mind. He swung his eyes to Blaine's with a level gaze and the slightest grin. "Oh yeah? Come on then. An extra gun might come in handy. I know you can shoot."

"Yesiree, I can," Blaine said. "And my horse can git."

Chapter 25

The bathhouse at the Twin T. was a marvel to all who had ever used it, and became a deeply appreciated benefit to all who ever worked at the ranch. Cowboys, who never bathed with anything approaching regularity before working at the T., developed schedules they held in reverence. Part of the schedule generally coincided with a cowboy's time off, which might include a trip to La Jara and a night at the saloon, or a go with one of the señoritas at Lupe's west end cantina.

Homer and Reuben had designed and built the bathhouse themselves. The log building had a steeply pitched roof and was situated between the ranch house and the bunkhouse. A hallway ran down one side and presented a door every ten feet, each of which was an entrance to one of the four separate bathing rooms. They special ordered the tubs and fireboxes and rigged indoor plumbing, employing a hand pump in each room and piping that carried used water through the floor and outside, down a slope to a rock pit fifty feet away.

Inside each room were wall lamps, stacked firewood, a chair and table with a washbasin and small oval mirror mounted above it, and hooks for garments and towels. A cast iron bathtub sat one foot above the plank floor on steel rails, allowing it to be rolled forward from over a firebox when the water was good and hot.

To take a bath, one would light a fire in the firebox and pump water directly into the tub. When the water had reached a suitable temperature, the tub could be rolled forward of the firebox to a second locking position, and the bather could then mount a small platform and enter the tub. When the bather was finished, the plug at the front of the tub could be pulled and the bath water drained into the funnel-shaped end of a pipe that was positioned just below the tub drain.

The nearest bathing room to the main entrance was reserved only for the women on the Twin T., and they had adorned it with their own accoutrements. Homer and Reuben had the second room to themselves. The remaining two rooms were for the rest of the hands and saw the most action, as there were between a dozen and twenty hands on the T. at any one time.

Cowboys occasionally raced to the bathhouse to beat out a rival during unreserved time, which was first come, first serve. Sometimes, several of the cowboys returning from a long day of work would make a break for the tubs, resulting in a melee of shoving and tackling in the quest to be first.

On one occasion of returning to the T. at the end of a long day, young Bill Lohmeyer, who was particularly impertinent, announced about a mile out that he would be first to the tubs. He immediately broke into a gallop, whereupon Franklin Edward gave immediate chase. Franklin became particularly irritated that he could only keep pace but not overtake Bill's buckskin. So, in a maneuver worthy of a wild-west show, Franklin pulled his rope and lassoed young Bill from behind at a full gallop. Franklin reined his horse to a stop and young Bill was ripped from his saddle, landing with a brutal thud on the hard-packed sod with such force that his buttocks were purple and black for the better part of a month and he was unable to do any saddle work for a week. No more cowboy lassoing occurred after that. But the incident was recounted many times over, always resulting in unrestrained laughter and the continued humiliation of young Bill, who would cuss and stomp away whenever in the presence of the recollection.

Sammy sat soaking in the tub, absorbing the relief of the hot water on his tired and stiff muscles and tendons. It had been a particularly hard week of work. The room was hot from the firebox, and the steam of the heated water enveloped everything. All was quiet in the pre-dawn hours as he drifted in thought. He opened his eyes just a crack and saw the glow of the wall lamps through the steam like far off towns.

He thought about the coming journey and the unknown adventure of it and of all whom he might meet and the things that he might do. There were no firm pictures of these things, only a maze of images flowing in a rapid current that the excitement of possibility could not hold in place. He imagined his own ranch and what it would look like, where the house should sit and how the rest of the setup should be. And he pictured his own herd and the challenge of making all the decisions. The prospect of it excited him.

His thoughts drifted to his mother and father and brother, now so long gone. It was hard to recollect their faces and voices. He wondered what might have been if not for Providence. He said a prayer for their souls and prayed he would meet them again. Then he imagined having his own family.

An owl hooted nearby. Sammy knew daylight was close. Five minutes later, he was dressed and walking to the ranch house as one of the roosters began crowing. Sammy was headed for town today.

Lucilla was cooking a tortilla to add to the pile that was already done. Two giant skillets of eggs mixed with potatoes and onions sat on the stovetop next to a pot of pinto beans. Two large coffee pots steamed on the adjacent stove. It was Saturday morning and the normal weekday routine of 6:30 breakfast gave way to the more relaxed routine of a breakfast window between 6 and 8, with the cowboys drifting in at their leisure. Through the winter, half the crew was off on Saturdays in a rotating schedule, and a few of those hands had made a dash for town the night before. The other boys on the T. would soon begin trickling in for breakfast.

Sammy looked at the cuckoo. It was 5:40. Lundy and J.P. were at the kitchen table making short work of their hand rolled burritos. Lucilla was humming a tune as she cooked another tortilla. Sammy listened to her humming and began to sing in the same melody. "Lu-Lu-Lu-Lu-Lucilla . . . muy bonita . . . por favor comida."

Lucilla blushed slightly and giggled. "You silly man, Mister Sammy."

"Yeah, ain't he the early songbird," J.P. said. "Say, you were bathin' in number one weren't you?"

"Yes, sir."

"I'll go take advantage of that fire you built 'fore she burns out," J.P. said. He quickly stuffed the last bite of burrito in his mouth and picked up his coffee cup to drink.

"You've already been beat out on that score," Sammy replied as he scooped breakfast onto his plate. "Knuckles was comin' in just as I was leavin. I don't guess he elected to build a new fire in number two."

"Noooo . . . I don't 'spect he did. Damn!" J.P. put his coffee cup down and pulled out the makings to roll a smoke.

"Well, yer looking nice and clean. Off to La Jara today, are you?" Lundy asked.

"Yep—gonna be on that trail in about fifteen minutes."

"Any particular meetin' in mind?" Lundy asked nonchalantly. J.P. stuck the newly rolled smoke in his mouth and smiled at Lundy, then struck a match and lit it.

"Oh, I don't know. Pickin' up some things I ordered a while back. Need cartridges too," Sammy replied. "You know . . . I've been eyein' a saddle over at King's. Goin' to Denver might be just the time to break it in. It's a beaut."

J.P. took a long drag and blew it out slowly. "Yeah, I seen that . . . expensive, but you're right . . . it's a beaut. There's a heap of beautiful things to be eyein' in town."

Lundy and J.P. smiled at each other.

Sammy looked from one to the other with a frown. "You two are just like a couple of old ladies . . . old mother hens."

Chapter 26

The morning was dark when Jenny rose. Twenty minutes later, she quietly entered the kitchen and lit the wall lamps, then prepared the stove and lit it. The kitchen was cold, and daylight had crept just enough to present a burgeoning, cloudless sky. She pulled the collar of the heavy wool sweater tighter around her neck and stood with her arms folded, gazing out the window with a rising sense of hope that it would be a nice day. The stove creaked as it began to heat the room, offering the reminder that there was much to do. Jenny began the preparation of the morning meal, knowing that the eight people currently residing at Watson's boarding house would soon be down for breakfast. Her morning would be very busy in order to complete the chores necessary for her to have the afternoon off, but the excitement of this day rendered the tasks nothing more than a pleasant diversion, and she buoyantly moved about the kitchen softly singing.

Jenny Simpson had been eighteen when she came to work at the boarding house two years earlier. Born and raised in Tennessee, her father had been killed at Shiloh fighting for the Confederacy when she was twelve. Her embittered mother, fearing that Jenny's two younger brothers would soon be forced into the fighting, sold the family farm and joined a wagon train that was making a westward exodus.

They settled in Albuquerque, where several tough years passed with her mother working as domestic help and her brothers working at the brickyard. Jenny took care of their small household, doing all of the cooking and cleaning and other chores to keep things orderly and running. Her mother eventually met and married a man whom Jenny found overbearing toward herself. But, he was good to her mother and he made a lucrative living in construction trades, so Jenny, being independent in mind and spirit, decided against her mother's wishes to move on. As it turned out, La Jara was only a hundred miles from Albuquerque and afforded the chance for she and her mother and bothers to occasionally visit each other.

Missus Watson, who had carried on with the boarding house after her husband's death, was a savvy businesswoman. She had quickly recognized the positive attributes and characteristics of Jenny; the girl was a great cook, hard working, and of unmistakably good character. On the down side, Missus Watson knew that Jenny's great beauty would bring her departure sooner rather than later, as the line of suitors respectively tried their luck. Someone would sweep the girl away. Missus Watson considered herself fortunate that she'd had Jenny in her employ this long.

Although Jenny attended church and dances and other social gatherings, a man had not yet wooed her. She worked diligently at saving her earnings toward some undertaking she was yet unsure of. Jenny was sure of one thing, though. Sammy Winds could be the man for her.

Missus Watson entered the kitchen as Jenny was pulling a pan of biscuits from the oven. "Good morning, dear."

"Good morning, Missus Watson."

Two years had not removed Jenny's formality toward her employer, and Ruth Watson had long since given up on trying to loosen it. Missus Watson retrieved her red porcelain cup with painted flowers and began to pour herself a cup of coffee. "It looks to be a beautiful day in the making. A little spring weather just before the season."

"Yes, ma'am," Jenny replied. "I'd be happy to see winter give way early. It's been very cold."

"Yes it has. It should warm up nicely today, though. It is very mild out right now and not a cloud in sight." Missus Watson stirred in a second scoop of sugar.

"I hope so," Jenny said with stark sincerity. "Missus Watson, you remember about me wanting to take this afternoon off?"

This was the third time in the last six weeks that Jenny had made such a request, and Ruth Watson was well aware of the reason. "Of course, dear. If you will wash the table linens after breakfast, you may be excused when you are finished. Have a wonderful afternoon, and please give my regards to Mister Winds, if you happen to see him."

Jenny blushed slightly. "Yes, I will. Thank you, ma'am."

Sammy pulled up to Parker Livery Stable at noon. The sun was bright in the sky, and a light breeze blew from the west. He dismounted and walked Dobe through the double barn doors. The proprietor, Jed Parker, was shoeing a Dun who was restless with the procedure and moving enough to make Jed's job more difficult than he wanted. "Damn it to hell! Hold still you puss bucket!"

Sammy chuckled. "It just so happens I want you to shoe Dobe while I rent your buggy for a few hours . . . if you think you're up to it."

"I'm up to kickin' your ass if that suits you better." Jed hammered in the shoe nails, the horse having steadied momentarily.

"Glad to see you haven't lost your sense of humor."

"Nope . . . that's all I got left at this point. The buggy's 'round back. Get old Blister out of the corral. He needs the exercise."

"Blister?"

"Yeah . . . he's the paint. Don't worry. He ain't blistered nothin' for at least ten years."

"Will he work? I'm goin' out by Lobo Pond."

"Oh hell yes. He'll high step all the way. The ole boy'll love it.

"Okay, boss. I'll be back around five."

"Put Dobe in that last stall on the left. I'm damn sure he won't give me half the trouble this flighty bastard has."

Jenny was sitting in the parlor looking out the window when the buggy came into sight. She picked up the wicker picnic basket and blanket and hurried out to the front porch.

Sammy reined to a stop in front of the boarding house. He jumped down and moved quickly to her. "Hello, Jenny." He took her hand in his and helped her up into the buggy.

"Hello, Sam. It looks like the right day for a picnic."

"It sure does."

They had planned the picnic several weeks before on a date when they sat together in the parlor of the boarding house, talking for hours, the weather too cold and windy to do much of anything else. Now they headed out of town and drove on the Lobo Pond trail that wound through pinion pine and juniper and gamble oak, then through massive groves of aspen and birch, whose buds swelled toward the bloom soon to come. They talked of events that had taken place for each of them since their last meeting. Their conversation was easy and alluring, with each listening rapturously to the other's words and intonation, as though their voices were the embodiment of what each felt.

The two-acre pond reflected the sun and the sky and the trees, and its surface was still with a sheen that was occasionally interrupted by the movement of a fish. Sammy spread out the blanket beneath the spruce trees near the shore. They sat together in the filtered sunlight. "Are you hungry, Sam?" I fried chicken and made cornbread this morning, and I've got some boysenberry jam."

Sammy was hungry, but hadn't given any mind to what might be in the basket. Jenny's presence overcame any such trivial thoughts. But now that she'd asked, his stomach was brought back to the moment and he felt his hunger. "Fried chicken and cornbread?" He almost noticeably salivated. "Yes, Jenny, I am hungry

. . . now that you mention it."

She knowingly smiled at him and began unpacking the basket.

"Oh, just a minute," Sammy said, getting to his feet and retrieving his canteen and a small satchel from the buggy. He sat back down and reached in the satchel. "Would you like some wine, Jenny?"

"Wine?" She looked slightly surprised.

Sammy was suddenly unsure. "Or, I have water here too."

"No, I'd love some wine. I just haven't seen any in quite some time. Aren't you resourceful."

"Not really . . . but my employer is. Reuben gave this to me." Sammy proudly held up the bottle. "He said no picnic was complete without wine. I think it's expensive . . . from back east somewhere. He has quite a collection at the ranch."

"It looks wonderful. Let's have some, Sam." Jenny smiled excitedly. Sammy produced a corkscrew and a moment later he filled each tin cup.

"Let's toast," she said, holding up her cup. "Here's to your safe journey to Denver."

Sammy held his cup up. "And here's to us."

They touched their cups together and drank, and then Sammy leaned forward and kissed her. Soft and perfect was her touch. Their lips held as if the lingering sweetness of a ripe season. When they parted, she looked deep into his eyes and he into hers. She leaned toward his embrace as the passion of the moment unfolded and their feelings for each other swept them together.

Birds serenaded the afternoon. Behind the cloak of the forest, black and brown bears were shaking off the sleep of hibernation while other wildlife and creatures acted out their rituals of survival. This first week of March brought the promise of spring bursting with renewal, as the snowmelt engorged the streams and rivers and the moist land spawned on with the sun's heat.

He held her in his arms and caressed her long hair as she nuzzled against him and kissed his neck. "I could stay like this forever," he said.

"Me too, Sam"

"You're so beautiful, Jenny, in every way a woman can be beautiful. I love you." She pulled her head away and looked at him, her violet-blue eyes studying each line and curve of his face and settling on his hazel eyes, which radiated happiness and pierced her soul.

"I love you, too."

They kissed and held each other in silence, each blissfully replete in the moment.

"When will you leave? Are you still thinking early April?" she almost whispered.

"If the days stay warm like this, then I think maybe just a few more weeks. They're driving the herd to Albuquerque mid May. I'd like to be back for that. With Blaine Corker leavin', and Lord knows who else between now and then, I don't wanna leave the Taylors short handed if I can help it.

"I'm sure they can find the help if they need it. Every cowboy in New Mexico knows of the Twin T."

"You're right about that. It's just that I owe those men everything. Lot of things can go wrong on a drive . . . even if it is a short one."

Sammy lifted his hand to her cheek and held it. "Jenny, the Taylors have offered me a chance at some of their land—good land. A chance to start my own ranch. It could be ours Jenny . . . our home. Will you marry me? Will you be my wife?"

Jenny held her hand up against his. She smiled and closed her eyes for just a blink and looked at him. "Yes, Sam, I will. But please . . . let's not tell anyone until you've returned. Would that be all right?"

"Of course. I guess folks are talking enough already."

They kissed again and again, and the day was warm with their intimacy. Later they ate the lunch and drank the wine, and he read poems from Emerson to her in the beauty of the remaining afternoon.

Chapter 27

Blaine Corker sat at the table in the dim light of a table lamp, cleaning his six-shooter. He'd made the coffee at 4 a.m. and was on his second cup when Sammy lumbered into the living room of the bunkhouse, his hair matted to one side and his eyes half-open. "Hey," Sammy said quietly as he crossed the room and headed out the front door into the dark on his way to the privy.

"Mornin'," Blaine replied and holstered his pistol. He got up and hung his rig on a hook, refilled his cup, and sat back down at the table.

Sammy returned a moment later and retrieved a folded paper from the top of a cabinet, then found his coffee cup and filled it. He sat down next to Blaine and unfolded the map, and moved the table lamp to the position of best light. The hand-drawn map showed the New Mexico and Colorado Territories with the position of the Twin T. Ranch toward the bottom and Denver toward the top. Various landmarks, mountains, passes, rivers, settlements, and other topographical features were depicted in great detail.

"Man! That there's a map," Blaine exclaimed.

"Yeah, ain't that somethin'? Reuben gave this to me Sunday.

Drew it himself. Said he knew a good deal of it on his own, and he pow-wowed with some reliable sources on what he wasn't sure of . . . meanin' Homer, Lundy . . . probably J.P. and Franklin, too . . . maybe some of those trappers he knows. Hell, knowing Reuben, his reliable sources might be bears and eagles and elk and such."

"I wouldn't doubt it. Whatever he tapped he sure did a job on this."

"Yeah, it's a good thing too. The maps I sent away for three months ago never showed."

"It don't appear we'd need anymore 'n this," Blaine concluded.

"Yeah, this oughta do it. Reuben told me the relative scale of distance between different points is likely off some, but he felt certain about the accuracy of compass bearings for it."

Blaine looked perplexed. "Relative scale? I figure I understand what you mean with accurate compass bearings, but relative scale done passed me by."

"That just means the relationship of distances between the things on the map probably ain't consistently right."

"Oh well, that's clear as mud now."

"Well look here," Sammy said pointing to a place on the map. "If we left Coyote and rode to Youngsville, figuring we'd gone about thirty miles, we might figure it was another thirty miles to Cebolla, because it looks to be about the same distance between Youngsville and Cebolla as between Coyote and Youngsville. But that might turn out to be wrong. It might be forty miles on up to Cebolla. So, the one inch on the map between Coyote and Youngsville might not represent the same distance as the one inch on the map between Youngsville and Cebolla—meanin' the relative scale ain't right."

Blaine looked at Sammy. "Yeah, I think I get it. I reckon it's like if my uncle Louis—he's a relative and a big ole fat boy—if he gets on a scale and it says he weighs thirty pounds more 'n me, but he really weighs forty pounds more. Then the relative scale is shitboned."

Sammy tilted his head for a moment and drained the rest of his coffee. "Yeah . . . that's about it."

"So, you got an idea 'bout the relative route?" Blaine asked as he broke out the makings and quickly rolled a smoke.

Sammy put his finger to the map and began to trace a route as he spoke. "I'm thinkin' we swing east around San Pedro Mountain, then head northeast to Abiquiu at the Chama River. From there it looks like a straight shot due north up through Los Brazos to Chama." Blaine watched intently and smoked while Sammy continued narrating and slowly running his finger along the map. "Then we veer northeast up through Cumbres Pass and on to Alamosa. Then we skirt these sand dunes on the east side."

Blaine leaned in a little closer. "Sand dunes? Like the kind with camels?"

"Yep, that's what it shows. I don't know about any camels, but look there . . . it says sand dunes. And they look pretty big on this map."

"Maybe we can trade our horses for camels when we hit Alamosa," Blaine chortled.

"Seesaw not built for sand, huh?"

"I ain't ever rode my horse through a land of sand. I got no notion 'bout how that might work out."

"The map looks like we wouldn't have to ride through it . . . just along the edge here till we hit the mouth of Mosca Pass. Look there at the little print. It says lowest pass of the Sangres—the Sangre De Cristo Mountains."

"Yeah," Blaine said, putting his finger to the spot. "Then up this valley here? The Wet Mountain Valley?

"Right," Sammy agreed. "Then on up there to Canon City, and on to Colorado Springs. Then trail straight north to Denver." Sammy leaned back in his chair for a moment and got up to refill his cup as Blaine studied the map. "Whadaya think?" Sammy asked, pouring coffee.

"She looks good on paper."

"Ain't that a fact," Sammy replied flatly. "Well, I guess we'll see what it looks like when we're ridin it . . . change what we want to."

"Or need to."

"Yeah, that too."

"You got any different thinkin' on when you wanna go?"

Sammy squinted in consideration of the question posed to him. "It's warmin' up nice lately, so I was thinkin' we could get goin' before the end of March. But nobody else around here thinks that's too good an idea."

"It ain't," Lundy said, limping into the room with the stiffness of an old cowboy who needed half an hour and a few cups of coffee to loosen up. "Was a lot of snow to the north this winter. Some of those passes are still treachery," Lundy opined as he hobbled out the front door, not waiting for a response or showing the slightest interest in hearing one.

Sammy looked at Blaine. "Heard that opinion about the passes a few times now. Homer, Reuben, J.P. . . . now Lundy."

"They likely got a good point," Blaine replied.

"I know it. I just want to get the hell goin' is all."

"Then what say we just set a date for early April and stick to it . . . come what will."

"All right. You got one in mind?" Sammy asked.

"What?"

"A date!"

"Nope. Anyways, it was yer party from the get-go. You pick it."

Sammy let his eyes wander around the room as if under the night sky looking for constellations, his mouth hanging half-open in awe of it. "April ninth is one month out. We'll leave then," he declared and gave a nod.

"April ninth it is," Blaine agreed.

Lundy came back in the front door a bit more upright and fluid. "We're leavin' April ninth," Sammy announced.

Lundy headed for the cupboard. "Good. Should be a better deal then. Course you could get stormed on whenever. You buzzards leave any coffee?"

"It's a twenty-cup pot," Blaine replied.

"Ahhh yes," Lundy said as he poured. He took a sip and his eyes perked a bit. "That's a dandy. Made 'er just right. You boys are up early. Scoutin' a route are you?"

"Yeah. Takin' a look," Sammy replied.

"That map'll get you there. You takin a pack horse?"

"No," Sammy replied. "Thought about it, but decided it'd just be one more thing to worry about. Looks like there's a fair number of towns the way we're headed. I'll take my fishin' pole and a hatchet with the rest of my gear. I can get all I need on Dobe."

Lundy nodded. "Yeah, that horse could carry three fat men while pulling a plow. You might want to stock up on food before you hit Cumbres Pass. Get caught thin up there and you could end up havin' to eat yer horses—or each other."

"I'll take plenty of salt," Sammy said.

The days stayed warm and the work hard, as spring brought the season's obligations of herding and calving and branding and all manner of ranch maintenance and ritual. Sammy was glad of the work and how it made the time pass. He attacked it like a contest of will and preparation to what was ahead. The other hands had to bust hard in the competition of keeping up with his feverish pace. Lundy and J.P. and Franklin had fun and mischief in spurring it on, and they marveled in remembrance of what youth on fire could produce.

In the mornings and evenings, Sammy and Blaine spent time committing the map to memory, quizzing each other daily on the minutest details. They speculated on what each area would yield in game and water and grass and terrain, and the unknown. The speculation poured over into the evening conversation of the bunkhouse, with most of the hands happily partaking, offering facts and opinions that they floated and debated like a salon of philosophes.

When news of a spring fandango hit just a week before it was scheduled, it replaced Sammy and Blaine's trip as the dominant topic of conversation. The young hands were grateful they wouldn't have to wait long for the social bonanza.

Chapter 28

T he paper machete globes had painted images on them and lanterns inside that made them glow like heavenly bodies against the darkening sky. Some had scenes of people dancing, and others showed things of the west. One had a stagecoach and another had buffalo running across the plain, while still another showed a wagon train and another showed a long waterfall. The globes hung on rope that ran from pole to pole and lit the large outdoor dance area on the backside of the Buckskin Hotel.

The warm evening bustled with scores of folks who showed up for the fandango, many coming from nearby towns and farms and ranches and settlements, eager to join in the renowned socials that the hotel sponsored four to six times a year. Skirts whooshed as boots stomped and twisted out the steps of the dances called. The crowd whooped and hollered to the music that filled the night.

The Miller boys played from a small stage at one end of the area, in the company of guitar, banjo, spoons, harmonica, and vocal harmonies that rang perfectly from years of performance. Along the back wall of the hotel were tables of food and drink with barbequed beef and pork and relishes and bread and potato and bean salads and pies and cakes and various confections. And there was cider and lemonade and coffee and beer, whiskey, tequila, and moonshine.

Sheriff Ritter collected firearms as people entered and kept them in a nearby wagon that two deputies took turns guarding. Chairs and benches formed each side of the area, with women on one side and men on the other, a custom that even the married folks mostly followed as each side preferred socializing with their own until they came together in dance or strolled away for a few private moments.

A few of the young Twin T. hands were congregating in a semi circle, cleanly shaven and wearing their best shirts with clean pants and attended-to hats. They had the appearance of roosters on the prowl, slightly puffed up with strutting movements and posture that suggested they'd been impaled up their backsides with fence posts. They were prideful and took comfort and cues from being part of the group, hands from the famous Twin T. Ranch.

Bill Lohmeyer stood with his left thumb hooked over his silver concha belt buckle and his right leg extended artfully forward like a matador. He sipped his first tequila of the evening, feeling the warmth radiate outward from his chest to his arms and legs like liquid heat. His eyes looked beyond those who were dancing to the other sideline, carefully appraising all the younger women as if determining an order of prospective partners. He took another sip just as he spotted her. "Whoaaa boys! Take a gander at that honey yonder in the purple dress."

"Where?" Jasper Dunlevy asked, almost shouting with his head bobbing and weaving like a turkey two days before Thanksgiving.

"I see her," Porter Loomis said. "Yeah, she's an ace. But looky there . . . that group of three to her left. They're *all* sunny side up."

"Where!" Jasper pleaded.

"Boys, there's a lot of handsome women here tonight," Ben Kettle said. "I figured that much out thirty seconds after we got here."

"Best get going while the night's young," Bill said. He drained his tequila and set the cup down on the bench behind him. He headed straight for the girl in the purple dress. A moment later they were dancing.

"Lohmeyer's faster 'n the pony express," Porter claimed admiringly.

"Man, that *is* a handsome gal he's turnin' with," Jasper said, finally zeroing in.

"Great fixin's they got over there," Knuckles Kopine said as he walked up to the group, still chewing the last of a mouthful and holding a cup of moonshine. "The barbequed pork is good as I ever et." He hoisted his cup and drank it all in one swallow, not flinching.

Porter looked at Knuckles. "I'll tell you what, Knuckles. If you can find a girl that's hungry enough, she can eat off your shirt while you're dancin' with her."

Knuckles pulled his chin in and looked down at his chest, which was strewn with bits of pork and sauce and other unidentifiable foodstuffs. "Oh, hell! Damn it to hell!" He quickly pulled a handkerchief from his back pocket. "Let me see that," he said, swooping the cup of whiskey from Porter's hand and preparing to dab his handkerchief in it.

"Hey. Wait a minute! Whiskey'll stain it darker!" Porter exclaimed. "Jasper's drinkin' that clear moonshine."

"Oh?" Knuckles said. He gave a closer look at the contents of the cup, and then drank it and handed the empty cup back to Porter. He looked at Jasper with a sly smile and an extended hand.

Jasper looked at Knuckles' hand. It resembled a small roast with fingers like salamis and knuckles that were huge and permanently swollen and disfigured from the many times they'd been broken. His hands looked like they weighed ten pounds each and were attached to wrists and forearms that looked more like a gorilla's than a man's. Knuckles was a notorious brawler who could slap a man and knock teeth out. Other than liking to fight and occasionally drink, Knuckles was a soft soul who was honest and hard working. Nobody knew his real name, but in the three years he'd worked at the Twin T., most of the boys had come to know not to provoke him.

"Go get some water. I don't want you dippin' your snot rag in my drink to clean your shirt," Jasper said, pulling his cup close to his body.

Knuckles gave a look of disappointment. "You ain't no fun at all." He abruptly left in search of water.

"Ya know, I think Bill had the right idea," Jasper said, looking intently across the area at a girl in a light yellow dress. "No time like the present. Down the chute!" Jasper put the cup to his mouth and gave a quick flick of the wrist while he threw his head back, as though it was the only proper way to ensure that it would all get down his throat. He swallowed in two forced gulps and suddenly pitched forward coughing hard. Ben and Porter instinctively backed up a step, unsure of what Jasper might launch in their direction. Jasper straightened up, his eyes as wide as lily pads and his face flushed. He took a deep breath. "That stuff is strong!"

Ben and Porter laughed. "You gonna make it?" Ben asked.

"I'm gonna give it all I got. Wish me luck, boys." Jasper handed his cup to Ben and strode off toward the girl in the yellow dress.

She saw him coming her direction and wondered if the slim cowboy with his hat pulled low had her in mind. He stopped in front of her and removed his hat, holding it over his heart as if the moment were a sacred ceremony, with her being worthy of the deepest honor and respect. "May I have this dance?" A vapor cloud of moonshine wafted into her face and she hesitated for a moment. But his straight blond hair was combed and his clothes were clean and he was a picture of politeness and sincerity standing before her.

"Yes you may," she replied and held out her hand.

Jasper put his hat back on and smiled at her. He took her hand and led her out to the dance area. "I don't know too much about dancin,' ma'am."

"Then why do you want to dance?"

"'Cause you're so pretty, and I didn't rightly know how else I could talk to you."

She laughed. "I think you'll be fine if the spirits don't overcome your balance and good manners."

"Oh don't fret about that, ma'am. I could ride my horse backwards with a half bottle of whiskey in me, and my mama taught me to always be polite. Besides, if I hadn't had a drink, I'd a been too nervous to ask for a dance."

"It seems your nerves are calm now. What's your name?"

"Jasper Dunlevy, ma'am. . . . and yours?"

"Crystal Alloway."

"It's nice to make your acquaintance, Crystal"

"And yours too, Jasper."

He held her close and they whirled around with the rest of the crowd.

Sammy took a long pull off his beer as beads of sweat rolled down his face. He and Jenny had danced four straight. He was happy for the beer and the break and a moment to watch all that was happening. Many of the Twin T. boys had found their way to the dance floor, while others were talking and drinking. Lundy and Franklin and J.P. were standing stoically together with drinks in hand, watching the action like the council of the wise.

Sammy could see Reuben at the makeshift bar with a cup in one hand and a bottle of whiskey in the other, his hands moving very animatedly as a group of men stood around him listening to the prophet of the night. Reuben paused to drink and inspect the level of the other men's cups, refilling those he deemed not sufficiently full and ignoring those who attempted to wave off any refill. He poured anyway. Then it was on with the story.

"Hey, Sammy," Blaine said as he walked up. "What a party, huh? Looks like you danced up a sweat too."

"Yeah, I'm not much good at it, but I'm gettin' lots of practice tonight."

Blaine took his hat off and wiped the sweat from his forehead with a pass of his forearm, then replaced his lid. "Buncha them girls came over from a college in Stratford . . . just started up last September. They's studying to be teachers."

"Where'd you hear that?"

"I been twirling with that sweet thing yonder in the blue dress. She told me. She's one of 'em."

Sammy looked in the direction Blaine was motioning. "She looks like a sweet thing."

"Two wagon loads of 'em come over. They got chaperones with 'em. Some of the teachers that teach 'em, she said. They're campin' down by the river tonight."

"Yeah, there'll be a bunch of folks campin' tonight . . . most of 'em drunk."

Blaine laughed. "Yep, I'll be one a that crowd. Fact, I might just camp down by the river myself . . . make sure them girls is looked after."

"Well, you won't be alone. Those boys who work the sawmill over in Cuba are here tonight. Between them and our outfit—and who knows who else—I'm guessin' that river will be a right popular spot once word gets around those gals are campin' there."

Blaine suddenly looked serious. "Well don't tell nobody! I don't want a herd a goofy bastards tryin' to horn in."

Sammy laughed. "They won't hear it from me."

"Where you puttin' in tonight?"

Sammy didn't answer. His attention was on Jenny. He could see her at the front tables where the food and soft refreshments were. She was shaking her head, as if to say no, and taking a step back from a man who was six foot four and thin, but strongly built. The man had advanced a step when she stepped back. She was looking to the side, not wanting to make eye contact with him.

Blaine was a little surprised when Sammy abruptly left and walked like a bull on the prod toward the food area. He peered ahead and spotted Jenny and the man who stood over her in a menacing manner. "Uh oh," Blaine said aloud to himself.

Sammy slowed his stride as he approached, not wanting to be obvious in his haste and attract undue attention. "Hello, Jenny," he said as he arrived. He immediately stepped between Jenny and the stranger, with his face to Jenny and his back to the man. "Is everything all right here?" he asked softly, searching her eyes.

The voice from behind came at once. "What the hell you think you're doing, Mister? I'm talkin' to her. Hit the trail!"

Sammy ignored him and looked at Jenny. She spoke quickly in a near whisper. "He wouldn't quit after I told him I didn't want to dance . . . but it's all right. Just walk me away. Let's not make trouble here."

The big hand grabbed Sammy's shoulder and pulled him around. "I told you to hit the trail!"

Sammy looked up several inches and knew he was one of the boys from the sawmill. "The woman doesn't want to have any further conversation with you . . . so let it go," Sammy mildly replied.

"I didn't hear that from her."

"I'm speaking for her now, and that's the way it is."

"Who the hell are you? Is she your wife?"

"No."

"Then you got nothin' to say. I'll whip your ass right here and show her who the man is!"

Sammy could feel the attention that the scene was drawing. People in the immediate vicinity were watching and listening. He leaned in close and spoke quietly. "All these folks are havin' a good time. Let's walk up that alley right over there where we won't disrupt these folks . . . and you'll get your chance, tough man."

The man shot a look at Sammy that had a hint of surprise and reappraisal of the smaller man standing before him. "Let's go," he finally said with as much confidence as he could muster in his tone. The tall man began to make his way toward the alley.

Sammy turned to Jenny. "I'll be right back," he said.

"No . . . don't go. Please stay here."

"I'm just gonna talk to him. It'll be fine. Don't worry and wait for me here." Sammy wheeled and started after the man.

Blaine could see the action developing as the tall man made his way through the crowd, saying something to a few other men along the way. They were sawmill boys, and they began to trail slowly toward the alley in a procession that Blaine sized up as unfavorable odds for Sammy. Blaine walked over to where Lohmeyer and Knuckles were standing. "Come on boys . . . we got a partner in need."

"In need of what?" Knuckles asked.

"Our help more 'n likely," Blaine replied. "Sammy's about to have it out with some tall dude. I think he's one a them sawmill boys, and I saw him signal some of his friends on the way out. Looks like a stacked deck."

"Let's go reshuffle it. We're followin' you," Lohmeyer said.

The men played down their pace, making their way through the crowd.

"Where you boys goin'?" Porter Loomis asked as his path leaving the dance floor intersected theirs. "The bar's the other way."

"Yeah, but the beatin's this way," Knuckles replied.

"Come on with us," Lohmeyer said.

"What the hell is this about?" Porter asked as the boys continued on their path without offering an answer. He fell in behind them. "Looks like I'm in," he announced to himself as he followed.

The foursome exited the party area and followed behind the group of five sawmill boys who were trailing Sammy and the tall man. The weird procession looked like it was on a march to the moon, which was nearly full and hung directly at the end of the alley like a beacon beckoning forth the spirits of the night.

One of the sawmill boys glanced back over his shoulder and saw the Twin T. boys trailing them. He elbowed one of the others, and a moment later all of the sawmill boys looked behind them. Knuckles was smiling at them.

Sammy and the tall man turned the corner at the end of the

alley and were out of sight when the sawmill boys stopped. They turned to face Knuckles, Blaine, Bill, and Porter. The sawmill boys fanned out slightly with the saltiest looking one stepping out in front. "Where do you boys think you're goin'?"

Knuckles stopped directly in front of him. "That ain't none of yer business unless yer planning on helpin' yer partner up there. Then we'll be doin' business together." Knuckles' smile was a portrait of sarcasm.

"There's only an ass kickin' waitin' up there for you," the leader said.

"Yeah?" Knuckles replied with mock fear. With lightening speed, Knuckles threw a thunderous punch to his abdomen. The leader crumpled to the ground. "Looks like the ass kickin' was right here for you."

A haymaker from the blind side caught Knuckles directly on the ear and sent him staggering into a fall on one knee. Stunned, and seeing stars flashing in twinkling bursts with sound fading in and out like some sort of bizarre storm, he rocked back and forth on one foot and one knee until his head cleared. He looked up to see where the punch had come from just in time to see the boot-kick coming at his head. Knuckles ducked and avoided a direct hit, then bounded to his feet as Blaine Corker threw a left hook that connected squarely on the boot master's chin. The man was limp on the way down.

Knuckles sensed another sucker punch coming from his right backside and wheeled hard, rocketing his right hand back in a flattening splat to the nose of the would-be thumper. The man stumbled back, putting both hands over his nose, the blood pouring into his hands and running between his fingers like a levee that had given way.

Knuckles swung his head around from side to side, wanting to avoid being further waylaid by anything he couldn't see coming. He saw Porter Loomis and Bill Lohmeyer slugging it out with a couple of the sawmill boys, and then he saw Sammy and the tall man. They had come back upon hearing the commotion and now appeared to be watching the show as spectators.

"Hey! Damn it! Stop that fightin' now! And I mean right now!" Sheriff Ritter bellowed as he arrived, slightly out of breath and with one of his deputies in tow. The action ceased, and the men stood in the moonlight, bewildered like cattle after a stampede.

The sawmill boy who Blaine had hit was just coming to and was helped up by one of his friends. The man that Knuckles had backhanded had a handkerchief pressed to his nose. "What the hell is wrong with you boys?" Sheriff Ritter exclaimed with unrestrained puzzlement. "You're all hard workin' young men with some time off. You oughta be laughin' . . . gettin' to know each other . . . tellin' stories . . . dancin' with all those nice looking young gals instead of beatin' the hell outta one another. What started this fracas anyhow?"

Some of the men shifted uncomfortably and looked around at one another in the dark. The big man finally spoke up. "This cowboy here didn't like me talkin' to his girl. Wanted to make somethin' of it."

Sammy wasn't having any of it. "Ahh! This blowhard is spoutin' bullshit. She didn't want to dance with him and he didn't wanna to hear it."

Blaine cut in, "This bunch followed Sammy up the alley. Ain't exactly sportin' odds, so me 'n' the boys here were just lookin' after our own."

"They was just comin' to watch," the tall man shot back.

"So was we," Knuckles said. "Then these boys tried to stop us. We weren't lettin' that happen."

"Yeah, well if any of you start anything more, I'll lock the bunch of you up for a week. Now go on and get!"

The men began drifting back down the alley toward the dance. Bill Lohmeyer walked up beside the tall man who was sauntering slowly with two other sawmill boys. "You're lucky that worked out the way it did. He killed the last hombre that wanted to tangle—stabbed him to death after the dude had shot him in the chest. Yep, you really didn't want none of that." Lohmeyer suddenly veered away and melted amongst the dark silhouettes of the other men. The big man grunted and the two men beside him didn't say anything but just looked at one another.

An hour later, Blaine and Knuckles and Bill and Porter drank and laughed with the sawmill boys. They told tall tales to one another about their work and their lives, and they felt the kinship of young men of the west.

Sammy and Jenny had left the dance for their own secluded spot. Sammy was leaving in two days, and this was their last night together for some time.

Chapter 29

The barn lamp threw a dull light that cast looming shadows on the wall as Sammy and Blaine saddled their horses and packed on their gear. Neither of them had gotten much sleep, but both were now wide-awake. They had said their goodbyes and well wishes to all at the Twin T. the night before. Now they worked quietly in the still of the early morning with each man lost in his own thoughts. The time to leave was finally upon them.

Sammy slipped the 44 Henry rifle into the scabbard and strapped on his gun belt, holding a pair of Starr Double-Action Army 44 revolvers. He had a Colt Navy 36 in his saddlebags along with two hunting knives and additional cartridges for each firearm. He rechecked all the cinching on his gear, then looked over at Blaine who had finished up and was lighting a smoke. "Ready?" Blaine blew out a cloud of smoke. "Yep."

Sammy walked over and blew out the lamp. Both men led their horses through the blackness to the barn door. Sammy pulled it open, revealing a faint light in the east that peeked over the dark, jagged horizon of hills. The morning dew hung heavy in the air.

Homer, Reuben, and Lundy were standing in the yard in a semi-circle, smoking and drinking coffee like sentries posted to inspect all who were coming or going. "Here come the two mus-keteers," Reuben said.

Sammy and Blaine led their horses over to where the men were standing. "To what do we owe this honor?" Sammy asked. "Are you gents the happy trails committee?"

"No, we're the hold-up committee," Reuben replied. "You'll have to hold up a minute until Jacqueline comes out with some breakfast she's got for you. She didn't like it much when you told her you wouldn't be in for breakfast before you left."

The kitchen door creaked and light poured out of the door-way as Jacqueline emerged holding two bundles, each wrapped in a red and white-checkered cloth. Sammy shook his head, slightly embarrassed. "We didn't want to be any trouble for you this morn-ing, Jacqueline. We've got plenty to eat packed with us."

"Well it's not hot, and this is." She gave Sammy and Blaine each a bundle. "You can eat it in the saddle."

"Thank you, ma'am," Blaine said. "It sure has been a pleasure eatin' your cookin'."

Jacqueline hugged Blaine. "Take care of yourself, Blaine. Good luck to you."

"Thank you, ma'am. I reckon I will . . . take care of myself, I mean."

She turned to Sammy with her eyes glistening and hugged him, holding him tight for several seconds. "You be careful. Don't dally up north too long."

"I won't be long."

She turned and walked briskly away, back into the kitchen, closing the door behind her.

Homer shook hands with Blaine. "If you don't like what you see up north, come on back. We've always got a job for a good hand."

"Thank you, Mister Taylor. I'll remember that."

"Time to ride," Sammy said.

"Yeah, there's plenty of that ahead of you boys," Lundy said. "Keep a sharp eye and pour the spurs to 'em if you see any Indians or banditos."

Sammy and Blaine mounted up and headed east out of the yard at a trot toward the pale light of the coming day. A mile out, they slowed to a walk and ate the warm tortillas rolled around eggs and beef and beans, burrito style. Then, as if called by the sun that was yet still hidden, they broke to a canter.

The valley rolled out in front of them, with the green of spring grass amid sage and rabbit brush, and wildflowers with blooms of lavender, orange, and white. Sammy and Blaine knew the land well. It would be the better part of the day gone before they would clear the eastern border of the Twin T. Anxious to see new territory, they clipped on in the cool of the morning.

At noon, they stopped in the low foothills to let their horses drink and crop grass at a deep stream with grassy banks. It ran through a grove of aspens and was about twelve feet wide with swift water and dark color. A boulder that jutted out from the bank across half the stream created a pool that looked to Sammy to have good prospects. "I think I'll give this a go for a few minutes. See if I can wrangle some trout for supper."

Blaine took it as a challenge. "First one to catch a fish gets the first pull of whiskey when we crack that bottle." He strode off toward the nearby aspen trees to cut a pole.

Sammy untied the two halves of his fishing pole and quickly assembled the rig, tying a hook to the end of the line. He put the pole down and moved slowly along the bank in a crouch, looking closely at the grass. With an easy motion, he pulled off his hat and held it at the ready. A moment later, he flicked it at the grass where the caddis fly had lit. The shot was a dead hit. Sammy retrieved his pole and carefully fed the fly onto the hook. He made his way to the pool just beyond the boulder.

Blaine quickly cut a five-foot aspen branch and trimmed it, then notched the end and wedged the string in. He was tying on the hook when Sammy made his first cast. From the corner of his eye, Blaine saw the fish hit Sammy's line. With a twitch of his wrist, Sammy set the hook. The big, silvery trout, thrashed through the water until it was propelled airborne as Sammy pulled hard over his left shoulder. It flew majestically through the air with color shimmering in the sunlight and landed fifteen feet back from the bank.

"Dammit!" Blaine said as he watched the two-pound rainbow flipping and flopping in the grass.

Sammy kneeled beside it and grabbed it tightly, then worked at removing the hook. "One more like this and we'll have us a fine supper."

"That weren't fair you castin' 'fore I was ready."

"I ain't waitin' on you . . . especially with that first fish, first on the whiskey deal." Sammy worked on the troublesome hook which was stuck in jawbone. "But being I'm the one with the good pole and charm that fish find irresistible, we'll start over right now. You best get movin' though before I get this hook loose, 'cause a head start and luck is the only chance you've got."

"That's more 'n I need," Blaine said. He started frantically looking for a fly to bait his hook, running along the bank and swatting at the prospects, but missing like a blindfolded child trying to hit a piñata.

Sammy finally got the hook loose and spied a Black Stone Fly on the grass just to the left of where he was kneeling. He pulled his hat slowly from his head and gave it the quick whip to the target. "You better hurry up. I'm fixin' to bait my hook."

Blaine stopped and looked with horror. "How'd you get that fly so fast? Only a pile of fresh shit could bring a fly that fast."

Sammy chuckled. "Yeah, well this pile of shit is gonna be fishin' in just a shake."

Blaine hustled over to his saddlebags. "It's time to go backwater style," he said as he pulled out some jerky and bit off a piece, then worked it onto his hook. Quickly, he moved down the bank to a spot where it cut sharply wider and the water slowed to a spiraling pool that was several feet deep. The overhang at the deepest part was where Blaine slowly worked himself into position.

He could see Sammy about thirty yards upstream, casting

again at the same spot he'd caught his first one. "Let 'em come up empty for just a minute, just a little bit," Blaine said to himself. "That's all I need 'cause I know there's a big one right under this bank . . . right under here." He lowered the hook with the peanut-size piece of jerky on it down a foot into the dark water, where it drifted under the bank. Blaine glanced upstream at Sammy, then turned his attention back to the task at hand and moved the line slowly down the bank. "Come on now. Come on." He eyed Sammy again and had a sinking feeling that he would hit any second. His gaze turned back to the dark waters just in time to see the silvery shadow darting toward his hook.

The force of the strike almost pulled the aspen branch from his hands. "Whoaa!" Blaine yelled as he quickly regained control of his pole and tugged upward. The fish was a four-pounder, and broke the water flailing and snapping, creating slack and then tremendous jerk on the line. Blaine quickly swung the big fish for the bank, but it whipped hard and suddenly came loose of the hook, falling like a ghost toward the water. It landed on the bank a foot from the edge and began flopping wildly toward the water. Blaine dove for the fish at the instant it flipped over the bank on the way to the freedom of its universe. His hands clamped onto the middle of the slippery fish as his body hit the edge of the bank, with more of him hanging over than on firm ground. He tumbled into the water, submerging completely with his arms outstretched, clutching the fish as though nothing else in the world mattered. The icy-cold enveloped him and rolled into his boots, searching out his toes as the last to be swallowed. With no arms to steady himself, Blaine squirmed and maneuvered to get his legs under him, then rose triumphantly with the fish fighting, but firmly in his grip.

He stood waist-deep in the water and stared at his prize for a moment before flinging it twenty feet up onto land. "See if you can flop your way back from there."

Blaine sloshed his way over to his hat, which floated at the edge of the pool, about to make its way into the main current.

"You in there invitin' 'em to supper?" Sammy yelled.

134

"Hell yes!" Blaine yelled exuberantly. He hustled out of the stream and over to the fish, then held it over his head like a trophy. "This one wants to sit at the head of the table!"

Sammy's eye's widened. "Lord almighty! That monster came outta this stream?"

"He sure did. I had to bulldog 'm outta the water, but I was gettin' hot anyways."

"Well, let's clean 'em up and get ridin'. We've got us a feast now."

Chapter 30

The long day's ride was better than fifty miles and ended at the southeast base of San Pedro Mountain, well beyond Twin T. territory and alive with surroundings new to both men. They made camp on a creek that fronted an open meadow and gave view to the north toward the canyon that would be the compass point for the following morning's ride.

Trout sizzled on the spit while the horses fed on lush meadow grass, their tails occasionally flicking at flies. Blaine smoked a cigarette and turned the spit, gauging the remaining cooking time. His stomach rumbled with hunger. He looked to the west, admiring the towering cotton-ball clouds with underbellies coated in the orange and red of an arrived sunset. It would be dark within the hour.

Sammy kneeled at the creek and washed the trail dust from his face and neck. The water felt refreshing, and it soothed in a way that made him aware of how tired he was. He walked back to the fire and squatted down to inspect the progress. "Man, that's smellin' good."

"If yer anywheres as near hungry as me, we might finish it all."

"It'll be close. Better eat it all or get shut of it or a bear might show up for a midnight feedin'."

"Might show up no matter what, but I'll be nuzzled up with all my artillery."

"Yeah, Dobe will stir if he catches scent of somethin'."

"Seesaw too. Good thing, 'cause I reckon I could sleep through a buffalo stampede tonight."

"Yep, me too."

Sammy and Blaine gorged themselves on fish and each ate a biscuit for good measure. They staked their horses in close and built the fire up, then rolled smokes as the last of the daylight faded like a receding gray shoreline. "Let's have us a bit of that whiskey against the night," Sammy said.

"I'm for that." Blaine reached into his saddlebag and pulled out the bottle wrapped in an extra shirt. "Here ya go," he said, extending the bottle to Sammy.

"Oh no . . . that first pull is all yours . . . fair 'n' square."

"Well, all right then." Blaine pulled the cork and took a long pull. "Oooohhhhh. It ain't too smooth, but it's right for the night," his raspy words rang. He handed the bottle to Sammy who took a long pull and then a deep breath.

"Yep, that'll bring the stars out." He handed the bottle back to Blaine, who corked it, and both men lit their smokes. They sat quietly for a moment, watching the fire burning brightly in the dark, cool breeze.

"Ya know, I figured you'd a made this trip with one of the Taylor brothers or maybe Lundy," Blaine said.

Sammy flicked his ash. "Each of 'em offered . . . damn near insisted. Got mad about it when I said no. But I didn't care to be obliged. Just wasn't the way I wanted it to happen."

"Yeah, I can see that."

Sammy took a drag and blew out a thin, slow line of smoke. "When you told me you were movin' on and headin' to Denver . . . well, that's a different deal."

"Yeah, seems I get the itchin' dust down my back every year or so. Only thing cures it is movin' on. Two years at the T was a record, save when I was a kid. I'm sparked up about Denver. Might just hang on there fer a bit. Get to know some a them city gals," Blaine smiled to himself. "Who knows . . . maybe open up a whorehouse 'n' reeetire to a different feather bed each night. Spend all my profits in my own business, 'less I can make it a condition of employment for my fillies—one night a week each for the boss."

"Your nuts would shrivel up and fall off before you were thirty."

"Maybe . . . but what a way to go."

"That's what they all say till they're on the way out."

Sammy laid out his bedroll, then rolled himself another smoke and reclined with his head on his saddle. Blaine did likewise, and the two men lay out under the stars speckling the sky like a handful of white sand strewn over black marble. "How 'bout one more taste of that whiskey?" Sammy suggested.

"You know it." Blaine handed Sammy the bottle. He took a swig and handed it back to Blaine who hoisted it and knocked back a slug. Both of them lit their smokes and lay back looking up at the sky.

"Moon's a little late gettin' up tonight. Havin' trouble climbin' over that ridge. The dark sure makes them stars jump out," Blaine said.

"Yes, sir. There's a few of 'em out there."

"Ya know, it's just hard to figure there ain't no end to it—or that there is an end to it. It just stupefies my pea brain. Blaine took a drag and gazed at the sky. "You believe in God?" Blaine asked.

"Yep. You?"

"I reckon I do. Hard to figure anything else that could account for all this. Some folks got different ideas. When I was over to Santa Fe those years back, I heard this dude . . . called hisself a doctor—not a medical doctor—a doctor of science or some such thing. He was street preachin', but it weren't religion. Said man come from apes . . . and apes had slithered outta the muck . . . being one thing, and then another, and another . . . over a long time, until finally they was apes . . . and the apes finally becomin' man. Said there isn't a God—just science and this deal called 'evolution.' He said when man can build a powerful enough spyglass, the secrets of the universe will be unlocked, and we'll know all there is to know. It made me kind of wonder, though. If we came from apes, how come there's still apes runnin' around? Maybe they's just the slow ones. You ever heard of that kinda stuff before?"

"Yeah, people who don't believe in God are called 'atheists.' I don't follow that line of thinking, though. The way I see it, science is only the means of our existence—not the cause or the purpose of it."

"Whadaya mean by the means?"

"Well, it's sort of like our horses being the means of us getting to Denver, but the cause of 'em going there is us wantin' to go there. . . . And the purpose of us wantin' to go there is a whole different pot of beans. Science accounts for the makeup of every physical thing in this world, and all in the sky above and beyond, but that's it. The makeup and the maker are two different things. The maker makes the makeup. It's God's creation. I don't believe man has given any purpose or meaning to anything in science. That would be like saying the purpose of gravity is to keep us from floatin' off into space . . . or the purpose of a volcano erupting is to let off pressure. That stuff's just action and reaction, or cause and effect, based on scientific laws. It don't include purpose. So science just *is*. It's just the means. And it ain't ever gonna be purpose or meaning. The way I see it, science must be subordinate to purpose."

"What's that mean, 'subordinate?'"

"It means 'under' or 'beholdin' to.' It means it ain't the boss."

"Yeah, but I think that dude in Santa Fe thought there wasn't no such a thing as purpose."

"Well, it exists for man. Hell, the preamble of the United States Constitution is nothing *but* a statement of purpose. If you think about it, you can give purpose to the physical structure of man too—and other livin' things for that matter. Like the purpose of your teeth is to chew. Or the purpose of your intestines and asshole is to get what you need from food and crap out the rest."

"I might crap out something shaped like a fish tomorrow."

Sammy laughed. "I know it." He took the last drag off his cigarette and flicked it into the fire. "Yeah, man will learn more facts about science, but not purpose. Ain't no telescope gonna reveal God or His purpose unless that's His plan. Absolute knowledge ain't in the cards for man. That's where faith comes in. Absolute faith exists because absolute knowledge never will."

"I never thought of it that way."

"Me neither, I think. Must be the whiskey talkin'. But you know, it'd be a sorry ass deal without God. The deepest and darkest despair—the most vile and indescribable anguish of people would be without grace or mercy or hope . . . or redemption. Pointless . . . like science. Now *that's* evil. Somehow I don't see that as the upshot of science and evolution, 'cause it ain't. Instead, it's part of God's creation, where the blackest of black is eclipsed by the brightest of light."

Blaine took a final drag from his smoke and snubbed it out by his side. "I don't reckon I understood half of what you just said. But if you ever decide to give up on cowboyin', I believe you could make a go of it at preachin'."

"Yeah. Amen."

A shooting star fired across the sky, and two miles upwind, a six-hundred pound black bear foraged in the night.

Chapter 31

The morning broke cold with a breeze that carried frigid mist and an occasional snowflake. Thunderheads to the southeast swelled ominously as they rolled northward, betraying spring and carrying forth the coming storm like the unsettled account of winter not yet vanquished. Sammy and Blaine quickly broke camp after a breakfast of hardtack and jerky, not bothering with a fire for coffee. They saddled up and rode hard to the north, knowing that time was against them.

"Looks like this one's gonna catch us before we get up that canyon," Sammy shouted as they galloped toward the mouth of Coyote Canyon with the wind picking up and flakes beginning to swirl a bit more than minutes earlier.

In long coats with gloves on and hats pulled low and tight, they raced across the last of the open plain to the beginning of the canyon, their horses breathing hard. "We better be right about this canyon," Blaine yelled into the ever-stiffening wind. "Ridin' up a box canyon right now could be a bad deal if it storms like I got a bad feelin' it might."

"We're right. The compass heading looked good, and that sure as hell was the southeast corner of San Pedro Mountain where we camped last night. You see anything else around here that could be that canyon?"

"I reckon not. We best get on up it 'fore we can't see anything."

The canyon was about ten miles long with an easy ascent and width that varied from a quarter to half a mile. Granite ridges rimmed the top of each side, with the last hundred feet up being an impassable, steep, sheer face. Juniper, pinion, and ponderosa pine dotted the mild slopes, rising gently up and out from the terrain of the bottom, which was mostly rock and sand that became a river of runoff during severe thunderstorms.

They started up the canyon at a trot, riding along the open bottom. Within minutes, they faced a roaring headwind howling along the chute of the canyon floor like a cyclone through a straw. It carried tiny hail that pelted their faces with stinging ferocity. Both men ducked their heads while their horses flinched, turning from side to side as the blitz hit like icy sand being blown from every direction.

"Let's get to them trees upslope!" Blaine yelled.

"Yeah!" Sammy instantly shot back. They reined their horses uphill and quickly climbed their way up to a stand of pines.

Weaving their way into the middle, the assault subsided as quickly as it had beset them. "How'd that wind get in our face so fast, blowin' that shit devil hail!?" Blaine yelled.

"She sure got in front of us in a hurry. Look on down there now. . . . That hail already gave up."

"The wind didn't—and now it's snowin' pretty good."

"Let's stay up here and trail on through the trees. Slower goin,' but not too steep."

"I'm for that," Blaine said, then he pulled his gloves off and fished out one of his cigarettes he'd rolled in camp the night before.

"That looks just right," Sammy said admiringly. Blaine handed him the cigarette and retrieved another from inside his coat. "Let's see if we can get 'em both on one match," Sammy challenged, maneuvering Dobe next to Blaine and Seesaw as a wind block. Blaine struck the stick match and both cowboys got their smokes lit. They held their smokes between the thumb and forefinger, cupping it to the inside of their hands and taking drags as they rode on, meandering through the trees with the wind and snow blowing around them in directionless swirls. They rode on for several miles, the heavy, wet snow becoming thicker, with the wind blowing it by like a mask of white camouflage.

Blaine was watching to his left and caught the movement as he passed a slight break in the trees that afforded a view across the canyon. For a moment, he was unsure of what he'd seen. Then, in the lapse between the convulsions of blowing snow, he saw it again, moving on the other side of the canyon. Blaine reined Seesaw to a stop behind one of the pines and looked back at Sammy who was trailing just behind him to his right. As Sammy looked at him, Blaine nodded toward the canyon. Sammy quickly reined up alongside Blaine. "What's doin?" Sammy asked.

"I think I seen Indians. Couldn't tell how many. Whoever it was, they're moving north too—on the other side of the canyon a little south of us. Maybe half a mile, I reckon."

"You think they saw us?"

"Don't know. It was pure luck I spotted 'em. Snow let up for a second and I seen 'em. What in the hell would they be doin' out in this mess anyways?"

"No telling. But we better figure out if they're stalking us."

Sammy rode forward a few steps around the tree, where he thought he wouldn't be in view, but could get a look. He pulled the spyglass from his saddlebag and started scanning where Blaine had indicated. "Damn snow's blowin' so hard that it's hard to see anything." He kept looking, and then he saw them. He stared hard for several seconds. Then he knew. "They're comin'. Seven or eight maybe. Apaches, looks like. Must have been huntin'— deer or elk flanks lashed on with some of 'em. Headed right for us now and makin' tracks."

"Well, this ain't no place to be sittin," Blaine said anxiously.

"You got that right. . . . Let's get! C'mon Dobe! Heaww!" Sammy snapped his reins and put light heels to his horse. The appaloosa bolted into action, with Blaine and Seesaw right behind. The men rode through the trees at a gallop, weaving back and forth with hooves pounding and the wind blowing the snow to near blindness. Each man gave his horse free rein, trusting their instincts to avoid the trees. They hung on and rode low on the necks, hitting branches that sent snow flying in small explosions. On and on they rode, unable to hear any pursuit in the howling wind and having no idea how close the Indians might be.

The wind and snow suddenly became fiercer, and all visibility ended as a whiteout erased everything. The horses slowed and then stopped. Blaine could just make out Sammy, who was less than ten feet from him. He pulled up alongside him with snow blowing everywhere like some mad blizzard in a closet. He leaned in close to Sammy so they could hear each other. "We gotta keep movin'," Blaine said. "Best to put as much distance between us and them while we can."

"Yeah, they sure can't see us or track us in this. But they may not quit on it . . . not as close as they were. Might be best to get up along the wall of the canyon."

"You think? We can't ride over the top."

"I know it. But it's an easy slope up, and if we hug along the high line, there's likely better defense with rocks up there. We wanna be holdin' the high ground if the shootin' starts. They wouldn't be able to flank us or get behind us."

"Hell, we couldn't see *what* they was doin'."

"Then they can't see what we're doin', either. It should be only a few more miles till we're outta this canyon."

"Okay. Let's get movin'."

"We gotta stay close. We get separated, and we won't be able to find each other."

"I'm right behind you."

Sammy reined Dobe up slope and they started out at a brisk walk with Blaine and Seesaw just off the left flank. Still unable to see anything other than sheets of whizzing white flakes, they knew they were headed toward the wall of the rim. Up the easy slope they climbed, each man straining to see or hear anything beyond the storm's fury. Nothing else existed.

After several minutes, they came to a juncture where the terrain suddenly became very steep. "I think this is the base of the rim wall," Sammy said loudly enough to be heard over the wailing wind.

"All right, lead on. I got the rear."

Sammy reined Dobe to the left and headed north, keeping the canyon wall snug on his right as a guiding line. They rode on at the best pace they could keep while maintaining a heading along the rim wall, but it was slow. The blizzard was unrelenting, and the whiteout continued. Time piled up against a wall of will and reason, as both men grew colder and thoughts of pursuing Indians began to be displaced by their odds of survival if they remained in the open of the storm. They were quiet against the wailing storm, riding on stubbornly with both of them focused on the base wall, straining their eyes in search of something they could duck in or under for shelter.

"Them Indians gotta be worried 'bout their own scalps by now. They surely ain't givin' chase to us no more," Blaine yelled to Sammy.

"Yeah, we gotta get outta this weather. I've been looking for anything that'll do along here."

"Me too."

"Keep lookin."

"Yep."

Two pines standing next to each other emerged out of the whiteness like looming green detours, causing Sammy to veer right and pinching him between the trees and a granite wall that became visible only as he was quite suddenly brushing along it. Blaine followed Sammy's lead, and they rode directly beside the wall for a hundred feet or so until Sammy reined to a stop. "There's some kind of corner here!" He yelled. He eased Dobe around the fold of the wall and could make out another granite wall about twenty feet ahead. To his right was a corridor between the two walls. He eased into the corridor and then stopped suddenly, holding an open palm back toward Blaine, who was right behind him. Both men dismounted. Blaine took several steps forward before he saw the object of Sammy's attention.

The horse dung was fresh. An area where horses had been tied was unmistakable. Though mostly covered with snow, they could make out the indentations created by horse hooves.

"Them looks like unshod pony tracks," Blaine said.

"Yeah—and that looks to be a cave opening ahead."

"You thinkin' what I'm thinkin'?" Blaine asked.

"Yeah. It could be they never saw us. I saw 'em comin' at us and figured they had. But they might have just been crossin' the canyon there to get to this side. They may not know about us."

"They sure as hell will if stay here too long."

"Maybe we oughta fight 'em for it."

"For what?"

"The cave. . . . Might be better odds than headin' back into that storm."

"You been drinkin' that whiskey this morning?"

"I mean it. If they don't know how many of us there are, and we shoot at the first couple comin' in, the rest might just vamanos on outta here."

"Hell, we don't know there's not more of 'em in there right now," Blaine said, the incredulity thick in his voice.

"Hold the horses for a minute. I'll find out."

"We ain't got time for that!"

"We rode hard for quite a while. I'll bet we've got twenty minutes on 'em."

"I reckon you're bettin' our lives."

"We'll hitch 'em here and go look together."

"All right, goddammit! But let's hurry up!"

Chapter 32

S ammy and Blaine made their way silently down the corridor toward the cave opening with rifles ready and the sound of the storm retreating. The scent of wood smoke hit them as they drew closer, and then they saw the flickering of light against the inside of the cave wall. They flanked the opening, hugging each side as they cocked their heads around the edge to peer inside. A fire burned in the middle of the chamber with smoke rising some thirty feet to a small hole through which a hint of light appeared. Several torches fixed in wall crevices threw a dancing glow along the upper walls.

An Indian sat cross-legged near the fire, intently cutting a hide with his knife. He wore buckskin pants and moccasins, naked from the waist up except for a poultice on his side and necklaces of beads, game teeth, and bear claws. His long black hair was shoulder length, flowing from beneath a leather headband with carved symbols. He was a young man.

But all of that was lost as Sammy realized what he saw on the other side of the fire. Three women sat huddled together, their western dresses filthy and torn in places, and their hair matted and unkempt with dirt and debris. Each wore a pair of dirty socks, above which Sammy could clearly see ankle shackles. Their faces

were dirty, but there was no mistaking that they were white wom-
en. The oldest appeared to be in her early thirties, and the youngest was no more than sixteen. The other was about Sammy's age.

The hair on the back of Sammy's neck stood up. He could feel
his blood rising as a wave of anger rolled over him like the fires
of hell. Blaine looked at Sammy's face, seared in contempt, and
knew what was coming next. Sammy stepped into the opening of
the cave and swung his Henry 44 level at the Indian's head as he
cocked it. "Blaine—get our horses and bring 'em in here," Sammy said, walking toward the Indian who held his side gingerly as
he got to his feet.

The Indian held the knife low and did not assume a posture of
fighting or defense, understanding that to do so would be to die.
The white stranger had him cold.

"Drop the knife," Sammy said, motioning with his rifle barrel toward the floor.

"Mente hoh dae cuna," the Indian said with expressionless
eyes before he pitched the knife several feet. Sammy could see the
dried blood on his side that had soaked through and under the
poultice.

Blaine led the horses into the cave, their hooves clicking on
the intermittent patches of rock floor. "What are we doin' with
this injun?"

"Tie him up—hands and feet and arms and legs." Sammy held
the rifle on him while Blaine quickly roped the Indian into a co-
coon, then pushed him to the ground and dragged him to the sidewall where he rolled him face down.

The horses drifted to the back of the cave, where a brook could
be heard running. They began to drink. Several travois, an army
strongbox, and all manner of looted goods from ambushed wagons and travelers were strewn about the main chamber. There
were also two tunnels that led somewhere else.

Sammy knelt before the women and looked into the pleading eyes of the oldest, whose face bespoke her anguish. The other two were looking down in apparent fear. "Don't worry, we're

going to help you . . . get you back to your people. Are there any more of you?"

The other two looked up at Sammy with sudden hope, mixed with the present terror of their ordeal. "They killed her," the oldest one said as she began sobbing. "Her name was Sally Hemmings, and they cut her throat for trying to escape. They killed her in front of us. She was the only other one. Please help us! Please get us out of here!"

"We're gonna get you out of here." Sammy quickly examined their shackles. There was eight inches of chain connecting the two cuffs of each set. They were stamped U.S. Army. "Do you know where the key is for these?"

"He has it. I saw one of them give it to him before they left," said the oldest, nodding toward the Indian.

Blaine was to the Indian as soon as she'd finished her pronouncement. Rolling him over and pulling the key from his pocket, Blaine tossed it to Sammy, who began working at getting the women free. "I'm gonna see about these tunnels," Blaine said. "Whatever the plan's gonna be, we better get 'er figured 'cause they're comin' soon."

"That one on the right leads to a small room with no other exits from it," the oldest said. "I think the other one must lead outside. I've seen some come back in that way after leaving through this big entrance."

"How many Indians are there?" Sammy asked.

"Eight, including him. They all have guns and knives."

Blaine moved quickly toward the tunnel that the woman had said led outside. "I'll see where it ends up if, it ain't too long," He disappeared into the dark opening.

"I'm Sammy Winds, and my partner's name is Blaine Corker. I need you gals to do what we tell you when we tell you. You understand?" They nodded their heads in unison. "All right, I want you all to move into that room you just mentioned. Is there any light in there?"

"Yes, there's a lamp I can light . . . but why don't we just leave!?

There's more of them than you two. We'd be trapped in there!"

"Ma'am, there's a bad storm outside, and we don't have but two horses. You're just gonna have to trust me. Now let's get movin'."

Sammy helped each of them to their feet, then pulled a torch from the wall and led them through a short tunnel of just several paces to the smaller chamber. It was circular shaped and about fifteen feet in diameter. Buffalo hides covered most of the dirt floor, and assorted household goods were piled along the wall. The air was dank with a putrid aroma. He handed the torch to the youngest. "Hold this," he said. "Light that lamp. I'll be right back."

Sammy went back to the main chamber and dragged the Indian by his feet on his belly toward the other chamber. The Indian moaned lowly along the way as his poultice was rubbed off, re-opening his wound. When they reached the other chamber, the lamp was lit and the women stood in the middle of the room. Sammy pulled the Indian alongside the wall, then quickly rummaged through some of the looted goods. He found cloth and ripped off three long strips, wadding up the first and stuffing in the Indian's mouth. He wrapped the second strip over the Indian's mouth and tied a knot at the back of his head. Then he tied on the last strip as a blindfold. The Indian lay on his belly with his head turned sideways and his cheek on the dirt. He breathed hard through his nose, causing little dust clouds to rise in front of his face each time he exhaled.

Sammy removed the pistol from his left holster and handed it to the oldest. "Do you know how to use this?"

"Yes, I do," she said, then pulled back the hammer to the first click to check the action. She used both hands to let the hammer back to the non-cocked position as she pressured the trigger. "All the way back when I want to shoot," she said as a statement rather than a question.

"Yes ma'am. All the way back to the second click. You're gonna hear some shootin' out there soon. Just hold steady. If any Indians come through that door—anybody other than my partner or me—shoot 'em. And if this one gets outta line somehow, shoot him.

She looked over at the Indian. "He's the only one of them who hasn't assaulted us."

"Well, he'll likely kill you now if he gets the chance."

Sammy walked over to the wall and picked up a tea kettle-sized rock. "If he starts tryin' to make noise, one of you take this with both hands and hit him right on top of the head—hard!—until he stops. What's your names, ma'am?"

"I'm Emily Evans . . . and this is Margaret Lew and Claire Studdard." The two younger ones looked at Sammy, but did not speak.

Sammy nodded his head at each. "Emily. Margaret. Claire. We're in this together now, and we'll get out of it together. Stay strong and quiet. I'll see you all in a little bit."

And then he was gone.

Chapter 33

Ten Loco slid gracefully off his horse and tied it. The hunt
was successful, and he and his men were relieved to be out
of the brutal storm and back at the cave that had served
as their winter camp. Ten Loco and his men were all Chiricahua
Apache, who had left the tribe a year earlier. He had been named
Ten Buffalo for his hunting prowess, but was eventually dubbed
Ten Loco for a series of transgressions that led to his banishment
from the tribe. The other braves, each partially involved in Ten
Loco's crimes against Apache custom and etiquette, decided to
leave with him rather than face Apache justice.

With Ten Loco as their chief, the renegades had made their
living attacking and murdering anybody unfortunate enough to
be traveling as a small party. Their plunder, among other things,
had netted a decent stake worth of gold, which Ten Loco used to
trade for rifles, cartridges, and other goods from a corrupt army
provisions agent. His braves particularly liked the whiskey that
came with each transaction. Ten Loco always carried his gold
with him in palm-sized leather pouches that hung from the back
of his waist sash like so many counter balances.

The women of the cave had been plucked separately during
ambushes on single wagons and buckboards, shattering the lives

of folks who had been calling on neighbors or going to town for supplies. Claire Studdard saw her young husband shot dead off their buggy as they traveled to a neighbors cabin for Christmas day supper. When Claire arrived at the cave, Sally Hemmings had already been there a month. The others came soon after. When Ten Loco savagely cut Sally Hemmings' throat in front of the other women, he left her body at their feet for a day, and they were not allowed to move from it.

Ten Loco carried a rifle in his right hand as he moved toward the cave opening. The others were untying the two elk that had been butchered down to prime cuts and tied among six different horses. Ten Loco was almost to the entrance when he saw the partial hoof print in an area under the overhang where no snow had fallen. He stopped. It was the partial print of a shod horse. He looked closely at the area for any other tracks, but saw nothing. Then he noticed the unnatural pattern of dirt, and he knew what it meant. The area had been rubbed over to erase tracks.

Ten Loco slowly backed up to his men, his eyes warily scanning all around as he moved. With hand signals and gestures, he silently communicated the threat and directed three of his men to scout and enter the other cave entrance. Ten Loco and the remaining Apaches moved toward the main opening with two on each side.

At the cave's edge, he motioned for the others to stay concealed behind the outside corners, and then he dropped to his belly with his rifle and slithered forward to where he could see inside. The fire burned strongly with fresh fuel and the wall torches were in place, but no one was in sight. His eyes slowly surveyed the interior, which was some seventy-five feet deep and cast in darkness at the rear. He strained his eyes to see, but could not make out the back wall or the small alcove at the rear of the cave where the brook ran. A boulder inside the cave to his right could conceal one man at best. All else seemed normal, and the many contents of the cave appeared to be undisturbed.

Ten Loco trained his eyes on the other entrance and waited for his men to appear. It was halfway back on the left side and close to the passage where the women were hiding. He watched intently for several moments until his men materialized like ghosts at the edge of the tunnel. They were looking over at him. He gave several head nods signaling for two to break to the left and the third to go right. Then, like a spider that moves in any direction with equal grace, Ten Loco slid backwards out of the entrance and leapt to his feet. He and his men moved into final position. Hugging tight to each side of the opening, the Apaches slid around the corners and were quickly inside the cave.

Ten Loco did not like the dark veil at the back of the cave and swung his rifle toward it just as the deafening blast reverberated forth and the bullet took him through the front of the neck. The next bullet came an instant later and ripped into his chest and through his heart, exploding it to pieces. Ten Loco was dead before he hit the ground.

The muzzle blasts continued from the darkness like a lightening storm in the night, flashing a halo around Sammy with each shot and then returning him to blackness for the briefest respite as he levered his Henry 44 like a machine. Caught in the open, the other Apaches with Ten Loco swung their rifles wildly toward the phantom shooter of the darkness and fired hastily. They missed. Sammy killed two more before either got off a second shot. Fright overtook the other Apache who had been next to Ten Loco. He dove for the entrance and quickly crawled out of the cave and the line of fire.

Blaine Corker was thirty feet to Sammy's left behind the boulder that Ten Loco had wondered about. As soon as Sammy fired his first shot, Blaine levered his Winchester at the three Apaches at the other entrance directly across from him. He killed one with his first shot and hit another in the shoulder just as the Apache fired back and quickly backed into the tunnel from which they'd come. The third Apache darted into the passage leading to the women. A moment later, a shot echoed from the passage. Then another, and another. Sammy ran to the passage yelling before he entered, "It's Sammy Winds comin' in. Sammy Winds!"

Emily Evans held the pistol at the ready, but lowered it upon seeing Sammy. Her face was a mixture of rage and fear. The room was smoky and overwhelmed with the acrid smell of gunpowder. Sammy looked down at the dead Apache. He'd been shot three times: twice in the chest and once in the head. Sammy looked to the other Apache who'd been tied up. He'd been bludgeoned, and the pool of dark blood beneath his skull had mostly soaked into the dirt. He was dead.

"Hold tight. I'll be right back," Sammy said, and bolted from the chamber.

Blaine was checking the last of the Apaches when Sammy reappeared. "They all right?" Blaine asked.

"She put three holes in him, and they stoved in the tied up one's head."

"Good."

"These ones all dead?"

"Done for. My heart's poundin'."

"Yeah I know. Let's get after the two that's left. I don't wanna be worryin' about them.

"I hit the one 'fore he lit up this tunnel."

"The other ain't hit. He went right out the front. Hope he didn't scatter their horses—we need at least one more. How do you want to play it?"

"I'll take the tunnel. You take the front."

"All right. Fire your pistol twice or yell if you're up against it. I'll do the same."

Blaine headed slowly into the tunnel without a torch, deciding it would make him a clear target if the Indian were still about. Hugging tight to the wall with his cocked pistol out in front of him, he moved as quietly as possible, putting each foot down with great care to avoid crunching anything. It didn't seem possible that the Indian would still be in the tunnel, but he didn't want to die being wrong. Now in complete darkness, he moved slowly, knowing from his previous trip up the tunnel that a corner was coming up. It would be a likely place for a surprise. His heart pounded like a blacksmith's hammer rapidly hitting the anvil, so much so that Blaine worried the Indian could hear it if he were there. Inching along the wall, he felt for the corner, as sweat rolled down his forehead, and he wondered how that could happen in such cold. The corner was suddenly there beneath his hand. He readied himself for an encounter, straining with all his being to smell anything or hear anything other than the faintest sound of the storm. He snaked around the corner, and there was nothing.

Now he could see the dim light about thirty feet ahead of him where the tunnel turned to the last leg that eventually led outside. Blaine stepped forward with more confidence that the Indian was long gone. The silhouette suddenly appeared at the turn ahead. It took an instant to realize it was not Sammy. The flash from the muzzle accompanied the thunderous boom and was followed by the sound of a double ricochet. Blaine felt the searing pain in his thigh as he flattened against the wall and fired his pistol again and again. The silhouette jerked, but the muzzle flashes continued from the other end of the tunnel. Then he heard the more distant but unmistakable report of a Henry 44. The figure at the end of the tunnel was blown to the side and collapsed.

"It's me, Sammy! Don't shoot!"

"I hear ya! Come on in!"

Sammy made his way past the dead Apache and down the dark tunnel where he found Blaine holding his thigh. "You all right?"

"I'm shot in the leg. Damn ricochet got me. I think it's bleedin' bad."

"Let's get back in the cave. I can't see anything here. That other Apache got away. I don't think he's comin' back—knows it's only him left. He scattered all but two of the horses. I think they came back on their own."

Sammy helped Blaine down the tunnel and back into the cave, where he got him seated by the fire. He could see Blaine's pants were soaked with blood. "We're gonna have to tend that right now. Work at getting your britches off. I'm gonna bring those horses in." Sammy strode quickly to the chamber where the women were. "You can all come out now. My partner is injured. Shot in the leg. We need boiling water and clean cloth. I'm goin' outside to get some horses. I'll be back directly." He turned and disappeared.

Emily was overcome with a sense of hope and relief more powerful than any she'd felt in her life. "Oh girls! We're going to be saved!" They all looked at each other, tears instantly welling up like a dam held back by terror and fear for so long. Emily caught herself. "There are things to do. Margaret, you find suitable cloth for bandages. Claire, get a pot and collect some water. I'll set up the cooking rig." The women broke apart and hurried toward their tasks.

Sammy brought in the Apache's two ponies and tied them in the alcove at the rear near Dobe and Seesaw. Then he brought in some of the elk the Apaches had left behind and set it near the fire where water was heating and Emily was cleaning Blaine's jagged wound. Margaret and Claire watched. "This storm is a bad one. We're here for tonight and we'll ride in the morning," Sammy said. Then he moved around the cave and dragged each of the bodies outside, piling them together after taking several of the coats. He took Ten Loco's leather pouches of gold and stacked the Apaches rifles at the rear of the cave. Then he returned to the fire.

"The bullet is still in my leg," Blaine said. He had skivvies on and a blanket covering his lower half. He held a wad of cloth against the wound to stem the bleeding. Blaine was initially embarrassed about being pantless, but his modesty had given way to the gravity of the situation. Emily had helped him get his second boot off and then his pants.

"There's a sewing kit here," Emily said. "I'll see if I can get that closed up some."

Sammy examined the wound on the front of Blaine's left thigh. "Roll over. Let's see if we can find that bullet." Blaine rolled over and Sammy could see the purplish bruise on Blaine's hamstring where the bullet had stopped. "I can see where it is. Not too deep on this side, I don't think. Almost made it all the way through. It has to come outta there," Sammy said, pulling his knife and holding it in the fire.

"I'll get the sewing kit," Emily said.

"Claire, would you hold this in the fire some more. I need to get something," Sammy said.

"Get the damn whiskey! I reckon I'll need it," Blaine said.

"That's what I'm gettin'."

Sammy returned a moment later and handed the bottle to Blaine, who promptly took a big swallow. "Easy on that. I'm gonna need it to clean these wounds when I'm done carving on you."

"Carvin'! Hell, I ain't a damn turkey!"

"You won't be any more useful 'n one if we don't get this bullet out."

Blaine took another pull at the bottle. "Then get to carvin'!"

Sammy looked at the young girl. "Thank you, Margaret. I'll take that knife now. You girls hold his leg tight down there on his calf. Emily, you hold that lamp in close." He held the knife with its tip glowing red and poured a little whisky over it, then moved it to just above the area he intended to lance. Sammy took a slow, deep breath. "Okay, hoss . . . here we go."

Sammy pressed the knife tip up against the purple distended skin, taut as a swollen melon. He applied pressure and moved the knife slowly and evenly for several inches, the incision rolling open easily because of the swelling.

"Mmmmmmmmmmm!" Blaine trumpeted without opening his mouth—a bronchial roar that sounded like a strange melodic note, resonating a wall of will against the pain.

Sammy held the incision partially open with the knife's edge and saw the glint of metal deep in the meat. He used his left thumb and forefinger to spread open the incision as best he could and then cut directly around the metal, peeling back the tissue which quickly vanished beneath the pool of blood that filled the incision. Sammy put the knife down and reached in with his fingers, rooting around to get a grip on the bullet that had been transformed to a jagged shard.

"Ahhhhhhh!" Blaine yelled with as much restraint as he could manage.

Then, like a prospector who had seized the prize, Sammy held up the bloody metal trinket and showed it to Blaine. "That's sure enough a ricocheted bullet," Blaine said, looking relieved at having it out of his leg.

"Yep," Sammy said, and tossed it into the fire. "Here comes a little whiskey." Sammy poured the golden spirit into the gaping incision.

Blaine grunted. "Too bad that hole can't swallow."

Emily sewed up Blaine's leg and tied on bandages while Claire and Margaret cooked elk and made fry-bread and coffee. Sammy rummaged through some of the looted goods and found paperwork that he tucked away. Then he sat where he could see both entrances to the cave and studied his map, the thought of their circumstances upon him. He had an injured man and three women who needed to be returned to their families, if they still had any, or at least to civilization. He knew it was likely to be a tough conversation, but a plan could not be shaped until it occurred.

Blaine slept, and the rest of them took their meal around the fire when Sammy opened up the conversation. "Where are you women from?"

They all looked up at him, but it was Emily who spoke first. "I live outside the village of Abiquiu with my husband and two sons. But I don't know where that is from here or how far. They took me from my own yard when I was bringing in wood. My husband was out hunting that morning with our boy, Grayson. He's eight. Torbin, our five-year-old, was inside. They never went in, I don't think. They blindfolded me. It was January eleventh. We've all been here through the winter." She paused and looked at Sammy as if for help making some sense of it.

"Abiquiu's not too far from here—mostly east—maybe twenty, twenty-five miles," Sammy said.

"We rode many hours—close to a day, I think," Emily replied.

Claire suddenly spoke out. "They killed Jonas . . . my husband! There's no one else." She began to weep.

"She has family in Texas," Emily said. "Isn't that right, dear?" Emily grabbed Claire's hand and squeezed it.

"Yes . . . but . . ." Claire did not finish the sentence.

"She and her husband lived by Santa Fe," Emily said.

Sammy considered that. "These renegades covered some territory. That's two or three days from here." Sammy looked at Margaret. He thought for a moment about the resiliency of youth versus the ordeal she'd been through. "And you, Margaret. Where are you from?"

She looked at him with pause, as though gathering her thoughts from a place she cared not to delve. "We live in Cordova," she began. "I was on a stagecoach with my father on the way to Santa Fe. They killed him and the other men. My mother and brothers are still in Cordova . . . I hope."

"I'm sure they are," Sammy said confidently. "My partner and me were headed for Denver. But tomorrow we'll make for your place, Missus Evans. From there, we'll head for Santa Fe. We'll see that you get back to your family in Cordova." Then Sammy looked into Claire's eyes. "And ma'am, we'll get you to wherever you decide you want to go. I'm not sure about the timing of all this yet. My partner's lost a lot of blood . . . not sure how he'll do."

"You all can stay with us as long as you want," Emily said.

"Thank you, ma'am. I appreciate that. We'll see how it goes."

After they ate, Sammy built a fire next to the brook at the rear of the cave and strung up some hides as a curtain. The women were grateful, taking the opportunity to bathe the best they could. The two cowboys moved back to a position in the shadows, and Sammy took up watch while Blaine slept again in a sort of delirium. When Blaine awoke, Sammy served him up some elk and frybread with coffee. Blaine had struggled to get up, his leg swollen and stiff beyond use. "Stay put. I'll get you a plate."

"I gotta get up sometime to piss."

"Well, if it ain't right now, you might as well lie there and eat."

"Yeah, maybe I'll wait a little." Blaine felt a rush of dizziness and half fell, returning to a lying position. As he ate, Sammy told him about where the women were from and what he figured they needed to do. Blaine agreed. They talked about the weather and the terrain of the new routes and the way they'd mount up with four horses. Then they talked about a watch schedule for the night and about Blaine's leg.

"You'll need to see a doctor about your leg."

"I reckon. But I'll be all right for now. You just wake me after a spell. You're gonna need some sleep too."

"Yeah."

Chapter 34

The storm quit early in the evening like a vanishing act, leaving behind a still, cloudless sky of twinkling orbs looking freshly polished. Sammy let Blaine sleep most of the night, watching the restless nature of it brought by the pain. When Blaine did awaken from his diluted sleep, he quickly sat upright and grabbed his rifle. "Go on and get some sleep now," he said, half irritated. "You were supposed to wake me."

"You need the rest more than me. You bled out like a stuck hog . . . bound to be a little weak."

"Anymore of that coffee? That's all I need."

Sammy poured him a cup. "All right. I'll be up in an hour. If I'm not, wake me," Sammy said, and hunkered down.

Sleep came instantly to him, deep and dreamless like a necessity of exile. He awoke exactly an hour later feeling refreshed and anxious. He looked over at Blaine, who sat stoically pondering. "I'm goin' out and take a look around," Sammy said as he got to his feet and pulled on his coat and hat.

Blaine got raggedly to his feet. "I'll go with you." He limped badly for several steps, but then improved slightly as if learning how best to compensate for his condition.

The night was stark and crisp and all was quiet as they looked around the canyon blanketed with snow. An owl hooted. "It'll come light in another hour," Blaine said.

"Yeah. We need to ride out of here before then."

"I hope that red bastard ain't out there just waitin' to take a shot at us when we leave."

"I know."

The women were up, and eagerness permeated their demeanor and their every move. "We can make breakfast quickly," Emily said.

"We don't have time for that. We'll take some of that cooked elk with us and eat later," Sammy replied.

"What can we do?"

"Be ready to go in fifteen minutes. We're ridin' out of here while it's still dark . . . and we'll be movin'."

"We'll be ready."

Sammy and Blaine saddled their horses as the animals stamped and snorted. Sammy reached in his saddlebag, then came to Dobe's head and slipped his open palm with the biscuit on it under his horse's mouth. "You'll be eatin' more soon enough." He tossed a biscuit to Blaine.

"Is this for me or my horse?"

"I wouldn't give the horse a choice if you really want it."

Blaine shot him a straight look. "Yeah, you're probably right on that." He took half of the biscuit in one bite and fed the other half to Seesaw.

They rigged halters on the Apache horses and tied lead lines to each. Emily mounted double with Claire on the back, while Margaret sat on the other with Blaine taking her lead line. The women were bundled in buffalo hide coats and looked deadly serious about departing the place that had been their hell on earth. "All set?" Blaine asked. The women all nodded.

Sammy looked back at them. "Claire, you hold on tight to Emily. All of you lean forward and low the best you can. I don't believe that Indian is anywhere near, but we don't wanna give him too good a target if he is. If me or Blaine go down, you keep goin'.

These lead lines ain't tied. Now we ain't leavin' at a gallop, but we'll keep a fast trot or a canter goin' till we're clear of this canyon. Any questions? Ready?"

"I'm ready," Margaret said.

"Me too," Claire followed.

Emily looked from Blaine to Sammy. "I don't think any of us have ever been more ready in our lives," she said.

The horses crossed the cave at a walk and continued out the entrance, past the pile of Apache corpses and on down the outside corridor to the canyon. Sammy looked at Blaine and nodded the signal to go. Each gave the reins a light flick, and the horses came alive. All was visible as the last of the moon spilled across the snow like a canvas of incandescent light. The horses loped forward into the stillness, snow crunching beneath their hooves and their nostrils cycling the air as their muscles contracted and expanded in the lithe flexing that propelled them on seamlessly between the drifts of snow and through the trees.

The night was vacant, but the riders were weighted with unease that accumulated like the haunt of escaping an unending peril. They rode on, tense and anxious, hoping a shot would not ring out. Each minute that passed offered a greater chance, one way or the other. Finally, the dim light of approaching daybreak saw the canyon's mouth give way, flattening out as a grand exit onto upper plains that rolled wide open. They turned to the east and rode at a canter.

An hour later, the sun was up, warming their faces as they squinted against the intense glare. Sammy saw a stand of cottonwood trees. "Let's pull up over there for a minute. Give the ladies a break. I need to get a compass heading."

"Okay," Blaine agreed. He looked pale, and Sammy knew he was hurting. A herd of fifty elk trotted from the trees as they reined up. "Looks like we just ran 'em outta their hotel," Blaine said

"Storm's over. Checkout time," Sammy replied, glad to see that Blaine still had a sense of humor.

"They're beautiful," Claire said, as the herd trotted single file across the open expanse like a wagon train leaving Independence.

Sammy quickly dismounted and helped the women down. Blaine made a rough dismount and stood for a moment, waiting for the blood to return to his leg so that he could move on. Margaret whispered in Emily's ear and then all three women began making their way into the trees. "We'll be back in a minute," Emily said.

"All right," Sammy replied. He unstrapped his canteen and took a long drink, then walked out to where he had a full line of sight and pulled out his compass. Blaine hobbled out after him, smoking a cigarette. Sammy glanced at Blaine's pants. The bullet hole in the fabric was surrounded by stiff dried blood that appeared undisturbed. "How's your leg doin'?"

"Well it ain't bleedin', I don't think."

Sammy stepped around and looked at the backside of Blaine's pants where he'd cut the bullet out. There was a small bloodstain. "How's it look?" Blaine asked.

"Looks pretty good. I'd say that gal is quite the seamstress. Sewed you up good and tight."

"She tied them bandages on good and tight, that's for sure. I don't reckon any blood could get outta there if it wanted to."

"You need to get 'em loosened?"

"Naw. They's better off tight."

"We oughta be there in a couple more hours . . . Emily's place. Then I think you and me should head into Abiquiu for the night. It'll be a tender reunion. I don't wanna be a crowd."

"What about them other gals?"

"Well, they can stay with her or go with us. We'll ask 'em in just a minute. Tell 'em our plans. I gotta hunch Emily will insist they stay with her. She may insist we all stay, but I'm not stayin'. Too personal."

"Yeah, could be a mite uncomfortable. If that town don't have a hotel or a boarding house or something, we'll bunk for the stars."

"Yep. That may help Claire and Margaret make up their minds. I'm sure they've had enough of sleepin' on the ground if they can avoid it. I'm gonna stake 'em the gold I pulled off that Indian."

"Gold?"

"Yeah, maybe a thousand dollars or so. If you've got no objection, I'll give it all to them and they can split it up, or whatever."

"Hell no, I got no objection. Those gals been through it."

They stood in a circle with a half-foot of snow on the ground and ate biscuits and elk, and passed two canteens around. The sun grew warmer by the minute in the brilliant blue sky. "We'll be headin' in to Abiquiu for the night after we reach your place, ma'am," Sammy announced as they ate.

Emily frowned. "Oh no, you must stay with us."

"Thank you, ma'am . . . but no. We'll be back in the mornin'. Is there a hotel in town?"

She shook her head. "No, not a proper hotel. There's a saloon, Tomingo's, that has some rooms they rent."

"That'll be fine," Sammy replied.

Margaret and Claire looked at one another, suddenly unsure of the situation. Emily instantly sensed it. "We have the room— an extra bed. You girls will stay with me . . . please."

"That would be best," Sammy interjected.

"Thank you, Emily. We'd like that," Claire said.

"Good. It's settled then," Emily replied.

As they prepared to mount up, Margaret suddenly rushed to Blaine and hugged him tightly. "Thank you for saving us," she cried. Blaine stood surprised and uncertain with his arms out, but then brought them around her and patted her reassuringly, looking slightly uncomfortable. "I'm sorry about your leg," she said.

"It's all right. Don't you worry. I'm just real glad we happened on that cave."

Then she let go and ran to Sammy and hugged him.

As if taken by the moment and the need to acknowledge their saviors, Claire and Emily followed Margaret's lead and hugged Blaine, both at once. "We prayed for help," Emily whispered as Blaine held both women.

"Yes! We did!" Claire followed. "God sent you!"

"Uhh, I'm just a cowboy, ma'am. I reckon God woulda sent an army. We're sure glad we could help, though."

Then Emily and Claire went to Sammy and hugged him. "Thank you. Thank you," they said as they all held each other.

"Like Blaine said, we're happy we could help."

Chapter 35

The log cabin had a covered porch across the front with two rockers on it. There was a small barn adjacent with a chicken coop along the side and a corral in the back. The modest spread sat on a rise backed by elm and cottonwood trees and was fronted with an easy slope that gave view to the southwest across good grassland. A creek meandered close by. It hadn't snowed much there. Most of it had already melted as the temperature soared to nearly seventy degrees by eleven in the morning.

Grayson Evans had his little brother on his back, running around the front yard playing ride the wild stallion, when he noticed the riders. He stopped and looked for a moment, then ran up on the front porch with his little brother still aboard. "Paw, there's somebody coming!" He yelled in the front door in a strange, muted tone, brought on from being choked by his brother, who held on to the stallion for all he was worth. "Let go! You're chokin' me!" Grayson yelled hoarsely as he ripped at his little brother's throat grip and shook his body to get loose.

The boy slid off. "Sorry. I was gonna fall when you jumped on the porch."

Their father came out holding a Winchester at his side and looked appraisingly at the riders who were a quarter mile off, approaching from the west. He could see two women doubled up on one of the horses and one woman on another horse. Two men flanked the women. They were coming on at a walk when the horse mounted double began to trot. Then he heard it faintly. "Daniel! Daniel!" It was instantly familiar, but he wasn't sure if it could be real. He strained to sort out any imperfections in his hearing and thinking. Then it came again. "Daniel! Grayson! Torbin!"

The little boy stepped forward. "Mama?"

Daniel began running toward the approaching riders. His boys began running after him. "Emmy! Is that you? Is it really you?" He could see her red hair now, and she had put the horse to a gallop with Claire clutching onto her.

The distance quickly fell away. She reined the horse up next to where Daniel had stopped and dropped his rifle. She put her arms out and fell from the horse into his. "Daniel! Daniel!" She cried as they held each other and kissed every inch of each other's faces.

"Emmy! Oh Emmy! I thought I'd lost you."

The boys arrived and began hugging their mother, and she kissed them wildly. Then they all melted to the ground in a heap and held each other and kissed each other.

Chapter 36

Tomingo Saloon sat in the middle of the long row of adobe buildings that made up the one-sided street of Abiquiu. A fifty-foot oak tree grew directly in front of the saloon, throwing a shadow that slowly moved like an eclipse from building to building, one end of the street to the other, as the sun moved across the sky. Sammy and Blaine tied their horses to the hitching post and made for the archway entrance with Blaine moving in more of a hop than a walk.

The wall behind the bar had a long mural painting of vaqueros driving a herd of cattle. "Buenos tardes. Good afternoon," came the greeting from the short, portly Mexican bartender. He was middle aged with thinning hair and a well-manicured, waxed mustache that was twisted into points on each end. His white cotton shirt was collared, accented by an ivory bola shaped like a bull's head with inlaid turquoise eyes.

"Hello," Blaine said as he made his way to a table against the wall by the front window. He sat down and set his injured leg up on another chair.

Sammy walked to the bar. "Hola, señor. You have rooms for rent?"

The bartender slapped his hands on the bar. "I can do that, señor. One or two?"

"How much for each room?"

"One night?"

"Yes."

"One dollar each room. Is less if you stay longer."

"Just one night," Sammy said as he put the silver dollars on the bar.

"Hey there partner, I could use a little pain relief," Blaine said from the table. "How 'bout pickin' a bottle of somethin' good. I'll pay the man when he brings it."

"Mescal, señor? Is the best I have," the bartender replied to Blaine.

"I reckon you oughta know. Bring it on."

"I will bring it, señor. Go and sit," he said to Sammy.

Sammy walked over to the table and sat down. "Pain relief, huh?"

"Yeah, she's throbbin' pretty good. Plus, I could just use a drink. Gunnin' down half a tribe of Apaches in close quarters ain't exactly a everyday thing."

"No, it ain't."

The bartender came with a bottle and two glasses. "You want to eat?" he asked.

"Later. I wanna drink for now," Blaine said.

"Yeah, I'll wait for a while," Sammy followed.

The bartender looked at Blaine's leg. Blaine saw him looking. "Is there a laundry house here . . . wash my pants?"

"I can do that, señor. Wash and fix: one dollar. You want a bath?"

"A hot bath? Caliente?"

"Si, señor. Hot. Big tub. One dollar."

"Maybe later. I'll get you my pants in a minute. I gotta get my other pair to put on." Blaine poured two fingers worth in his glass and drained it.

"I didn't see a livery when we rode in. Is there one around?" Sammy asked.

"What do you want, señor?"

"I wanna get my horse fed, watered, brushed, and stabled for the night."

"I can do that, señor."

"One dollar?"

"Si . . . I have a barn around back. I am Enrique Tomingo. Anything you want, I can do that. Okay señors?"

"Alright, Enrique. I'm Blaine Corker and this here's Sammy Winds. You can take my horse, too, but I'll stow my own gear. Everything but my saddle will stay in my room with me. Okay?"

"Si, Señor Blaine. You want your things in your room now?"

Blaine looked surprised. "How's that gonna happen?"

"I can do that, señor."

"One dollar?"

"No charge, señor. But you can give the boys something if you want."

"They can get my gear too," Sammy chimed in. "You better get his stuff. He's not in the best of shape on his feet at the moment."

"Si, señor. Right away." Enrique turned and yelled at the doorway behind the bar. "Juan! Ernesto! Come here!"

Two boys about ten years old walked quickly from the doorway and came to attention before Enrique Tomingo. "Yes, Papa," one of them said.

"Go and get everything but the saddles off the two horses in front, and put it in rooms one and two. Now."

"Si, Papa." The boys wore harachi shoes with brown homespun pants and white blouses. They hurried out the front of the saloon. Sammy and Blaine watched through the window as the boys quickly and expertly removed the saddlebags and other gear from Dobe and Seesaw.

"Your sons?" Sammy asked.

"The taller one is my son. His friend Ernesto works for me on Saturdays. They are good boys, señor."

"Yeah, it is Saturday. I reckon I'd be drinkin' 'bout now anyways," Blaine said as he poured another one and threw it back.

"Yes, señors. The piano player will be here soon and many people will come tonight. There will be card games too, if you like." Blaine shifted his leg slightly on the chair and grimaced. "We do not have a regular doctor, Señor Blaine, but there is a old medicine woman I can get if you want for your leg. She is very good with dressings and healing paste. She knows all the plants and how to make the paste from them."

"Thanks, Enrique. My amigo here and a good woman did a nice job already. It's just sore is all. Could I see her in the morning if I wanted?

"Si . . . I think so. I will inquire of her."

"Okay. How much for the mescal?"

"One dollar."

Blaine put five dollars on the table. "Here's for the mescal and my pants and extry good care for our horses. You can give any leftover to your boy and the other young man."

"Gracias, Señor Blaine."

The boys came back in the saloon carrying the gear and walked through to a back hallway. Blaine gingerly pulled his leg down from the chair it was propped up on and stood up, pausing momentarily before beginning to hobble after the boys. "I better change these pants while I'm still sober enough to do it."

"Give a holler if you can't manage it," Sammy said.

"Oh I can manage 'er now. I got mescal management in charge," Blaine replied as he disappeared into the hallway.

Sammy poured himself a drink and took a sip. He knew from the bottle that it was homemade, but was surprised at the quality. Most of the homemade stuff he'd tried tasted more like turpentine or kerosene than alcohol, except for the whiskey that the Taylor brothers brewed at he Twin T. They knew how to make it right. He drank the rest in one swallow and felt the wave of warm calm descend on him. Sammy poured another and drank it, then another. The ordeal of the previous day kept entering his mind as something that needed to be recognized, and then released to burn in the fire of the spirit he now consumed.

He relaxed and looked around the saloon, taking it in and appreciating the atmosphere. An upright mahogany piano resided at the back near a pot-bellied stove, and a dozen tables with chairs filled sat on the multi-colored tile floor. The plaster walls were adorned with brightly colored serapes, spread and affixed at intervals. Three old men occupied a table at the other end of the room and were presently eating.

Blaine limped back into the room and over to the bar holding his wadded-up bloody pants and his right boot. "Here ya go, Enrique."

"They will be ready first thing in the morning, Señor Blaine." Enrique took Blaine's pants and disappeared into the room behind the bar.

Blaine made his way to the table and sat down breathing hard. "I couldn't get my damn boot back on. Leg's too swollen to bend enough. How 'bout a hand."

"I can do that, señor. One dollar," Sammy smiled, his eyes glazed and half open.

Blaine looked from Sammy to the bottle on the table, which held noticeably less than when he'd left. "Are ya sure?"

Sammy got up and grabbed the boot from Blaine who extended his leg up as Sammy pushed the boot on. "Forget the dollar— give me some makins," Sammy said.

"I'll go ya one better. I'll roll it for ya. You pour."

The men sat and drank and smoked and talked of all that had happened in such a short time. And they talked of the women and their tribulation and of the detour to Santa Fe and of what was ahead. They drank and smoked as the late afternoon faded into evening.

They didn't pay any mind to the medium-height thin man with the sombrero, who floated easily by them like a breeze toward the back of the saloon. Then the alluring melody of a Mexican folk tune lifted from the piano keys as his fingers danced with precision. Juan and Ernesto appeared from the back and lit wall lamps and two overhead chandeliers that had previously been wagon wheels, and people began to drift in.

Out of nowhere, she stood before them. Her thick, black hair was long and tumbled over her bare shoulders with the lustrous sheen of misted silk. Her skin was pure like almond ivory, and her large brown eyes peered at them from an angelic face with refined features. She wore a blouse and long skirt that fit loosely but could not hide the rare and sensuous figure that generated instant heat in men. She was beautiful and completely voluptuous. "Do you want to eat now?" she asked.

Sammy and Blaine both sat transfixed, staring at her with mouths slightly open as if observing one of the world's wonders. Her eyes widened and her eyebrows rose slightly, signaling that she was in search of an answer. Sammy regained some semblance of awareness and smiled as his head fell back a little. "Yes, ma'am. The mescal appears to be all gone, and I believe we're hungry. What do you have to eat?"

"Carnitas, beans, and tortillas. Very good."

"Yes, ma'am. We'll have it! And a pitcher of water too, por favor."

She smiled at them, then turned, and was gone. "Did I just see that?" Blaine asked. "Did I just see the most beautiful woman I ever seen . . . right here in whatever the hell the name of this town is?"

"Yep, you surely did."

They ate like drunk, ravenous men, each having a second plate. Soon after their meal, the mescal and fatigue took its toll. The evening was festive at Tomingo Saloon, with music and card games and dancing as the piano player played to a large crowd. But Sammy and Blaine were not there to see it. They had turned in and slept soundly through the noise of the night.

Chapter 37

After breakfast the next morning, Sammy bought two old saddles and tack from Enrique Tomingo for a small piece of Ten Loco's gold. The cowboys packed on their gear and the extra saddles, and were down the trail toward Emily and Daniel's place before eight. Smoke came from the chimney, rising against the blue sky of morning, as they reined up in front. "Hellooo the cabin," Blaine yelled as they prepared to dismount. The door opened and Emily and Daniel stepped out on the porch. Their boys came out just behind them and closely flanked their parents, the youngster's eyes wide with interest and curiosity about the cowboys' every move. "Good morning," Daniel said.

"Mornin'," came the almost simultaneous reply from Blaine and Sammy.

"Come in and have breakfast," Emily said.

"Thank you, ma'am, but we just ate. We're gonna saddle up those Indian ponies and we'll be in," Sammy replied.

"They're in the corral around back. I can help," Daniel said.

"No need."

"Can I show 'em, Paw?" Grayson eagerly asked.

"Me too!" His little brother pleaded instantly. Daniel looked at Sammy and Blaine, trying to detect whether or not they wanted the company, knowing that his boys would be full of talk and questions.

Sammy sensed it. "We'll take all the help we can get," he said.

Daniel looked down at his sons. "Okay boys, but don't be meddlesome, and stand clear of those horses while they're saddling them."

The boys jumped off the porch and stood in front of the cowboys, awaiting further instruction. "How is your leg this morning, Mister Corker?" Emily asked.

"About the same, ma'am. Not any worse I don't think. So that's good." Blaine's answer sounded more like a question.

"I can change those bandages for you," she said.

"Changed 'em out this mornin', ma'am. Poured some whiskey on too ta kill any germs. But thank you. I *would* favor a cup of coffee, though, if ya have any made."

"I do."

"Well, we'll be there in two shakes."

"Which way men?" Sammy asked of the boys.

"Follow me," Grayson said, and he began to march off toward the corral. He noticed his brother wasn't in proper formation. "Get in line!" he ordered.

Little Torbin quickly fell in behind his older brother and marched in-step as they had practiced many times before while playing soldier.

Sammy looked at Blaine. "Guess we better follow the general," Sammy said.

"I reckon so." They fell in line, leading their horses behind the boys with Blaine pulling up the rear at a limp.

After they finished, they went in and had coffee and visited for a while. Margaret and Claire were in good spirits, and their hair was freshly washed and combed. They wore clean dresses that Emily had given them. Emily made up a bag of food that had chicken and biscuits and oatmeal squares for their trip. "Here's some food to take with you. I hope it lasts you for awhile," she said

177

as she placed the canvas bag on the table.

"Thank you, ma'am. We'll be fine. We've each got a lot of jerky and hardtack. We even picked up some tortillas this morning," Sammy said.

"Sammy here's a pretty fair hand with his fishin' rig too," Blaine said. "And we'll sure enough see game."

Sammy reached into the pocket of his long coat and pulled out four small leather pouches and put them on the table. "I took this off one of those Indians . . . their leader I think. It's gold. We want you ladies to have it. I used a little to buy saddles for those ponies, but the rest is yours."

The women looked at one another, and there was momentary silence until Daniel spoke. "Emmy and I don't want it or need it. I have my wife back and our boys have their mother again. You give it to these gals here, Claire and Margaret. I'm beholding to you men for my wife's return. I can never repay you for what you've done."

"I didn't mean to give offense, sir," Sammy said, suddenly aware of the possible affront to Daniel's sense of honor and now feeling a little stupid for having broached the subject in this particular setting. "We just figured they should have it. But we'll give it all to Claire and Margaret if that's what you want."

"No offense taken," Daniel said. He extended his hand to shake Sammy's, then Blaine's. "Please, give it to them."

Claire suddenly felt very awkward, and Margaret looked anxious. "I don't want it," Claire said.

"Me neither," Margaret followed.

Sammy felt the dumb ass and was determined to extract himself from the situation as quickly as possible. "Let's figure this out latter on," he said, putting the pouches back in his coat. "We oughta get goin'."

"Yeah, we oughta," Blaine seconded.

Sammy and Blaine brought the ponies around front as Claire and Margaret said their goodbyes to Emily. The women cried as they hugged each other. They promised to write each other. Then Emily led them in one last prayer as a group, something they had done together many times during their months of captivity. The men respectfully stood back and watched the scene unfold, aware of the intense bond between the women.

The women held hands and prayed. They stood silently clutching each other, as if summoning strength from each other against the emotional scars that each knew would confront them in their lives ahead. Then Emily hugged Blaine. "I'll never forget you, Mister Corker . . . either of you. I wish you Godspeed. If you're ever this way again, you always have a place to stay."

"Thank you, ma'am. You take care."

Emily went to Sammy and led him away from the rest of the group as they said their goodbyes. She faced him, keeping her back to all so as not to be heard. She spoke softly. "I believe Claire is with child."

"Ma'am?"

"She's pregnant. So if anything should overtake her, you'll know why. She'll need that money. You make her take it."

"I'd already planned on it."

"She's got nobody else in Santa Fe—just her home. She said her folks in Texas disowned her when she ran off and got married. They didn't like the boy. She doesn't feel like she can ever go back—that she'd be shamed. Now with an Indian baby on the way . . ." Emily shook her head in worry and continued. "If Margaret's mother has moved on for some reason, you leave her with Claire. The place she lives, Cordova, is not too far from Santa Fe. She's only sixteen."

"We'll make sure she's in a safe circumstance before we move on."

"Thank you, Mister Winds." She hugged him. "God be with you and bless you."

"And you too, ma'am."

The cowboys helped Claire and Margaret get mounted up on

179

the Indian ponies, now replete with saddles and blankets and the buffalo coats tied on. They all waved as they rode out of the yard at a trot toward the southeast into a light breeze. The mid-morning sun was warm, and the pastel sky was swept with brush strokes of wispy clouds that hovered innocently and victoriously as witness to the glorious spring day.

The high plain was mostly flat, affording the chance to make good time on the fresh horses. They rode for several hours at a steady, easy lope, abreast of each other, the women in the middle with Blaine and Sammy on ends. Both the cowboys observed how well the women sat the saddles and held the reins. After a brief stop to eat and rest, they started out again at a walk. Claire asked Sammy, "Would you be riding faster if we weren't with you? You're not taking it easy on our account, are you?"

"Well . . . no."

Claire turned her head and looked at Margaret, who was keenly interested in Claire's comment. "Come on, Margaret. Let's see what they've got!" Claire kicked her heels to the horse and leaned forward as the animal leapt to a full gallop. Margaret instantly followed Claire's lead, and the soft sod flew as the Apache ponies galloped with all they had.

Blaine looked over at Sammy, noting the vacant space between them. "I reckon they wanted some wind in their face."

"Yeah, well no doubt they need it."

"Should we give chase?"

"Nah, let 'em run. We'll keep 'em in sight. Sure looks like they can ride."

"I know. They look like they're goin' to a land grab."

Run they did. The feeling for each of the women was exhilarating and liberating, as if an act of purging the horror of the cave. They raced on, with the only sound being the steady drumbeat of hooves rumbling over the ground in a concussive drone as the air rushed by and the expanse of the moving plain melted into a massage of the soul. Claire and Margaret were both smiling.

"They ain't gonna be in sight much longer," Blaine said several minutes later.

"Yeah, they're getting small quick. Those ponies have some stay. We better get."

Dobe and Seesaw received their master's commands and took off in a full gallop.

The cowboys' horses ran with the spirit of chase, knowing instinctively they were after the ponies that had a head start, but running as if they were only yards behind rather than facing an insurmountable lead. On they galloped, with the specks they were chasing growing no larger after a long run. "They can't keep that pace goin'!" Blaine yelled.

"Neither can we! They're carryin' less weight!"

They kept their horses running full out for another half mile, then finally backed off to a lope again. "I'm not runnin' my horse lame tryin' to catch 'em," Sammy said.

"Yeah, I guess we'll catch up when they want us to."

After two more miles, they caught up to the women, who had their horses at a walk. "I reckon you'll be able to outrun anything that's chasing ya," Blaine said as they pulled up alongside.

"Aren't they wonderful! They can really run!" Margaret exclaimed with an exuberant smile.

Claire looked happy too. "That was grand!" she said.

"They're good horses. They're yours now," Sammy said.

Margaret leaned forward and rubbed her horse's lathered neck. "I'll call him 'Windchaser.'"

"I think he done caught it," Blaine smiled.

Margaret laughed. "How much more will we ride today?" she asked.

Blaine looked at the sun. "It's gettin' on now."

Sammy glanced up. "Yeah. It looks like another two hours across this plain to that forest ahead. We'll camp there if you gals have some travelin' left in you."

"Don't worry about us," Claire replied.

"Easier said than done, ma'am," Blaine mused.

Chapter 38

They made their camp in a clearing of trees with an hour of daylight left. The temperature was mild, and Blaine collected fuel and made a fire while Sammy stripped and hobbled the horses. The women laid out bedding and prepared coffee and the meal. They sat on the ground around the fire and took their supper, eating off tin plates and drinking coffee from tin cups. Blaine also drank from his new second canteen, filled with two bottles worth of mescal from Enrique Tomingo. He asked Sammy if he wanted some, but Sammy declined, saying that the previous night's bottle still had him feeling "fogged."

"I need the fog. The day's ride got this throbbin' somethin' good," Blaine said, feeling the relief as he ate and alternated sipping coffee from his cup and mescal from his canteen.

"Anybody else want some mescal?" Blaine asked, his leg feeling better from the medicinal effects and his current position on the ground.

Claire looked up from her plate. "I think I would like to try some, Mister Corker."

"Would you please call me Blaine, ma'am. I reckon we've been through enough together."

"All right, Blaine, but you must call me Claire."

"Well all right, Claire. Give some a this a whirl," he said, and passed the canteen to Margaret to pass on. "Can I call you Margaret?"

"If I can call you Blaine."

"You better."

"Call me Sammy," Sammy offered. "In fact, let's just agree we're all on a first name basis."

"Yes let's," Claire said, as she poured some of the mescal into her cup."

"Okay, Sammy and Blaine," Margaret said.

"Goooooooood," Blaine said. He pulled out the makings and began to roll a smoke.

Margaret decided to ask. "Can I have a little bit of the mescal, Blaine? Not very much. I'd like to try it."

"Sure you can. But careful, it's potent."

She poured a little in her cup as Claire had done and handed the canteen back to Blaine. "Thank you, Blaine."

"Right in with the coffee, huh? Well, let's see how that does," Blaine said, as he poured some into his own coffee.

Margaret and Claire took their first sip cautiously. "Oh . . . it made the coffee better," Claire said.

"I think it's making his leg feel better too," Margaret said.

Sammy smiled. "It's making him feel better, and his leg's goin' right along with it."

They drank their spiked coffee and Sammy had his regular. Claire asked about where Sammy and Blaine were from, and the cowboys told the women all about the Twin T. and Homer and Reuben and the hands and Jacqueline and Lucilla and Raquel. The young women sat mesmerized, listening and asking occasional questions about something, but mostly just reveling in hearing about normal life and people.

The conversation played on for a while, and then during a pause Claire grew thoughtful for a moment and changed the subject. "How were you able to kill all those Indians? There was only the two of you."

Sammy glanced over at Blaine, who suddenly looked a little more alert. "We opened up on 'em. Surprised 'em," Sammy said.

"This man right here can shoot," Blaine said, motioning toward Sammy.

"We can both shoot. Lucky in our shootin' too. It just worked out for us. One of 'em got away. You gals took care of those other two."

Claire had a look of recollection on her face. "Emily shot the one who came in. She was off to the side in the shadows. He never saw her because he was looking at us. She didn't hesitate for a second."

Then Margaret spoke. "I hit the other one in the head with the rock—a couple of times. He was there when they killed my father and the other men. He was part of it. They ambushed us. My father was still able to kill one of them before he died. I'm not sorry I killed him. I hope God forgives me."

"It's them that needs forgivin', but first they needed killin'. You done the right thing," Blaine said.

"That's right," Sammy agreed. "Don't you let that prey on you. They killed a lot of innocent people, and would have kept at it. You saved somebody's life—somebody who would have been innocent. You were brave to do what you did. Now it's time to get on with livin'. That's what your father would have wanted. That's what you'll do."

The morning ride was slow going through mostly forest with occasional stretches of open meadow. They saw deer and elk and several different bears that paid them no particular attention other than passing glances. In the early afternoon, they came across a trail that was well worn by horses and wagons. It looked to Sammy to be heading in the general direction of Española. He hoped they'd make it by sundown. They turned onto the trail and alternated between a lope and a trot.

It wasn't far down the trail before Blaine took a turn for the worse. He continually shifted in the saddle in search of a position that would yield relief to his leg. He grabbed his mescal canteen and took a long pull, then slumped for a bit before hitting the canteen again. Sammy pulled up alongside him and could see the sweat on Blaine's pale face. His eyes were glassy and bloodshot. Sammy suspected Blaine was feverish, which meant infection was setting in. "How you doin?" Sammy asked. "You wanna rest for a while?"

"Damn leg feels worse today than ever. But let's keep goin'. If I fall out of the saddle, then I guess we better stop for a rest. How much farther ya figure?"

"Couple more hours. If you wanna stop before then, let me know."

"Okay."

"You look to be runnin' a fever. Might wanna take it easy on the mescal."

"Ah, bullshit! It's keepin' me goin'."

"All right, hoss."

Sammy dropped back by the women, who had been watching Blaine's erratic posture in the saddle. "He's not well," Claire said.

"No, he's not. I need to get him to a doctor as soon as I can. He looks to have a fever. I think his leg is infected."

"Maybe we should stop and let him rest," Margaret said.

"Yeah, he needs it. But the more we stop, the longer he goes without proper attention. We'll ride until he says he needs to rest. We should make Española in a couple more hours. Maybe they have a doctor there."

"I know Española," Claire said. "There might be a doctor. But if not, it's only several hours farther on to Santa Fe, and I know a good doctor there."

They kept up a good pace as the afternoon wandered on. Sammy took frequent compass headings and was certain of the trail's destination. He also watched Blaine and worried over his friend's condition. Blaine drank water, but continued to work at the mescal to fight the pain. He was finally overcome with nausea and delusion, vomiting just before toppling from his horse in a slow motion roll. On the way down, he pawed at his saddle and the horse's neck, attempting to slow his descent toward the ground. He landed on his back with a thud. The sky above spun in a sickening whirl, and he turned his head to the side and vomited again. Then he blacked out.

The Evening Star glistened in singular solitude against the dark blue sky of twilight. Blaine focused on it as his eyes slowly opened. He felt the cool of the wet cloth on his forehead and became aware of his surroundings. His head was cradled in Claire's lap as she sat propped against a cottonwood tree holding the cool compress on him. His pants lay beside him. A blanket covered him from the chest down. Margaret was cooking meat over a nearby fire. He looked up at Claire, whose face was silhouetted by early evening. Her long hair hung down near his face and moved gently with the easy wind. He thought for a moment he was being held by an angel. She was looking down at him and reached for the canteen next to her when she saw he was awake. "Here, you must drink some water," she said, holding the canteen to his lips and gently tilting it to deliver the cool liquid to him. His thirst overwhelmed him at the first sip, and he brought both hands up from his side to take control of the canteen, gulping several mouthfuls, then pausing to get his breath and drinking more. He finally stopped and looked at her, wondering how he came to be resting his head on her.

His voice was raspy and not much above a whisper. "What happened?"

Claire moved the cool compress around his face as she spoke. "You passed out. You have a fever, and I dare say it didn't mix well with the mescal. There is some infection in your leg, but I don't think it's too bad yet. We cleaned it, and Margaret made a poultice that's wrapped on. It should help."

"Margaret made a poultice?"

"Yes. Sammy told her what to do. She boiled some yucca plant with elm bark and charcoal and flour."

"Ain't he just a bag of know-how. I'll tell ya, that boy's smart. How long have I been out, anyway?"

"Three or four hours. Are you hungry? Sammy shot a turkey, and Margaret is cooking it right now."

"No. I don't reckon I could eat."

"That's the fever," she said.

Sammy appeared from the trees with both arms so full of wood that it nearly covered his face. He walked cautiously toward the fire peeking around the side of his balancing burden. When he got near enough for comfort, he pitched the load forward and it crashed to the dirt with prolonged rumbling as each piece wrestled in the clump for its ending position. "That oughta do for the rest of tonight and the morning," he announced with the tone of certain calculation.

"I think the bird is close to done," Margaret said.

"All right, Margaret. Let's see how our patient is doin', and then we'll get to supper."

"Good . . . I'm hungry," she said. "It sure smells fine."

"Well, that's cause you've done such a fine job cookin' it. Just like you did makin' up that poultice."

She smiled at Sammy and he could see the joy the young girl took in the simplest of compliments.

Sammy walked over to the tree and looked down at Blaine, who had a blank stare. "Hey, amigo. Feelin' alive?"

"That's about all. But I sure am a lucky one for the care I been gettin'."

"That's a fact. We'll see about a doctor in Española in the morning. If they don't have one, we'll make a run for Santa Fe. Should make it by the noon or so. Get you to the doctor as soon as we can."

"I'll be ready to ride," Blaine said without hesitation.

Sammy and Claire and Margaret ate a supper of perfectly roasted, succulent turkey with biscuits, while Blaine continued to sleep. Claire took him a small plate later and woke him, imploring him to eat to keep up his strength. He wasn't hungry at all, but ate a little bit anyway to make Claire happy. He vomited a few minutes later. Claire felt badly about it, and took up her position against the tree with Blaine's head in her lap. She continued to administer the cool compress against the fever that would not yield. Later in the evening, she asked Margaret to bring her a blanket. She spent the rest of the night talking to him, cooling him, singing to him, waking him to drink more water, and sleeping for periods herself.

Chapter 39

Blaine opened his eyes and listened to an owl hoot as the night sky began to give way to the morning light. He smelled the coffee and lifted his head to look at the fire.

Sammy was sitting by it, drinking his first cup. He looked at Blaine when he saw the cowboy's head come up, nodding to him, but saying nothing. Margaret was sleeping near the fire, and Claire had rolled from sleeping in a sitting position against the tree to being curled up on the ground just above Blaine's head.

Blaine moved quietly and grabbed his pants, then worked at getting them on. Sammy watched the ordeal and thought it looked something like a man trying to stuff himself into a potato sack. A minute later and out of breath, Blaine completed the maneuver and pushed himself to his feet using his arms and one leg, while his injured leg stuck out to the side like an errant rowboat oar. He limped off into the dark to relieve himself. A moment later, he returned and retrieved his boots.

Blaine limped over to the fire where he dropped his boots and fell forward, landing on his hands and then flipping to a sitting position in a rather acrobatic move. He was able to get both his boots on with no assistance. Sammy took the whole episode as a sign of improvement. He poured Blaine a cup of coffee, and the two men sat quietly by the fire as daylight crept upon them.

The women were up soon after. Claire came over to Blaine and felt his forehead and face. His fever was still present, but she thought it seemed a bit better than the night before. "I'm all right, Claire," Blaine reassured. "Thanks for looking after me, and thanks for the poultice, Margaret. It must be helping 'cause my leg feels better."

"Really? It really does?" Margaret asked.

"Yes, ma'am. I'm ready to ride today."

Two hours later, they rode down the main street of Española, made up mostly of mud huts. "Hold up here for a minute." Sammy stopped them in front of a small frame building with pine siding and white painted letters: GOODS. "I'll be right back." He jumped down from Dobe and tied him to the hitching post.

"You want us to just sit here in the street?" Blaine asked.

"You can all get down if you want. I was just gonna check to see if there's a doctor in this town. Won't be but a second, and I didn't figure you were partial to using that leg if you didn't have to."

"I see your point. I'll be waitin' here."

"We'll wait with Blaine," Claire said, sensing Sammy's desire to be fast.

Sammy returned quickly. "The doctor comes once a week from Santa Fe—on Fridays."

"Well, I reckon we better get on to Santa Fe then 'cause this don't look quite lively enough to wait for a couple of days."

"It's only a few hours more," Claire added.

"Do you ladies need to stop for a break?" Blaine asked.

"I don't," Margaret said.

"No, let's keep going," Claire said. "We're so close now."

"Onward, Mister Winds," Blaine declared in a tumbling phrase.

Sammy looked appraisingly at Blaine, knowing he was hurting and ever so nimbly delusional. His fever looked to have picked up some. He knew he could get worse fast, or maybe he would hold on and make the ride easily. "Let's make dust. The trail we want is out the east end," Sammy said, putting Dobe to a trot.

As they cleared town and came upon the trail, Blaine undid one of his canteens. Claire feared he might be getting ready to have a go at the mescal again, but then the pale cowboy pulled his hat off and proceeded to pour water all over his head. It ran down his face and over his ears, soaking the top of his shirt from front to back. He took a deep breath and shook his head to clear the excess. His dark brown hair was matted slick and sheen. Smiling, he put his hat back on and re-hung the nearly empty canteen. "Now that I'm wet, I reckon I'll make a little breeze for myself. Get up, Seesaw!" His horse jumped to a gallop along the flat, straight trail.

"It appears he'd like to get there sooner rather than later," Sammy casually remarked.

"Me too!" Margaret said. "C'mon, Windchaser!" She put her heels to the horse and was gone in a burst.

Sammy looked over at Claire, who was still in a trot beside him. She looked knowingly back at him. "Ladies first," he said. She smiled, and then put her horse to a run. Sammy continued on at a trot, watching the parade of horses galloping ahead, throwing up a dust trail that mixed with the scent of pine and wildflowers. Dobe snorted and twitched. "You tryin' to tell me we oughta get on after 'em? Heaaaaaw!"

The Plaza was sodden with late morning sun that warmed the many adobe walls. Santa Fe sat at an elevation of seven thousand feet and had a population of some three thousand. Wagons, horses, and buggies were thick on the main avenue, and the boardwalk bustled with people, some moving with the pace of commerce while others strolled in the melody of looking. The young crop of alfalfa grew on the Plaza Square, presenting a lush foreground and vibrant contrast to the textured brown adobe of the Palace of the Governors and San Miguel Mission. A cathedral with Corinthian columns of Roman architectural influence was being constructed and looked oddly singular in style to the other buildings. Alongside the construction site, several dozen men worked in a large mud pit for making the adobe. Vendors lined the square with their carts and wagons selling jewelry and artwork and pottery and baskets and weavings and hats and clothing and foodstuffs and leather goods and potions and perfumes. The people on the Plaza were mostly Spanish and Mexican, but there were also Anglos and some Indians and Asians.

A stagecoach stopped at a corner of the Plaza. The weary-looking occupants climbed stiffly out into the bright sunshine. One of the travelers, an older woman, began to beat the dust from her dress, but stopped and looked with fascination and slight disdain at Margaret and Claire, riding western style in dresses.

Sammy was behind them, alongside Blaine, now slumped in the saddle as if he might fall any second. Blaine had displayed stoical grit and determination on the ride from Española, but now he was played out. His fever was well up and the pain was unrelenting. He'd stayed away from the mescal, knowing he'd never make it if he began drinking. But he hadn't held off the delirium. He'd seen the Indian from the tunnel flying around in the treetops, and engaged in rambling conversation with his long deceased grandmother and several of his boyhood friends during the last half hour before hitting town.

"It's right up here," Claire said over her shoulder as she reined up in front of the Exchange Hotel. The sign on the low one-story adobe building next to the hotel simply said: MEDICA. Sammy pulled up, jumped off Dobe, and helped Margaret and Claire dismount. He turned to give Blaine a hand, but the cowboy was already dismounting and was halfway off when he blacked out and fell to the ground.

Several people stopped and looked, some just thinking it was a drunken cowboy.

"You gals tie the horses off," Sammy said as he quickly moved over to where Blaine lay in the street. Blaine's eyes opened as slits squinting against the sun. He began to try and sit up. Sammy kneeled down and got his arms around Blaine's upper torso, lifting hard to help his friend to his feet. "Come on, hoss. Let's go see the doctor."

"That horse can't dance proper," Blaine slurred.

"You can teach him later," Sammy replied. He pulled Blaine's arm around his neck and began to walk him toward the building. "Lead the way, Claire." Sammy half-dragged Blaine along. Margaret hurried to Blaine's other side and took his free arm, doing the best she could to help.

Two old Mexican women were sitting in the outer office when Claire opened the door. Sammy, Blaine, and Margaret followed her inside. The old women glanced at Blaine then looked away. He was pale with chalky lips. Beads of perspiration ran down and around his hollow, red-glazed eyes. His blue cotton shirt was dirty and clung to his shoulders and chest, soaked with sweat.

There was no one at the reception desk. Claire was just about to knock at the door when it opened and Dorian O'Malley emerged with his assistant and a patient. He was dispensing some final words to his patient in a heavy, Irish accent when he caught sight of Claire. He stopped cold. "Missus Studdard?" he asked, shocked.

"Yes, Doctor O'Malley. . . . It's me."

"My dear! You're back. No one knew what happened. Your husband . . . Robert . . ."

"Yes, I know, Doctor. I was there when he was murdered. They took me, and these men saved us a few days ago." Dorian O'Malley looked over his spectacles in a state of bewilderment at Blaine and Sammy and then to Margaret. Claire wasted no more time. "This man is injured and sick. He needs your help immediately."

"Yes . . . of course, of course." The doctor looked at the old women who had been waiting. "Un pocos minutos, por favor."

"Si. Si," they both said, apparently understanding the urgency of the situation and waving the backs of their hands as if to say don't waste time standing out here.

"Muchas gracias," Blaine said to the old women in a slow, slurred drawl.

"Si, gracias," Sammy added while dragging Blaine through the door to the examination room.

"He's got a bullet wound in his left thigh, Doctor," Sammy said as they helped Blaine get situated on the examination table. "It didn't go all the way through, but I was able to get it out from the backside. It looks to be infected where the bullet entered. I don't think it is on the backside where I cut it out."

"I see. Well, he's very feverish, so I would say infection is a certainty."

Blaine's head rocked to the side and he opened his eyes. "I reckon this pain is a certainty. You got anything for it, Doc?"

"Yes lad, I do. Alice would you bring me the laudanum?" Doctor O'Malley turned to Claire and Sammy and Margaret. "Why don't you folks come back later on. We've got several beds in the back for patients, and unless there's some dire emergency, I think your friend shouldn't move any farther than one of those beds. I'll know more in a bit. The hotel next door is the best in Santa Fe if you need accommodations."

"Yes, I know that doctor," Claire said with surprise.

"Well, I didn't know if you had been by your home yet."

"No, not yet. We came straight here. What do you mean?"

Doctor O'Malley looked a little uncomfortable. "I think someone is living there."

Chapter 40

Outside in the street, Sammy could see Claire was shaken at the news of her home. "We'll get this straightened out about your house, Claire. We'll go first thing in the mornin'. But for now, let's check into this hotel, get cleaned up, and see about Blaine."

"They can't do that—just move into my house!" Claire said, her confusion suddenly turning to anger.

"They sure as hell can't!" Margaret followed. "That's just not right!"

"We bought that land, and Robert built that house! It's ours! It's mine!"

"Yes it is," Sammy said, gently putting his hands on Claire's shoulders to calm her. He looked in her eyes. "I'm telling you not to worry. You understand? It's going to be all right. Now here, you take this. And Margaret, you take this." Sammy gave them each a pouch of gold coins. "I'll give you the rest later. Keep it where you know it's safe. Don't tell me you don't want it. You're takin' it, and I don't wanna hear anymore about it. Now go and check in and have a bath and something to eat. And go buy whatever you need. I'm taking the horses to the livery and I need to do a few things. I'll catch up with you later. If you go out, stay together."

"All right," Claire said, feeling more composed.

Sammy walked the horses down to the livery stable and then found his way to the post office. He wrote two letters, one to Homer and Reuben, and the other to Jenny. He wrote about what had happened and that he wasn't sure how long he'd be delayed, but he'd get word to them of his progress. Then he went back to the doctor's office.

The two old women were gone, replaced by a young mother and her child in the waiting room. The doctor's assistant, Alice, was not at the reception desk. Sammy knocked at the door and a moment later Alice opened it. "Can I come in and see my friend?"

"Just a moment." The door opened a few seconds later. "You can go in," she said as she returned to the reception desk.

"Thank you, ma'am."

Blaine was laid out on the table in his shirt and skivvies asleep. Doctor O'Malley was finishing bandaging Blaine's leg. "How's he doin'?" Sammy asked.

"Time will tell. The front wound is infected, but the poultice helped keep it from spreading . . . for now. Did you do that?"

"N○, the young girl did."

"She did a good job. It was effective. There were a few bullet fragments left in the front side, but I think I've removed all of them."

"Damn. I should have looked better in the first place. It was a ricocheted bullet."

"You did remarkably well. The spot where you cut in appears to be doing all right, so I'm quite sure you got all that was there. Now we wait. If the infection worsens, he could develop gangrene—then he'll lose that leg. Or, it could kill him. I had to take some tissue out of that front wound, so there was no sewing it up. I've packed it. He has to stay in bed and keep completely off of it for several weeks at the least. We'll know which way this is headed in the next day or two. Help me carry him to the bed in the next room."

"Sure doctor. By the way, I'm Sammy Winds and your patient is Blaine Corker."

"Pleased to make your acquaintance. I'm Dorian O'Malley."

The two men shook hands and then carried Blaine to a bed. Sammy saw the bedpan on the floor and was reminded of his own feeble condition just six months earlier. He wanted to change his thinking quickly.

"Have you ever met Homer or Reuben Taylor? They own the Twin T. Ranch west of here. Irish brothers . . . came to America when they were boys."

"No, I've not had the pleasure. But I believe I've heard of the Twin T. Are you acquainted?

"I work for them. So does Blaine . . . or he did."

"How is it you came to the aid of Missus Studdard and the other girl? Did Indians take them?"

Sammy paused for a moment. "Well, Doctor, no offense, but I'll let Missus Studdard tell that story if she cares to."

The doctor tipped his head down just a bit and looked at Sammy over the top of his spectacles, appreciative of the young man's discretion. "Of course. Forgive the question."

Sammy looked down at Blaine who was out like a light. "He's sleepin' like a log."

"It's the laudanum. It kills the pain and will make him sleep, which he needs."

"I'm glad of it. What about at night?"

"Missus Martinez lives in the back. She'll be looking in on him."

"Much obliged." Sammy dug out some money and held out ten dollars to Dorian. "Will this cover for now?"

"Yes, that's more than enough."

"I'll settle up with you when this is played out, if that's all right."

"That will be fine."

"Can you tell me where Claire's house is?"

"Oh, why yes. It's certainly distinct compared to the adobe

houses. It's just out the north trail. You follow this avenue east and turn at Rosario's Wagon and Repair, then on out of town about a mile. It's the white house with green trim to the east of the trail. It's a beautiful place. Robert was a carpenter."

"Thanks, Doc. Say, do you happen to know a man named Willis Burk?"

"I don't know him, but I know of him."

"Do you know if he's still around?"

"As far as I know."

It was late afternoon when Sammy rode out the north trail to Claire's house. After a visit to the courthouse, he was certain of the law on claiming abandoned property. No one had filed a petition to claim the house as an abandoned property, and no one could without evidence that it had been abandoned for at least six months. There was a recorded deed for the land with no liens or mortgages. Sammy figured it was probably somebody from the area trying to be opportunistic.

It sat back off the trail about a quarter mile, facing southwest on good grassy ground. It was frame construction with lap siding and a steep roof with two dormer windows, indicating an attic or loft or second story. The house was nicely painted and had a covered porch that ran the width of the front, providing shade for two large front windows. Tall ponderosa pine and blue spruce grew to the sides and rear of the house at a distance that provided an acre of open yard. A two-story barn and other outbuildings had the same lap siding with white and green paint. The whole spread gave the appearance of a small estate. There was neither visible livestock nor horses, but smoke trailed from the red brick chimney that stretched skyward on one end of the house.

Sammy reined up in front and dismounted, tying Dobe to a hitching post in the yard. He wore his gun-belt with both pistols.

"Hellooooo the house," he yelled, loud enough to be heard without sounding as if he were shouting orders. All was still. He remained in the yard, looking at the front windows for any sign of movement within. There was nothing. "Hellooooo the house," he yelled again, this time a little louder. Again, there was no response. He waited another half minute, then walked up on the porch and rapped on the door. "Helloooo," he yelled as loud as he could, not caring what he sounded like now. Sammy heard movement inside and several voices, but he could not tell what was being said. He rapped once again, and finally heard boots on a hardwood floor approaching the front.

The door opened. A white man about forty years old, with thinning hair and bad teeth, looked at Sammy as though he'd been rudely disturbed from some favorite pastime.

"Yeah, what do you want?" It was more of an accusation than a question.

Sammy could see from the man's expression and tone that he was probably going to be a hard case about it. He decided any politeness would be a waste of time. "Since you put it that way, mister, I want you and whoever else is in this house out of here in the morning. And you'll be takin' only what you came with." Sammy had his right hand resting on the butt of his gun and casually eyed both windows. A woman and three boys and two girls were peering out at him.

"Who are you?" the man asked.

"I represent the owner of this property, who is presently in town and will be here in the morning to take possession of her home. Look mister, you and I both know this isn't your place and you don't belong here."

The man looked unsure. He rubbed the stubble on his chin as if it were helping him to see the clarity of the issue. "We came by here a while back . . . on the way to California. My wagon broke an axle and I got no more money. We was campin' nearby. There wasn't nobody here in over a week, so we was looking after it. We been in here over a month and nobody's come yet."

"Well that's right neighborly of you to look after it, but now the owner is back. Did you get your wagon fixed?"

"Yeah, finally. It took all the money we earned locally."

"I'll tell you what. Seeing as how you're hard pressed for money, I'll give you fifty dollars for your trouble to pack up right now and leave."

"Fifty dollars? Right now?"

"Yep, right now."

The man rubbed his chin some more then scratched his head. "It could be you're just tryin' to get me outta here so you can claim it for yourself."

"Yeah that could be, but it ain't the case. If you want, I'll leave right now and come back in the mornin' with the sheriff and the owner with her deed. But you won't get a penny then. And if there's anything missing that should be here, you'll be accountable for it whether you're still here or not. And if you're not, we'll be comin' after you."

The man suddenly looked mad, but even more worried. "Hell, it could be somebody took somethin' before we ever got here!"

"Yeah, that could be. But it won't matter in the eyes of the law. You'll have been the last party in this house."

The man ran his fingers through his hair several times. "If we go right now and something is missin' from before we got here, what's to keep you from pinnin' it on me anyhow?"

"Well, I'm gonna stand right here and watch you pack up and go. So I'll know what you took . . . or more to the point, what you didn't take."

The man paused for a minute without rubbing his chin or running his fingers through his hair. He stood there slowly realizing that Sammy was on the level, and that his best chance for profit was to pack it up and get. Sammy knew he was close, so he got out fifty dollars of his own money and held it out to the man. The man looked Sammy in the eye and held his gaze for several seconds, then took the money. He turned his head in toward the house. "Amylou, start gettin' packed. We're leavin' . . . now. You boys go hitch the team up and bring the wagon 'round front. You girls help your mother."

Chapter 41

Claire and Margaret checked in to separate rooms at the Exchange Hotel and immediately availed themselves of the bathing facilities. The Exchange was the only hotel in Santa Fe that had such facilities as part of its offering. The rooms were the best in town, so most of the stagecoach traffic and other travelers stayed there. After they bathed, both the women slept for a while and then Claire collected Margaret and they went to the lobby, checking with the clerk to see if Sammy had arrived. When they found out he hadn't, Claire suggested they get something to eat in the hotel. "Don't you want to go out?" Margaret asked.

"No, not really. Not yet. Do you mind? It's just that I feel out of place. It's all so strange. I don't care to see anyone I know yet. They'll ask what happened. I don't want to talk about it right now . . . or ever, really." Claire's eyes suddenly misted up. She took Margaret's hand and squeezed it gently. "I miss Emily already."

"I know, I do too," Margaret said, suddenly relating to all that Claire had just expressed and realizing how difficult it would be when she returned home and saw people that she knew. What would they think? What would they say about her in the whispers and the gossip? What boy would be interested in her, knowing what the Indians had done to her? "That's fine that we stay

201

here," she agreed.

They found a table next to a window looking out at the court-yard. Several men pitched coins against the wall as the shadows of late afternoon stretched across the open ground. A waiter came and they ordered their meals. Claire also picked a bottle of wine. "Will you have some with me?" she asked Margaret.

"I've only ever tasted some once. Yes, I'd like to have a little."

"Good." Claire gazed thoughtfully out the window. "You know, Robert and I lived here nearly three years and I've never been in this hotel." Then she quickly changed the subject. "I wonder where Sammy is? It's getting late. We should go see Blaine after we eat. I hope he's back before we go."

"Do you think Blaine will be all right?" Margaret asked.

"Oh, I pray so. They're such good men."

"I think you were right when you said that God sent them."

"Now we'll pray that God heals Blaine."

The waiter brought the wine, and Claire and Margaret drank and talked as they waited for their meals. Margaret had been thinking about it, but was unsure of asking. With the sedation of the wine, she was a little more confident and went right to the heart of it. "Claire, could I stay with you for a while? I'll help out and work hard."

Claire had a slight look of surprise that quickly melted to a warm smile. "Of course you can. You can stay with me as long as you like. I'd be so pleased not to be alone right now. But what about your family, your mother and brothers?"

"I'll write a letter to my mother and let her know what happened and that I'm all safe. But I'm not ready to go back yet. Kind of like you not wanting to go out here and feeling strange. I feel like I need some time to settle. Besides, my mother and I are not that close. I love her, but . . . and my brothers are in their own worlds. I'll see them. I love them, but I don't know if I'll ever move home again now. I'll be seventeen next month."

They smiled at each other. Claire reached across the table and took her hand. "We'll make the best of it, together. You can go when you want, or stay as long as you want." Claire took a deep breath. "You know I'm pregnant, don't you?"

"Yes, Emily told me she thought you were. She said you'd tell me if you wanted to. I'm glad you wanted to."

"Well, it won't stay a secret much longer anyway."

"You're barely showing. I mean I can see a little difference, but that's because we've been together for so long. What are you going to do?"

"I'm going to give this baby a home. I think it may be Robert's. I pray it is. The timing seems about right. We were trying just before I was taken. I had morning sickness the day they murdered him. I'll just have to wait till it's born."

"Oh Claire, I'll pray hard for you . . . and I'll help do whatever you want me to."

"Thank you, Margaret. That means so much to me."

Sammy walked up to the table. "Mind if I sit down with the two best looking gals in the place?" Margaret smiled as if she'd just won a beauty contest. Claire scanned the room.

"We're the only two gals *in* the place."

"That'd make you the best looking gals then. But I was referring to all of Santa Fe."

"Nice to see you so chipper, Mister Winds," Claire said.

"I prefer it that way. I also prefer to eat when I'm starvin'. Did you eat already?"

"No, our food should be here any time now," Margaret answered.

Sammy saw the waiter walking by. "Would you bring me whatever they're havin' . . . twice."

The waiter raised an eyebrow. "They ordered different meals, sir."

"Then bring me one of each, and some water too, please."

"Yes sir. Right away."

"Polite hombre," Sammy mused. "Everybody I've met in this town has been polite. You can move back into your house anytime you want, Claire."

Claire's eyes met Sammy's directly, looking for confirmation of what she thought she just heard. "What do you mean? What about what Doctor O'Malley said about somebody living there?"

"They're gone now," Sammy said casually as he reached for a piece of bread from the basket.

"When did they leave?" Claire asked with a tone of wonderment.

"Not long after I asked them to."

"You were there?"

"Yep. Was a man and his family livin' there . . . 'bout a month. They were passin' through and broke an axle on their wagon. Also, I happened upon a neighbor. Pablo Hernandez I believe it was. He said that some other folks out that way, name of Grimes—they have your cow, some livestock, and a buckboard."

Claire'e eyes brightened. "Yes, I know Mister Hernandez, and the Grimes' are close friends. We were on our way to their place when we were attacked. Oh my. Thank you, Sammy, for taking care of that. It's such a burden off my mind. Thank you!"

"You're welcome, Claire. I'm just glad it smoothed out without a fight."

The waiter came with Claire and Margaret's meals. "Yours will be out in just a minute, sir."

"I'll be here," Sammy said, and stuffed another piece of bread in his mouth.

"We're planning to go see Blaine after we finish here if it's not too late," said Margaret.

Sammy finished chewing and took a drink of water to wash it down. "I saw Blaine earlier. Doctor O'Malley said it's wait and see. I won't lie to you. He said if the infection spreads he could lose his leg—or maybe his life."

"Oh no, no!" Margaret exclaimed.

Sammy shook his head. "Hold on. It hasn't spread yet. It seems to me there's a good chance it won't now. The doctor took out some bullet fragments and said the infection was still local, which I figure is a good sign, being that's its been four days now.

He's young and strong. Now he's sleepin' hard and gettin' good rest and care."

"Can we look in on him yet tonight?" Claire asked.

"I think so. The doc's assistant lives in the back—that side door off the courtyard over there."

Blaine did not wake up while Sammy, Claire, and Margaret stood around his bed in the room's dim light, talking about him in whispers. He woke up later after a dream about busting broncs caused him to move his injured leg suddenly when he was thrown from the horse. The pain was not severe, but it was enough to bring him to a groggy state of consciousness after having been asleep for nine hours.

The room was unfamiliar and nobody occupied the three other beds. He could hear the sound of people and activity coming through a small transom window high on the opposite wall. It was tilted open, but cast no light. Night, he thought, feeling as if still in a dream. He called out, "Hello."

A moment later the door opened and a middle-aged woman in a floor-length scarlet robe entered and made her way to his bedside. Her long hair was dark and streaked with gray and braided so it looked like heavy rope hanging to the middle of her back. "Good evening, señor," she said with perfect enunciation in a thick, Spanish accent.

Blaine stared up at her.

"Good evening to you."

"You have slept a long time. I will bring you food if you are hungry."

"No, but I am thirsty."

"I will bring you water. You must not get up." She took the bedpan from the table next to the bed and put it beside him. "Use this when you have to go. There is paper here," she said, pointing to the sheets on the table. "Do not get up. I will help you if you need."

"Thank you, ma'am. I'll manage that part myself . . . I hope."

"It is all right. I have helped many people. Your friends were here earlier tonight. You were sleeping. They will be back in the morning. They are staying next door at the hotel."

Blaine lifted his head and propped himself a little higher. "They were here, huh? They got a bar in that hotel? 'Cause I'd be in it if I wasn't here." He lifted the sheet and looked at his heavily bandaged thigh. "I don't remember the doctor workin' on me, but it looks like he did."

"Yes . . . you were sleeping then too."

"I been sleepin' a lot."

"It is the medicine. It is for the pain, and it will help you sleep."

"Well how 'bout some more of that medicine, 'cause now that I'm awake the pain is back."

"I will bring some with the water," she said, and disappeared through the door.

Blaine lay there listening intently as he looked up at the window. He could hear the Mariachis, who had started up with guitars and singing, followed by several whoops from the audience. It was a lively piece they were playing, painting a picture in his mind of the festive time somebody was having. "Sounds like where I'd like to be," he said to himself. Blaine's eyes slipped to half-mast as he floated in the spirit of the song and momentarily put the ache of his leg to the back of his mind.

The woman was back at his bedside without him realizing how she got there. She handed him a large clay cup and put the pottery pitcher on the table next to a washbowl. Blaine slugged at the water for several seconds, half emptying the vessel and then taking a deep breath. "Much obliged," he said as he placed the cup on the table. "We ain't been properly introduced. I'm Blaine Corker."

The woman pulled the small dark bottle and a spoon from the pocket of her robe as she spoke. "I am Alice Martinez, the doctor's assistant." She removed the cap and carefully poured the chocolate brown liquid onto the spoon. "Take this," she said as she held the spoon to his mouth, "and hold it under your tongue for a minute before you swallow." Blaine took the medicine. It had an alcohol base and tasted like extra strong moonshine to him. He held it under his tongue for the better part of a minute and then swallowed.

"Can I have a smoke to go with it? The makins is in my shirt pocket there."

"It is not good for you with a fever. But if you want . . . " She retrieved his tobacco pouch and papers and then wet a washcloth while he rolled a smoke. She put the cool compress on his forehead and pulled the wooden chair from the table. She sat down. "I will sit with you while you smoke. I do not want you to go to sleep and burn us down. The medicine is strong."

"Thank you, ma'am. I appreciate the company."

Blaine smoked and told her about when he'd been in Santa Fe several years earlier. By the end of his cigarette, he felt light-headed and wasn't sure if it was the medicine kicking in quickly on an empty stomach, or just the tobacco. He snuffed out his smoke and laid his head back on the pillow as Alice talked of things that had happened or changed in Santa Fe in the years since Blaine had last been there. Then he knew it was the medicine taking over as the pain began to subside and a blanket of warmth flowed over him. Alice's voice became a faint echo that slipped away as he began to dream of boarding a stagecoach pulled by golden horses.

Chapter 42

T he morning came, and he had another teaspoon of medicine dispensed by Alice before he ate a small plate of choriso and beans with a tortilla for breakfast. Sun poured through the transom and filled Blaine with optimism about his condition. He sensed some improvement. His leg ached badly, but he generally felt better, and Alice had said she thought his fever had come down some. He rolled a smoke and lit it, then sat waiting for the medicine to kick in.

Doctor O'Malley opened the door as Blaine was finishing his smoke. "Good morning."

"Good mornin', Doc."

"Missus Martinez tells me your fever has come down." The doctor walked to the side of the bed and put his palm on Blaine's forehead. "Ah . . . yes, better. Not gone, but better. How are you feeling?"

"A sight better 'n when they dragged me in here. Seems I been asleep all but about one hour since I got here. That oughta help some."

"Yes, well let's have a look." The doctor pulled the sheet off Blaine's leg. The center of the bandage was heavily blood stained.

"Should it be leakin' that much blood, Doc?"

"I don't think it's something to worry about. I had to cut out some tissue getting at the rest of those bullet pieces. I couldn't close it back up the same way, so you have somewhat of an open wound. It was bound to bleed some. That's one reason you have to stay off this leg—for several weeks, I suspect. You'll never get it healed if you're on it too soon. The real concern for now is the infection." The doctor started looking closely at the leg and feeling up and down from the spot of the wound."

"Whadaya looking for, Doc?"

"Red streaking, abnormal swelling and tenderness away from the wound, lines of discoloration." The doctor pulled out a pair of scissors. "Let's change this bandage right now." He cut the bandage and carefully removed it.

Blaine stared at the short gash in his leg that was packed with gauze. Suddenly, he felt the surge of wonderland as the painkiller of the small brown bottle hit him. He was grateful of it. His concern melted, and he watched with some glee as Doctor O'Malley extracted the packing and flushed the gapping hole with a clear solution from another brown bottle. "Those brown bottles are right handy," Blaine said, as if he were on a picnic.

Doctor O'Malley looked up at Blaine, taken with the whimsical tone and obvious departure of sobriety in his patient's last statement. "Well, I don't see any signs that the infection is spreading. So far, so good."

"Wonnnnderful," Blaine sang out, just as his eyes shut and the vision of himself swimming naked with eight ladies in a hot springs led him to another drug-induced sleep.

An hour later, Blaine heard the voices in the twilight of consciousness, and his eyes cracked open to slits. The blurry figures before him slowly came into focus. Sammy, Claire, and Margaret stood by his bed staring at him appraisingly, like he was beef for sale. He smiled slowly at the recognition of his friends. "Anybody home?" Sammy asked.

Claire walked up close and placed her hand on his forehead. "He does feel better," she said in a tone of confirmation.

"Yes he do," Blaine chimed.

"Hello, Blaine," Margaret said excitedly. "I'm so glad to see you awake with some color in your face."

"I'm glad to see you too, Margaret." Blaine extended his hand to hers and gave it a squeeze.

Sammy smiled. "You do look more like the living now."

"I been sleepin' like the dead since you hauled me in here."

"Claire wants to haul you out of here," Sammy replied.

Claire spoke up. "There's no sense in you staying here any longer than need be. Tomorrow we'll move you out to my place if the doctor okay's it. I've got the room, and we can look after you proper while you convalesce. Doctor O'Malley says by tomorrow he should have a good idea about the state of your infection. If it hasn't worsened, it will be all right for you to go."

"That'd be loverly." Blaine looked happy to hear the plan.

Sammy pulled the buckboard in front of Doctor O'Malley's office at one o'clock the following afternoon. Claire and Margaret both got down before Sammy could get around to help them, the women having decided they were perfectly capable of getting down themselves when a mission lie ahead. Sammy and Dorian carried Blaine and laid him out on the deck of the wagon with his head on two pillows just behind the seat. Then Dorian went inside with the women to give them instructions and materials for cleaning and re-bandaging and to tell them what symptoms to keep an eye out for.

Sammy stayed with Blaine, who took the opportunity to talk to his friend. "Ya know, amigo, I'm gonna take the doctor's advice and stay off this thing. Get healed up."

Sammy lit the cigarette he'd just rolled, then took a long drag and blew the smoke into a breeze. "I'd say that's sound thinking."

"There's a larger point," Blaine said, smoking on his own cigarette.

"Yeah?"

"Yeah."

"There usually is."

"What I mean is, you don't need to hold up on my account. Doc said a couple of weeks. If I was you, I reckon I'd ride on."

"I appreciate you sayin' so, but I'm not goin' anywhere this minute. We'll see how it plays out. I need to stay awhile and help these gals get set up. You can't help 'em right now. *There's* the larger point."

"Yeah, that's a large point." Blaine took a drag and blew it out and then got a glint in his eye as if something had just occurred to him. "Hey, how come you keep talkin' about gals, as in two of 'em? Ain't Margaret goin' home?"

"Not anytime soon. She asked Claire if she could stay with her. Claire was more than happy about it."

Blaine smiled. "Well whadaya know. We're gonna be one big happy family out at Claire's for awhile, huh?"

"Looks that way. Hope they can cook."

"Yeah, but back to my larger point. Anytime you wanna ride on, you just go ahead. I understand and won't take offense."

"Okay."

The door opened and Dorian came out with a wooden crutch. The women carried gauze and bandages and a bottle of antiseptic solution. Sammy walked around the wagon to help the women. Dorian walked over to Blaine and laid the crutch down beside him. "I only had one," he said. Then he handed Blaine a pint bottle of laudanum. "You shouldn't need this too much longer. I don't recommend ever taking more than a teaspoon every six hours. The dosage is written on the label. If you take too much, it can kill you."

Blaine's eyes widened. "I'll try to avoid that."

"Just letting you know, lad. It's easy to like, and easy to get carried away. I'd let Missus Studdard dose you, and stay off that leg. I'll be around to Missus Studdard's in a day or two to look in on you.

"Thanks, Doc. Much obliged. How much do I owe you?"

Blaine said, reaching into his pocket.

"Mister Winds settled your account. Good luck."

Claire had an idea that she would set Blaine up on the settee in the den. Sammy was bunking in the loft room and Margaret slept in the bedroom with her for now. The den was directly off the parlor and had a window with a pretty view to the south. She was sure he would like it. And like it he did. But there was a screened porch on the backside of the house that he preferred more. It had a table and chairs and a cot in the corner where Robert had liked to nap on warm summer days. "It's practically outside!" Claire had stated in objection when Blaine had suggested it.

At first he didn't want to tell her the reason he preferred it, being slightly embarrassed. But he didn't want to be disagreeable with her. Not in her own house. Not over where she wanted him to stay. Not without a reason she would understand. So he told her. "No offense, Claire, but I'm not gonna use a bedpan if I don't have to. I got too much modesty to have you looking after me that way. I ain't crippled. That privy is close by. I can get back and forth fine with this crutch."

"But it'll be cold on the porch at night and early morning," she said.

"Naaww, why that's just fresh air. It's the middle of April. I gotta good coat and two blankets. And I can come inside anytime, can't I?"

"Of course you can. Well, if that's what you want."

"Thank you, Claire."

Claire fixed up his cot with pillows and extra blankets and brought him a couple of Robert's adventure novels. Blaine found it to be quite the setup and sat cushioned with his back up against the wall so that he had a panoramic view of the yard and outbuildings. He spent his days reading and talking to Sammy and Claire and Margaret as they did outside work and chores, getting the place back in shape.

The women did washing and cleaning and tilled and planted

the garden. Sammy fixed the chicken coop and garden fence, retrieved Claire's livestock, and packed in food and supplies. Then he spent several days felling dead trees and using Dobe to drag them. He sawed logs and split wood, all while Blaine watched and talked and rooted him on, smoking cigarettes in a laudanum-induced haze.

Blaine was pretty handy on his crutch, using a swing-and-hop motion that kept him from ever bearing weight on his bad leg. He was careful not to use the privy or move anywhere else while the full effects of the laudanum were present. And he didn't do too much moving around because, even with no weight on it, just moving around made his leg throb. So he stayed put most of the time and enjoyed the mild weather and easy breeze of the porch as he begrudgingly endured his sedentary existence. The laudanum killed the pain and certainly made the time go by with periods of extended sleep. When he was awake, it was generally in a sort of trance in which he was unaware of time passing as the hours melted.

He did as the doctor had suggested and had Claire give him the dosage. He knew it had been the right move. With his vanishing sense of time and reality, he was quite sure he would have overdosed himself.

After a week, he made up his mind that he was done with the laudanum. He had begun to feel like a potted plant, content with sun and watering. In a rare moment of lucidity, he understood how far he'd slipped.

Claire brought him some fresh biscuits, eggs, and coffee, along with the teaspoon and the brown bottle. "No more of that," he said to her as she prepared to pour the dose into the teaspoon. "I feel like I'm livin' in a cloud. My brain's been pickled enough."

Claire smiled at him. "I'm glad to hear you've come around to that thinking."

"There's over half a bottle of that stuff left. If I don't come around to that thinkin' right quick, I reckon my brain'll end up down a wormhole."

She sat with him while he ate, and they talked of all that had been done at her house since they returned. The garden was in, the chickens were regular with eggs, the cow was regular with milk, supplies were in, and needed repairs had been done. Sammy had sawed and chopped enough wood to last well into the following winter. "We have plenty of wood now," Claire said. "We won't need any for heat for the next six months. Just for cooking."

"Sammy can swing an axe like he come from the cave of the north wind. That's for sure. I'm itchin' to do some work myself. I reckon I'd pay money to break a sweat workin'. This layin' here day after day is gettin' plumb miserable."

"You'll have no problem findin' work if you'll pay to do it. I'd bet my horse on that," Sammy said, walking into the porch and hearing Blaine's last proclamation. He pulled up a chair and sat down.

"I'll let you two talk. I've got work to do," Claire said, as she stood up and collected Blaine's plate.

"Thank you for breakfast, Claire"

"You're welcome," she replied, and walked back into the house.

"You chased all the women away. Now you gotta keep me entertained," Blaine said. He pulled out the makings. "Smoke?"

"Yeah."

Blaine had two rolled up inside of a minute. Sammy struck the match and held it to Blaine's first, then lit his own. He took a drag and exhaled. "I've done about all that needed doin' here, for the time being anyway."

"Yeah, you got it shaped up fine," Blaine said, sensing what was coming next.

"I'm ridin' tomorrow. I need to get this little adventure movin.' I'd like to be back on the T. before they make the drive, and I wanna have some time in Denver."

"Yep, I know. I'd like ta be goin' with ya, but this ain't ready yet. Won't be for another week or so, I reckon. And who knows. I might hang on here for awhile. Help out."

Sammy smiled. "Claire's a good woman. Good lookin' too."

"I did notice that."

"Hard not to."

"I ain't thinkin' that way, though. Could be she wants to get shut of me as soon I'm healed. Margaret's here with her now."

"I don't think that will last. Maybe. But she'll likely wanna see her family. She posted a letter to 'em. They might just show up here one day."

"Yeah. They might." Blaine took a drag and looked out at the yard. "What's your route now."

"Nothin' too complicated. Swing east over to Las Vegas and on north to Raton. Then over the pass and up the plains along the front range of the Rockies. There's a stage runs all the way from here to Denver."

"Whoa! That's a long haul. You're not ridin' that are ya?"

"Nope. But I heard there's a rail line that runs from Las Vegas up to Raton . . . and your horse can ride in a stock car. Dobe might like that."

"You gonna do that?"

"Maybe. I've never ridden a train. That would be somethin'."

"Yeah, me neither. I'd like to do that."

"It'd be easier on your leg."

"Once I'm healed up, the last thing I'm gonna be is easy on this leg. But I sure could make some time ridin' a train part ways. How long you reckon you'll stay in Denver?"

"A week, maybe two. Reuben told me there's a lot to see there. I'm gonna see it. He told me to stay at the Ducayne Hotel, so that's where I'll be."

"Well, Sammy, I hope I see ya up there. If not, I wish ya the best of luck. We sure ended up with more 'n we figured. I don't think I'd be drawing breath now if I'd a happened on that cave with anybody else."

"Neither one of us would be if you hadn't held up your end. If I see you in Denver, I'll buy you a bottle of whiskey and the biggest steak in town."

Chapter 43

T he night was moonless and black like coal. A dog barked several times at a passing skunk and then grew quiet again. Inside the small adobe house, the man slept deeply, snoring and exhaling a whiskey vapor that permeated the room. He did not hear the door whine ever so faintly as it slowly opened. Nor did he hear the floorboards creak as the intruder took slow, easy steps into the room and then stood still, waiting for his eyes to adjust.

The dark did not relent. The intruder made his way toward the sound of snoring, stepping lightly until he reached the bed and stood in the pitch black beside the slumbering soul. Then he quietly took the match from his pocket. A moment later a burst of light leapt from the darkness as the stick match fully ignited.

The intruder immediately saw the gun belt hanging from the bedpost near the man's head and grabbed the six-shooter from the holster, stuffing it in his waist while his eyes scanned the room for other weapons. There was a rifle on a wall rack just to his right, and a hunting knife in a sheath on the bedside table. He grabbed the rifle with his right hand and turned to the bed as the man in it opened his eyes and made a desperate grab for the empty holster. The rifle butt cracked the man's head with brutal force and he fell back onto the bed bleeding and unconscious. The match went out, but another one lit an instant later and was used to light the lamp on the table.

Willis Burk opened his eyes ten minutes later. He was lying on the bed on his side with his hands shackled behind him. His mouth was stuffed with a rag and bound over by another that was tied at the back of his neck. There was rope around his chest and arms as if he'd been lassoed. Moving his head, he felt the sticky ooze of blood between it and the blanket, then looked down at his feet that were shackled. Blood had flowed into his eyes and he blinked rapidly to try and clear his vision. What he saw struck him as oddly familiar. Then he realized that the shackles were army shackles. He blinked his eyes repeatedly and the blurry figure across the room began to come into focus.

A man sat at the table. He looked to be writing something. Willis Burk was having some difficulty breathing through his nose and attempted to yell, but it came out only as a muted and indistinguishable grunt. Sammy looked up from the table. "Shut the hell up," he said, and continued writing while Willis continued bleeding.

Willis grunted, but there was no one to hear him, even if he had screamed. His house sat on the eastern edge of town, a quarter mile from the other nearest building. As he lay there watching the man write, his mind twisted and turned over what this was about. He'd never seen the stranger before that he could remember, and he tried to piece together the possibilities. There were many. He knew that being bound by U.S. Army shackles was not a good sign. It led him to consider the illegal sales of army rifles, ammunition, and other army provisions to Indians and Mexican banditos. But he'd never had direct dealings with any of them. That's what his two trusted associates were for. He was insulated.

Willis Burk was a former army officer with a distinguished record who had landed a position as the civilian procurement and provisions agent for Fort Union just outside Santa Fe. His two trusted associates had been under his command as part of his platoon during the Civil War. In their present illegal activities, they arranged the sales and directed the deliveries, and Willis provided the goods to be sold. Willis ordered for the fort based on needs the fort's quartermaster submitted to him. He simply added on a little extra to the requisition form for his own enterprise before it was submitted up the supply chain. Then, when the goods arrived at the Santa Fe warehouse he oversaw, he removed his take and forged a new bill of lading before delivery to the fort. The newly-created bill of lading properly represented what was in the received shipment, so the fort got what had been ordered, and Willis embezzled the rest. Willis knew the whole operation could go south with a proper audit, but understood the lack of efficiency and oversight of the army, and of western forts in particular. And he certainly figured he'd have advance warning if any inquires began. Then he would simply vanish. His associates hadn't been compromised. If they had, he would have known about it before this man came in the night.

Sammy finished writing his note, folded it, and put in an envelope. He pulled his chair over in front of the bed and sat down. "You made a big mistake sellin' guns to renegade Apaches . . . and whoever else you sold to." Willis blinked hard and narrowed his eyes. "Those Apaches murdered innocent people with army rifles. I oughta cut your throat right here. Of course, if I'm wrong about this, I'd be real sorry. But I'm not wrong . . . am I, Willis?"

Willis grunted.

"That's what I thought you'd say. You see, I've got a bill of lading that I took from a cave where some renegades were livin'. It's for a shipment delivered to you. Got your signature at the bottom. Part of that shipment was a case of twelve rifles—even gives the first and last serial number of the lot. It's been circled with a notation that says: To T. L. And I've got this note, too. Looks like the same writin' as your signature. It says 'Ten Loco, noon at Hogback Butte.' Instructions for somebody, Willis?"

Willis laid still now, hoping his face didn't betray his worry.

"It so happens I brought one of those rifles back from the

218

cave—and you wanna take a guess at the serial number? It ain't good, Willis. You know what I can't figure, is how the hell that bill of lading and note ended up in that cave?"

That was exactly what Willis was trying to figure out as panic beset him.

"Sure looks like you or one of your friends was careless. I'm not sure how this will all fit together to barbeque you. But you and I both know those rifles never got to the fort. How'd you cover that up? Well, no matter. I'll give 'em what I got, and they can figure it out."

Sammy stood up and backed up a few feet, grabbing the lead rope from the floor, the other end of which was tied around Willis Burk's chest. "On your feet!" Willis swung his shackled legs off the bed as Sammy pulled on the rope. Willis rose with the momentum of being yanked, and then hop-stepped suddenly at Sammy with his head down like a charging bull. Sammy sidestepped him and watched as Willis pitched forward and crashed face first to the floor. "That wasn't too graceful, Willis. All right, we can do this the hard way." Sammy grabbed the rope with both hands and dragged Willis out the door and into the night.

Sammy stopped by the sheriff's house at 5 a.m. and beat on the door until he heard the stumbling movement inside. A moment later, a dim light shone through the window as the occupant got a lamp lit. The door opened and the sleepy man stood before Sammy with a pistol in his hand. "What is it, for Christ's sake?"

"Here you go, Sheriff." Sammy handed him the army rifle and an envelope that contained the bill of lading, the note, and a letter explaining all that had happened.

"What's all this?"

"This is about Robert Studdard and Willis Burk. It's all explained in the envelope. Burk's been selling army rifles to renegade Apaches . . . and others I don't doubt. I hope you convict that piece of shit. I won't be around for the trial. If you need any other questions answered, talk to Blaine Corker. He's stayin' out at Claire Studdard's house. You could talk to her too. She may be ready to talk about it now. So long, Sheriff."

"Whoaaa, you hold on. You're not just waking me up and droppin' this in my lap then prancing down the trail without telling me all there is."

"I gotta get goin', Sheriff."

"Look mister, you just handed me evidence which gives me the right to detain you until I hear all the facts from you—not read about 'em, or look at somethin'. You understand?"

"Yeah, I guess I do."

"Then drag your ass in here. I like a good story and company while I'm having coffee. You look like you can provide both."

"Fine, but can we finish this quick? I'd like to be ridin' when the sun comes up?"

"The coffee will be ready in fifteen minutes. The rest of it depends on how fast you can talk? What's your name?"

"Sammy Winds."

"I'm Mitchell Hunter. Glad to know you." The two men shook hands. "Now come in and tell me about that—how'd you put it— piece of shit? Yeah, I think that was it. That piece of shit Willis Burk. I gotta tell you kid, I know that piece of shit. Always suspected he was crooked. I love it when my instincts are proven right."

They drank coffee and ate some day-old fry bread as Sammy told the sheriff about stumbling upon the cave in the storm and all that happened afterward, including finding the bill of lading and the note, and their journey to Abiquiu and then to Santa Fe. The sheriff sat spellbound by it all and then grew curious.

"So you've been here nearly two weeks? How come you're just telling about this on your way out of town?"

"I've been busy working, helping Claire get her place back in shape. Besides, I'm not stickin' around for any trial. And I don't know for sure if there's enough there to prove he was in on it. I'd bet my horse on it, but I don't know what they need in court to make it stick."

Sheriff Hunter thought for a minute. "The fort should have some records of their own. If they do, I'm guessin' Willis has a problem . . . particularly if they were never reported stolen on his end."

They talked a few more minutes before Sammy finished his coffee and stood up. "I gotta get goin', Sheriff. I sure hope you can put it all together."

"With what you just gave me, I believe his goose is cooked."

A minute later, Sammy was mounting up in the pale of first light as the sheriff stood watching from his doorway. "I'll be paying Mister Burk a visit later today," the sheriff said.

"He's already waitin' at your office."

"There's nobody there now."

"That's all right. He'll be there." Sammy tossed the key down to the sheriff.

"What's this for?"

"You'll know when you see it," Sammy said. Then he put light heels to Dobe and the horse broke to a trot up the street toward the trail to Las Vegas.

Sunday morning broke clear and beautiful in Santa Fe, with the Plaza coming to life as people headed to San Miguel Mission for Mass. The sheriff's office was adjacent to the mission, and many people passed it on their way to church. They stared and spoke quietly to one another as they passed by the pitiful figure shackled to the porch post in his underwear.

The top of his forehead had a gash, and his face was bruised and scraped raw on one side from hitting the floor. Dried blood was caked in his hair and on his face, and down his sleeveless undershirt. A note with thick letters was pinned to the back of his shirt and read: The Scoundrel Willis Burk - sold army rifles to murdering Apache renegades.

Willis did not look at, or speak to, any people passing by, nor did anybody speak to him. Some privately speculated that the sheriff had run out of jail space or that maybe this was a new humiliation tactic to deter crime.

Willis was still there when Mass was over. Sheriff Hunter showed up at noon.

Chapter 44

Sammy rode the horse trail east as it crossed high mountain plains and led into forest, skirting the base of peaks that rose thousands of feet above the trail. Fast moving clouds swept the tips and blended with the snow high above. The April runoff ran full, and Sammy's pace slowed over the mountainous ground, busy with creeks and pine trees and groves of aspen and birch, thick with buds on the cusp. He kept a watchful eye and a brisk pace, aware that he rode alone for the first time in unfamiliar country. The forest occasionally gave way to patches of open meadow, but extended visibility was never present. It was perfect territory for an ambush.

At noon he stopped in an open meadow and sat at the base of a steep incline that commanded a good view of all that was in front and below. He ate cinnamon bread and beef that Claire had packed for him, and thought about the strange turn of events since he and Blaine had left the Twin T. It certainly hadn't been the adventure he had imagined in the months leading up to his departure. Now, he felt strangely alone, with a renewed appreciation for the unforeseen. His mind wandered back to Claire and Margaret and Blaine. They already seemed distant, even though the farewell had been just the night before. Emily's return to her family and the night in Abiquiu seemed a month ago.

He wondered if he'd ever see any of them again. Claire and Margaret had fought back tears and insisted that he write to them when he returned to the T. Both had promised they would write to him.

Blaine gave him the half-full bottle of laudanum as a going away present. "I'm done with that loco tonic. I can get some more from the doc if I really need it, but I won't. I'm healin' up good now. I reckon if the rest of your trip is anything like the first part, you'll be needin' it before me." Sammy chuckled to himself as he recollected some of the expressions on Blaine's face while stoned on laudanum.

He finished the beef and bread and drank water from his canteen as Dobe cropped grass thirty feet in front of him. The sun was warm, and tiredness descended on him like a thing not to be held off. He leaned back on the slope with his hat over his face and dozed. It was deep and pure and brief. Fifteen minutes later, he woke feeling as if he'd slept for hours, and with the sudden revelation that he wanted to get to Denver as soon as he could. "Come on Dobe . . . let's get movin'." He mounted up and took off at a gallop across the meadow.

Toward the end of the day, Sammy rode down a gradual decline that continued on through the woods for several miles before finally flattening out onto the open plains. He had a sense of relief on finally clearing the woods, knowing that Las Vegas sat on the plains and that he would arrive sometime the next morning. As the sun drew down in the sky behind him, the cowboy and his horse threw an eastward shadow that stretched out on the ground like a long finger pointing the way.

On the horizon he saw the shape ahead in line with the direction he was riding. It was a good ways off and rose above the flat plain like an oasis, with a thin stream of smoke trailing skyward. As he got closer, he could see it was a group of five wagons pulled into a circle formation next to a stand of cottonwood trees. The distant recollection of his own family and their murderous end ran through his mind, but he was brought back by the sound of barking dogs, who had spotted him coming their way.

Several men stepped out from the center of the encampment and pulled their hat brims lower against the setting sun to see the object of the dogs' interest. Women were cooking at a fire in the center of the camp, and young children played a game of chase. Several teenagers were attending to chores, but some stopped and walked out amongst the men to see the approaching rider.

Sammy slowed to a walk the last hundred feet up to the camp. "Hello," one of the older men called out as he stepped forward holding a rifle that was pointed down.

"Hello," Sammy called back. He reined to a stop.

"It's rare to see a single rider out here on the plains. You need help?"

"No. I'm headed for Las Vegas. Just came off the Thompson Peak Trail from Santa Fe."

"The trail to Santa Fe?" the man asked, confused.

"Yeah, one of 'em. It's not the stagecoach trail—not fit for wagons. It's a shortcut through higher country. Mostly forest. Rough ground. I don't know how much of a shortcut it was. First time for me. I've never been the stage route. That would be farther south of here."

"That's what we thought," the man said. "We're bound for Santa Fe. Started from Pawnee Point, Kansas, and got here by way of the Cimarron Cutoff. We passed Las Vegas earlier this afternoon. It's straight up that way," the man said, pointing northeast. "Another two hours. It's coming on dark. Why don't you get on down and have supper with us. You're welcome to camp with us too."

"That's the best offer I've had today," Sammy said as he dismounted. "I'll take you up on it." He held his hand out to the older man. "I'm Sammy Winds."

"Ronald Moore," the man said as he shook Sammy's hand. "Happy to know you."

The other men stepped forward and introduced themselves

one at a time before they all went to the center of the camp where the scent of fresh biscuits and baked beans wafted sweetly in the air. Sammy was introduced to the women and all the youngsters. It appeared to Sammy to be a group of families with about twenty-five people in all.

During supper, everyone sat around the fire. The teenagers were interested in the lone rider from the plains. "Let the man eat in peace," one of the men said after Sammy had answered a string of questions in a row.

"It's all right. I don't mind," Sammy said. Some of the women took his statement as an invitation and began asking about Santa Fe, its shops and services and eateries and the people. Sammy obliged the questions, answering them with informative and colorful descriptions that had everyone listening intently. And as Sammy was very hungry and delighted by the quality of what was on his plate, he ate with abandon, spooning the beans and biting the biscuits in a symphony of flowing narrative and synchronic ingestion.

"Would you like some more, Mister Winds?" a girl of about eighteen sitting near him asked, just after he ran his spoon around his plate to collect anything remaining.

"Thank you. Yes, I would if there's enough."

She quickly rose and took his plate. "There's plenty."

Sammy looked directly into her eyes and realized how beautiful she was. "All right. Thank you, ma'am," He looked away, aware that some eyes were viewing the interaction to see what they might.

"It's Melinda."

Sammy looked back at her. "Excuse me, ma'am?"

"My name is Melinda."

"Oh. Thank you, Melinda"

She smiled at him in a way that conveyed her interest. "You're welcome."

The evening wore down with an hour of after supper talk

around the fire, and then Sammy had taken his leave, thanking them all for supper and wishing them a good journey. The day's long ride and his early-morning reckoning with Willis Burk had left him tired and grateful at the prospect of hunkering down under the stars. Ronald had invited him for breakfast, but Sammy had told him he'd likely be gone at first light.

He laid his bedroll out by the far cottonwood and staked Dobe nearby after feeding him several pieces of hardtack and an apple. "Long ride today. Thanks for the lift." Sammy sat down against the tree and rolled a smoke, listening to the nearby camp activity as some folks still sat around the fire talking. Others moved over to their wagons for evening chores before bed. A guitar played softly from inside one of the wagons, and a woman sang a lullaby.

Sammy lit the cigarette and took a drag as he looked up at the star-laden sky. The night was mild and the air was still. He saw the silhouettes approaching and opened his eyes wide. There were two people coming directly at him. One of them was a woman. "Hello, Mister Winds," the soft, easy voice came. "It's me, Melinda."

"Hello, Melinda."

They walked up beside him. "This is my younger brother, Spencer," she said.

"Hi, Mister Winds," the boy said. "I met you before, when you got here."

"I remember." Sammy was unable to distinguish much about the boy's face, but knew he'd met everybody.

"At supper he heard you talk a little about that ranch you're from and wanted to ask you a few questions about being a cowboy," Melinda said.

"Well sit down and ask away."

They sat down and the boy wasted no time. "Is it exciting being a cowboy?"

Sammy took a drag. "How old are you, Spencer?"

"Eleven. I'll be twelve on my birthday—June fourth."

"I'll tell you Spencer, It's real excitin'. Lots of hard work, but that's what makes it excitin'."

"Really?" the boy asked quizzically. "'Cause we farmed in Kansas before the tornado, and I did lots of hard work. I didn't think it was too exciting."

Sammy laughed. "I never farmed, so I can't say. I've been cowboyin' since before your age. It's all I've ever known. It ain't all fun. Nothin' is. But it's a good life. Somethin' a man can hang his hat on. Anything a man does that he's good at, that he can make an honest livin at, is something he can hang his hat on."

"Yeah, but what's the exciting parts?"

"You want the most excitin' parts, huh? Well . . . bustin' broncs, ropin', roundups, drivin' a herd, huntin' predators, calving, brandin'. There's a whole world of it. Of course, the least excitin' parts is some of the same things. It all depends on how you look at it."

"What do you mean, how you look at it?"

Sammy took a last drag and snuffed his cigarette out. "A while ago I was injured—hurt bad. And I couldn't do much of anything save lie around. When I finally could work again, I looked at it a whole new way. I was so happy just to be able to work, I found the joy in all of it. I have a friend who's over in Santa Fe right now. He's hurt and on the mend. He told me just the other day he'd pay money to work again."

"He did?"

"Yep. That's a fact."

"He could do my chores and wouldn't have to pay me."

"I'll let him know."

"Did you ever shoot an Indian?"

"That's enough, Spencer," Melinda said. "You get on back to camp now. I'll be there in just a minute."

"Oh, all right. So long, Mister Winds."

"So long, Spencer. And remember, whenever you're working, find the joy."

"Okay. I'll be looking for it." The boy began walking back to the camp.

"That was nice of you. Those were good words," she said.

"Just words I know to be true."

She looked up at the sky. "You sure can see the Milky Way tonight."

"Yeah, the path of the gods."

"Path of the gods?"

"Somethin' like that. Path of the gods, road of the gods . . . so named by ancient Greek poets."

"You know about those things?"

"I know there's a lot of mythology—stories connected to the Milky Way and all the stars and constellations."

"Tell me about the Milky Way."

"Well, Greek myth has it that it was created when Zeus' son Heracles was suckling at Hera's breast. And when she pushed him away, some of the milk spilled. But different people and cultures have their own stories. The Cherokee call it The Way the Dog Ran Away, based on a story of a dog that stole some cornmeal and ran away to the north, spilling the cornmeal across the sky."

"Well, Mister Winds."

"Call me Sammy."

"Yes, Sammy. It sounds like you know much more than just being a cowboy. Missus Rupumond didn't teach us any of that when I was schooling."

"I've read a few books is all."

Melinda scooted close and sat right next to Sammy. "Are you married," she asked.

"No."

"Do you think I'm pretty?"

"Yes."

"I think you're a handsome man. I'm not trying to be forward. It's just that . . . I don't know what's to become of my life. Everything is so turned upside down. And here we are talking under the stars somewhere out on the prairie. Our farm was wiped out. Now we're moving to Santa Fe for some business prospect my pa's excited about. My folks had enough of tornados. Me too. It's the third time we been hit, and this last one took everything."

"I'm sorry."

"Me too. I wish it helped how I feel. I'm just not sure of much anymore. A lot of girls my age are already married."

"Maybe. But a lot of 'em ain't. How old are you?"

"Eighteen. How old are you?"

"Twenty-one."

"Will you ever go through Santa Fe again?"

"Ever's a long time. I'm sure I will. It's only a couple of days from the ranch I ride for."

"Will you kiss me once . . . here, this night . . . now?"

Sammy looked at her, and even in the dark he could see the despair and hope in her face. Life was as so many stars splayed across the galaxy, the possibilities always beautifully endless and forever frightening. He held his palm against her cheek and moved to her, kissing her deeply against the passion of it all.

They lingered for a moment. "If you come to Santa Fe again . . ."

"You'll be married by then. A beautiful woman like you won't last long."

She smiled and held his face, then she rose. "I have to get back. Good luck and goodbye," she said, and began walking back toward the camp.

"Goodbye."

Chapter 45

S
ammy stepped to the window of the small booth that stood alone with twenty feet of boardwalk in front of it, like glory road in the middle of the surrounding dirt. "I'd like to find out about the train to Raton," he said to the young clerk with the slicked-down, combed hair, wearing a white shirt and bowtie.

"Yes, sir. The train leaves at 10 a.m. and arrives in Raton at 1 p.m. The fare is six dollars."

"Three hours is all it takes? How far is it to Raton?"

"One hundred and ten miles."

Sammy's eyes widened. "That train rolls right along."

"Nearly forty miles per hour."

"I was told a man could take his horse too. Is that right?"

"Yes, sir. On a space available basis. And right now, there's space available. The horse's fare is eight dollars."

"It's more for the horse than me?"

"Yes, sir. The horse takes up more space."

"Yeah, he eats more too. Okay, one man and one horse."

"That's fourteen dollars, sir. You can load your horse at 9:30. Passenger loading begins at 9:40."

Sammy handed the clerk the money. "When's the train gonna run to Santa Fe and Albuquerque?"

"They're surveying now. It shouldn't be more than a year or two. There's talk of building a line over Raton Pass too."

Sammy looked down the track a quarter mile to where the train was positioned under a water tower. "Do we get on down there?"

"No, they'll pull up here in another half hour or so."

Sammy glanced again at the clock behind the clerk. "Is your clock right?"

"Wound it this morning."

He had an hour to wait before he could load Dobe, so he headed over to the main street in search of breakfast and more tobacco. The small hotel he came to had a dining room. After two helpings of biscuits and gravy, Sammy took in the store across the street and bought chewing tobacco, cigarette tobacco, papers, a western dime novel, and fifty cents worth of cherry hard candy that nearly filled a popcorn-size brown paper bag. "You must be riding the train," said the old-timer behind the counter.

"How'd you know?"

"Tobacco, readin' material, and candy. Just right for ridin' the rails."

"The candy's for my horse," Sammy said, as he reached in the bag and flipped a piece into his mouth. "Mmmm . . . that's good candy." Sammy quickly dispensed with sucking and went right to chomping.

The man raised his eyebrows. "Good thing there's enough there for the both of you."

"Maybe. Much obliged, mister."

Swollen, dark clouds began to pile up as Sammy stood outside the livestock car waiting for the ramp to drop. He held two pieces of candy in his palm under Dobe's mouth. "Well, ain't this a bit of timing." Dobe took the treat and nosily enjoyed it. "I believe we're gonna avoid gettin' wet." Just then, he felt a drop hit his hand. The ramp came down and the man at the top waved him up.

"You're first, so pick any stall you like," the man said. Sammy loaded Dobe into an end stall. The horse peered out between the slats with a calm demeanor that suggested he was all right with the experience, so far.

"There you go. Privacy and a view." Sammy exited down the ramp just as three men with horses and another with a cow showed up to load.

The train was only six cars long with one passenger car. Sammy walked the length of it, looking at each car. He stopped at the locomotive and stared in fascination at the sculptured mountain of iron and steel, with its great spoked wheels connected by steel rails. Smoke drifted from its stack. He could hear the furnace burning and sensed the power of it as the shoveler was loading it up. The engineer noticed Sammy looking and tipped his hat when the cowboy's eyes moved to the cockpit where he stood at the window. Sammy nodded back with a smile, then walked back to the passenger car as people began to arrive. He boarded and sat next to the window at the rear of the car. The raindrops became more frequent, causing a few folks to hasten their pace in boarding.

Sammy reached into his shirt pocket and retrieved one of the pieces of candy he'd stashed before he'd put the rest of it in his saddlebags. He rolled it around in his mouth, resisting the urge to chew it as he usually did, but wanting to make it last, and curious about how long it would if he allowed it to dissolve completely. He looked at the dime novel, its cover depicting a rancher in front of his cabin shooting at a lone Indian on horseback, as his wife stood in the doorway with a fearful expression and two young children pushed against the folds of her dress. *The War of Lazy W. Ranch* was the title. "Guess I won't be namin' my ranch the Lazy W. Looks like there won't be much lazy about his place anymore."

He read the first page and forgot about his quest to suck the candy, instinctually doing what came naturally. He chomped it. A few pages in, he heard the shout from the conductor and looked out the window. "All aboard!" An older couple hurried to board as steady rain began to fall, quickly painting the remaining dry spots on the boardwalk platform. Sammy put the novel down on the empty seat beside him, unable to concentrate in anticipation of the train's movement. He looked around the car, surmising it was about half full with thirty or so passengers. Couples sat together, and singles availed themselves of an entire bench where the opportunity presented itself.

The train's whistle gave three blasts. A moment later, the car jerked and began a slow roll, with the sound of the engine pushing out sluggish, intermittent blasts of steam that increased in tempo as the train picked up speed. Sammy listened to the melodic pitch of the steel wheels turning over the rails beneath, with the light clicking sensation as the connecting seam of each rail was breached. The train cleared the town, the speed increasing and the skies opening up in a deluge of pouring rain.

He sat contented, dry and glad in the comfort of the train car, whizzing along, excited by the speed and the sensation of it as he watched the rain pound down on the plains with such force that it appeared to be bouncing back up several inches. He rolled a cigarette and then smoked it, gazing out the window and reminiscing on all that had happened. It seemed easy to put in perspective with the calm of the moment.

The man at the store had been mostly right. Sammy didn't pick up the dime novel the rest of the trip, but he certainly did enjoy eating more candy and smoking cigarettes as he contemplated it all and rode the rails north to Raton, eager to get on to Denver.

Chapter 46

Nature's onslaught of rain played out like a concerto, ebbing and flowing through the ministrations of unfolding passion and necessity that finally spent its worth on the land, leaving behind a clearing sky and washed plains brimming with the unleashed scent of sage and feathergrass. The Raton depot was bathed in sunshine and heavy with humidity as the train slowed to a stop. Some people inside the car peered through the windows at folks in front of the depot, quickly identifying those who had come to meet them and putting forth a wave or nod of recognition. The Conestoga freight wagons were already lined up alongside the freight cars when Sammy climbed down and made his way to the livestock car to retrieve Dobe.

"Excuse me, sir. You ever been over Raton Pass?" Sammy asked an older man who was already waiting for the livestock ramp to drop.

"Yes, I have."

"Is that it—the first break on the left there?" Sammy asked, pointing north.

"Oh yes, straight north there," the man replied as he pointed toward the rising mountains whose canyon mouth appeared to be a couple of miles off. "Just follow the stage road. It's an easy climb—no switchbacks. A lot of stagecoaches and freight wagons run it. There's a cantina at the top. Teamsters and folks coming from either direction stop and rest their animals. Good food, too. That gal does some business."

"How far to Trinidad?"

"Oh, maybe twenty miles. It's the first thing you'll hit when you come off the other side. The stage leaves for there in about thirty minutes. You may want to trail with them. Banditos up the pass occasionally. They'll waylay single travelers."

Sammy adjusted his hat rim. "Banditos, huh?"

"Yeah, a lot of trees and cover up there, places to hide. If you're not moving on till tomorrow, some of those freight wagons will be going in the morning."

"I gotta check with my horse. I'm game to go now, but he may have a different idea. He oughta be ready to work. Been standin' around doin' nothin' for the last hundred and ten miles."

The man smiled. "Yeah, well good luck with that. The Rooster Box is the only hotel here if you end up staying. Just up the street there."

"Much obliged, mister."

Sammy unloaded Dobe and led him to a water trough where the horse took a long drink. "What say we get on over this pass to Trinidad. It's a fine afternoon now, and we got to sit out all that rain." Dobe gave him a noncommittal stare. Sammy pulled out a piece of hardtack and fed it to Dobe, then followed it with a couple of pieces of the cherry candy. The horse perked up, munching contentedly. "I'll get you fed up big tonight. But first you gotta earn it."

"What's his name?" asked a little girl about eight years old who had wandered over and overheard the one-sided conversation. Sammy turned and looked down at her, surprised that she had gotten within earshot without his awareness.

"His name is Dobe."

"Does he answer you back?"

"Yes he does, in his own way."

"What's his own way?"

"Well, that's the horse way. It's not words, but I can hear him anyway. Sort of like when you feel the heat coming off a stove or hear the wind whistle through the trees . . . or smell the wildflowers. He's got his own glow. I just listen harder to understand."

The little girl blinked several times in thought. "My dog, Georgie, talks to me. My mom says it's make believe."

Sammy smiled. "I'll bet Georgie doesn't think so. Besides, it only matters what you and Georgie think. I don't much care what other folks think about me and my horse because we've got an understanding that no one else understands like we do."

"Like a secret?"

"Yep, just like a secret."

The woman strode over hurriedly. "What are you doing over here, Cynthia?"

The little girl looked innocently at her mother. "I was asking the man about his horse."

"You are not to wander off like that. Do you understand?"

The girl blinked several times. "Yes, I do understand—much better now."

The mother gave a curious look to her daughter's response and took her by the hand. "It's time to go," she said, giving Sammy a quick glance.

He tipped his hat to them. "Say hello to Georgie for me," he said as they began to walk off.

"Okay, I will. Goodbye, Dobe. Goodbye, mister."

Sammy mounted up and headed north out of town at a brisk trot. He considered what the man had told him about banditos and his advice about trailing with the stagecoach over to Trinidad. But he didn't care to wait on the stage, and the warning filled him with a grim resolve laced with anger. "They better catch me sleepin' or they're gonna get whatever they plan on givin'," he said to himself, feeling his blood rise.

The ten-mile trip up the pass to the summit turned out to be an easy ride up a beautiful canyon, ripe with evergreen and White

Birch. He saw mule-tail deer and eagles, and listened to songbirds loud with springtime chatter. Below and parallel to the trail was a seasonal river that he heard ever present, rushing full in its banks. He caught sight of it from time to time through the occasional clearing of trees and brush.

Two small groups of wagons passed him going the other way, and the traveling parties of the Santa Fe Trail eagerly shouted out their hellos to him as they passed. "Is Raton still there?" one of the wagon drivers shouted as they passed.

"Bright and shiny after a good rainstorm. Another seven or eight miles," Sammy yelled back.

"Thank you, neighbor! Prosperous travels to you!"

"And to you and yours!" Sammy replied.

Chapter 47

The Jupiter Sky Cantina and Hotel sat precisely at the trail's crest, recessed a hundred feet from it and sitting up against a wall of granite four times its height. It was a long, log building with its name in flowing purple letters hanging above the double entrance door. The large, flat hard-packed area of dirt and crushed rock in front of the Jupiter Sky could easily accommodate three dozen wagons and scores of horses, although it had only seen that limit once during a fierce late-June storm that produced a foot of snow and drove the horde of people in the pass in search of its cover.

A hand-dug trail with flagstone steps left the back of the Jupiter Sky from under a sign that read: Stairway to the Stars. The path followed a natural ridge for a quarter mile, ending at a domed rock upon which a platform gazebo sat, revealing a full view of the southwestern sky and the distant plains twelve hundred feet below. A donation can to maintain the stairway, and its glorious experience, was pegged to a post at the beginning of the trail. It netted the proprietor an extra hundred or so dollars a year.

Sammy reined up in front and dismounted. A Mexican boy trotted out from a barn at the side of the Jupiter Sky. "I can water, feed, and brush your horse, señor. Good care for your horse, señor. Twenty-five cents."

"Feed him what?"

"Oats, señor. Good. Fresh."

"Okay, amigo." Sammy pulled out a silver half dollar. "You take good care of him . . . not *too* much with the oats." He held up his hands in the shape of the appropriate portion then flipped the coin to the boy, who looked at it for a moment."

"Fifty cents?" the boy asked.

"Si."

The boy reached in his pocket and pulled out some coins to make change. "No, amigo," Sammy said, waving off the boy's change. "Take good care of my horse. I'll be out soon."

"Gracias. Thank you. Gracias. Good care, señor!"

Just inside the door, a man wearing a leather apron sat behind a pedal-driven grinding wheel. "Get your knives sharpened and polished. Ten cents a knife. Done in ten minutes," he pitched as Sammy walked in.

"Okay, mister." Sammy pulled his hunting knife from its sheath and flipped two bits to the man. "So I can shave with it," he instructed.

"It'll be a throat cutting, hair splitting beauty in ten minutes," the man replied as he began to make change.

"Keep it. I've been tippin' big since I got here. Why stop now."

"Thank you kindly. I'll give it the extree special whomp-a-moo-boo cleaning."

Sammy squinted at the man quizzically. "Whomp-a-moo-boo?"

"Yipper . . . eee . . . iii . . . ohh."

She appeared from a hallway on his right with timing that suggested she knew he was ready for the next service. "Hello, mister. Would you like something to eat? A cold beer? Or perhaps some whiskey or tequila? Or our own Jupiter Sky gin?"

Sammy considered the choices. "Your beer is cold?"

She looked at him a moment then shook her hair ever so slightly. "Yes, it is. Kept in a rock cellar on the north end. And if you're hungry, we have the Triple B Plate—beef, beans, and biscuits. The best on the Santa Fe Trail, guaranteed. If you don't think it's delicious, you don't have to pay. Of course, if that happens, we'll expect you to haul your ass off our premises. But that shouldn't be a problem because everything here is the best. Everything." She gave Sammy her soft eyes.

He looked at her and marveled at her brash style, tied up in a pair of snug denim pants, boots, and orange cotton blouse that pulled tightly against her generosity and enticement. Her brunette hair had soft, natural curls that hung to the bottom of her neck and nicely framed her blue eyes, high cheekbones, and full lips.

Sammy smiled at her. "How could I say no to that? Yes, ma'am, I'll have a beer and the Triple B."

"Good, the beer is ten cents, and the Triple B is fifty cents. I'm Annie Jordan, the proprietor. If you decide to stay, rooms are one dollar. I have four of them. First come, first serve. I would be delighted to serve you."

"Thank you, Annie. I appreciate it. We'll see what happens, but I was kind of thinkin' on makin' Trinidad yet."

"Javier! A beer for the gentleman," she told the bartender. She gave her hair another mild toss and lifted her chin as she flexed her shoulders back to a more perfectly revealing posture. Her eyes fixed on his in a soft, penetrating look. "You know, it's another ten miles down the pass to Trinidad. What's your hurry? Besides, they don't have what we've got."

"Oh yeah? What's that?"

"Stairway to the Stars, cool sleeping on great beds, and the Jupiter Sky bar with its special atmosphere and own magic that comes from being at the top of Raton Pass. What's your name, cowboy?"

"Sammy Winds."

"I was right. You are a cowboy, aren't you?"

"Yes ma'am, Annie."

"One of the area ranches?"

"I ride for the Twin T. . . . south of the Chintah Range. A week's ride southwest of here."

"Oh. You're a long way from home."

He looked at her, trying not to stare. He guessed her to be in her late twenties. Though she wasn't beautiful, her appeal was seductively unmistakable.

"Well, you think about it, cowboy. I'll get your food. Sit anywhere you like." She walked away and he watched her, concluding her movement spoke a language all its own.

The barroom rolled out like a long story. The bar top was a center cut, forty-foot-long ponderosa pine, sanded and varnished so that it shone like smoky glass on the wood's grain. A buffalo head hung off the center wall behind the bar and was flanked by elk, deer, and bear heads, coyote pelts, and snake skins. They gave the appearance of a game convention, and served as extra company for anyone occupying a barstool. An older couple sat at one of the tables against the windows of the front wall. Sammy walked to the bar and took a center stool.

The bartender brought his glass. "Your beer, señor. Welcome to the Jupiter Sky Cantina. My name is Javier."

Sammy finished taking a long pull off his beer. "Much obliged, Javier. I'm Sammy. That's good, cold beer."

"Yes, señor. We make our own—and our own gin, too, with juniper berries. There are lots of juniper trees in Raton Pass."

Sammy considered it. "I can't say I've ever had gin."

"We have tequila and whiskey too, but we don't make it. Is more expensive. Imported."

"I believe I'd like to know what those juniper trees taste like when they're fermented. Help put the prime on my appetite before I mutilate the Triple B Plate."

"Señor?"

"Pour me gin, Javier, and another beer too," Sammy said, and drained his glass in relaxed, satisfying swallows.

"Ahh . . . yes, señor."

Javier poured the shot and Sammy took the glass and smelled

the aroma. Then he sipped it, considering the flavor and quality and finding the bouquet of the juniper berry to be as he had imagined. He took the rest in a swallow and waited for the kick. "Whoa," he exclaimed. "Rattle my spurs. That's got some bullwhip to it."

"Another, señor? Is ten cents a shot or one dollar for the bottle."

"Not yet. No telling where I'd end up if I had too much of that before I ride."

"Then stay, señor. Enjoy the Jupiter Sky."

"I've heard that before. Must be the company line."

"Señor?"

"Ahh—that means muchas gracias, Javier."

"Por nada."

Annie Jordan came with Sammy's plate piled high, smelling and looking every bit as appetizing as she had advertised. "Here you are, cowboy. If you want more, just let me know."

Sammy's eyes widened. "I'll break a sweat finishing this."

"I hope you like it. Javier, give Mister Winds a drink on the house. Whatever he likes. See you in a bit." She turned and started her furnace toward the hallway.

"Thank you, Miss Annie Jordan. I'll drink to your prosperity," Sammy called to her, watching her locomotion as she steamed across the room.

"Just keep adding to it and you'll be toasting a good cause."

"I think she likes you, Señor Winds."

Sammy dug into the plate and instantly knew it was as good as he'd ever had. The beef brisket was salaciously tender, having been slow cooked in molasses and spices that made it delectable. The biscuits were hot mounds of perfected batter baked to a flaky delicacy with a honeybutter spread. And the beans were tender pintos in a light garlic sauce with fresh cilantro, diced onion, and jalapeno. He tried to pace himself and make it last, but the pace was driven by how good it was. It went quickly. He slugged the beer down in long, steady pulls to put out the fire of the jalapenos.

"Do you want Miss Annie's drink now?" Javier asked.

"I'd better . . . I'm on fire! Another beer, Javier. Is she the cook?"

"Yes. There are two other women who work for her, but they follow her recipes."

"Man, she's got some know-how with cookin'."

"Yes, she is very good in business also."

The man put the knife on the bar beside Sammy. "Thar she is—ready to cut a trail any direction."

Sammy picked it up and admired how meticulously clean the handle was, and the blade gleamed with shine. "It looks like when it was new—five years ago." He held the blade to his cheek and slid the edge downward for an inch in a shaving motion, then felt the smooth where whiskers had been. "Just right . . . much obliged."

"And to you also. May your trail be clear of dead enemies and your full belly warmed by the sun," the man said, then walked away. Sammy thought on that for a moment now that his belly was full.

Two cowboys walked in and headed for a table near the window. One of them called out, "Javier, como estas? Two beers and a bottle of whiskey."

"Hello, Señor Frank . . . Señor Thomas. Is good to see you," Javier replied and began to draw the beers.

Sammy glanced back, certain from their dress and manner that they were ranch hands. They looked at him and sized him up the same way. He nodded and raised his beer slightly in a toasting gesture, then faced back toward the bar.

"Hey mister, do you cowboy?" the older of the two asked Sammy.

Sammy looked over his shoulder at him. "Yeah, I do."

"We ride for the Rolling R.S. Ranch a few miles west of Trinidad. Turned up short-handed recently. You lookin' for work?"

Sammy turned all the way around on his barstool to face them. "No, just passin' through."

"What outfit you ride for?"

"The Twin T.. a few hundred miles southwest of here."

"I heard of it. Must be a big outfit."

"Yeah, it is."

"What brings you up here?"

"I'm headed for Denver."

"You got another two hundred miles getting' there. Come have a drink with us. We got a bottle."

"All right. Much obliged." Sammy walked over to their table. "I'm Sammy Winds," he said, holding out his hand to the man he'd been speaking to.

"Frank Adams," the man replied as they shook hands.

"Thomas Hedgerton," the other said, shaking Sammy's hand.

Javier showed up with the beers and whiskey and three shot glasses. The men poured whiskey and Sammy began to roll a smoke.

"How many head you run down there?" Thomas asked.

"It varies. We average about ten thousand."

"Ten thousand! That'd be a sea of beef on a drive. How many hands ridin'?"

"That varies, too. Usually between fourteen and twenty."

Frank Adams looked amazed. "Hell, I thought we was big. We ain't but half of that. The boss knows his business, though, and he's a good man. It's a good ranch to ride for."

"Well here's to the Rolling R.S. and good places to stake on." Sammy held up his whiskey and threw it back in one swallow.

"Here's to the Twin T.. And to you, Javier!" Frank said, turning at the last to the bar, and then he and Thomas threw theirs back.

The stagecoach from Raton pulled up in front and the travelers climbed out. They made their way into the Jupiter Sky where a few went to the bar and quickly ordered drinks. The stage drivers and the others dispersed among several tables. With the arrival of the crowd, the two women working for Annie Jordan came out and took orders and served meals and drinks. The room was steady with chatter and eating and drinking for the next forty-five minutes. Then the stage loaded up and was gone as quickly as it had arrived.

Sammy and Frank and Thomas talked and drank through all of it as the afternoon meandered on and shadows grew longer through the trees, creeping up the long rock faces all about.

"Well, we better git while there's gittin' left," Frank declared an hour after the stage had pulled out.

"Let's git then," Thomas replied in a fermented, languid drawl.

Frank nodded at the bottle that was in its final quarter. "Mister Winds, please regard that bottle and dispose of it with our good wishes and horse luck."

"Yeah?" Sammy happily asked, feeling the afternoon's indulgence in glorious respite. It occurred to him that he hadn't seen Annie Jordan in quite some time, and he briefly entertained the idea of heading for Trinidad. But he knew the lateness of the day, and his present state, leaned toward taking an easy bed and enjoying the Jupiter Sky Cantina and Hotel. "Muchas gracias, amigos. I'll give 'er a go. Have yourselves a good trip to Raton."

"We'll do that little thing," Frank replied, then asked, "You stayin' here tonight?"

"I'm thinking on it. Another drink or two oughta settle it."

"I know which way. Did you meet Annie Jordan yet?"

"Yeah, she was wearin' pants and lookin' good doin' it. I ain't seen many women wearin' pants."

"I ain't ever seen her wearin' a dress," Thomas chimed.

Frank chuckled. "Well, there's been a lotta tryin' with her . . . pants or otherwise. One's I know of have come up short. Too bad. She could run some whores and do a helluva business."

Chapter 48

Sammy was halfway through a cigarette and looking out the window at Frank and Thomas disappearing from view on the trail heading south. She appeared like a fresh day. "Hello, cowboy."

"Helloooo, Annie. I was wonderin' what became of you."

"I had a few things to tend to, but I'm all finished now."

"Well sit down and have a drink with me. I owe you one."

"I'd like that. Are you going to spend the night with us?" she asked as she sat down. She could see that Sammy was mildly intoxicated and extinct of any shyness. She wondered how his manners would hold up.

"Yes, ma'am, Annie. I'm stayin' put for tonight. And call me Sammy." He smiled at her. "I like it more personal at this point. Like we know each other."

"Okay, Sammy. Now we *do* know each other."

"Well, then. What'll you have?"

"I like tequila."

"All right. Javier, bring Miss Annie a bottle of your best tequila!"

Javier raised his hands with a look of mock exasperation. "Is only one kind."

246

"The best it is then. She'll have it."

Annie looked at Sammy with amazement. "A bottle? That's pretty ambitious, Sammy. You'll have to help me with it."

"Well, as you may have noticed, I'm feelin' ambitious."

"Then we'll drink to ambition," she said.

Javier brought the bottle and fresh glasses and Sammy poured her drink and then his. "To the Jupiter Sky and you, Annie," He clicked his glass to hers.

She gave him a heated, soulful look. "Thank you, Sammy. To your ambitions and their fruitions."

"Fruitions?" Sammy chimed, slightly surprised. "Yeah, I'm for that. Fruition!"

Sammy drank his shot, and she drank hers quickly, but in two, equally large sips. "I'm glad you're staying. You got the last room. Close call."

Sammy was surprised to hear it was the last room. He knew other people had arrived since the stage had left, but had not paid much notice since he and the Rolling R.S. boys had been in the throes of storytelling and smoking and drinking. He glanced around at the other folks in the bar. "Good thing I decided now."

She picked the glasses up and started to rise. "Come on. I'll show you around. Bring the bottle."

"Yes, ma'am."

They walked out the front doors into the shade of the yard. The sun had dropped behind the west peak and the clear blue sky above was shading darker with evening coming. She walked toward the barn at a leisurely pace with Sammy in tow. "Your horse in there?"

"I hope so."

"Pepito!" she called to the barn.

A moment later the boy appeared in the doorway. "Si, señorita."

"This man is staying the night."

"Okay," the boy said. "Do you want me to pull your rig from the horse, señor? We have a storage room. I can put it in there, or

I can take your things to your room."

"Pull my gear and put it in the storage room, save my saddle-bags. Put them in my room."

"You haven't signed the register. You don't have a room yet," Annie playfully noted.

"You hear that, Pepito? Looks like I'll be sleepin' in the barn with my horse."

The boy laughed. "The hay is soft, señor."

"Put his saddlebags in my office. He'll pick them up later."

"Si, señorita."

Annie began to walk. "Come on. I'll show you Stairway to the Stars."

"On to the stars . . . on to the moon . . . across the Jupiter Sky!" Sammy cheered and walked with her across the yard and around the far end of the cantina. "You've got a lot of buildings here," he commented, noticing several smaller log structures to the side and rear of the main building.

"There are eleven people who live and work here. Javier has a wife and two boys. Pepito you know. That's my cabin right there."

"It looks nice."

She led him back to the granite wall where the sign announced the stairway and the worn trail led easily upward. "How did you come to be here, Annie?" he asked as they made their way up the trail.

"I had a man—a gambler he was. We weren't married prop-er, but hitched just the same. He won himself a big stake and we were headed farther west when we came through here nine years ago. It was a provisions store then, just the main building. Angelo, my man, loved the spot and had a grand vision for it: cantina, ho-tel, gambling parlor right on the Santa Fe Trail. He made an offer to the old German couple who owned it, and they took it. I don't think they had done too well. We were young and wild, and this was a shot at a real enterprise. Anyway, we added on and the Ju-piter Sky Cantina and Hotel was born. There's a wonderful spring here—I don't know how way up here, but it has all the water we could ever use."

"Where's Angelo now?"

"Dead. He was shot by a gunslinger over a card game down in Trinidad. Angelo beat him at cards and the man accused him of cheating. Angelo could play cards, but he was no match for a fast draw."

"I'm sorry."

"It's been five years now. I just kept on and built the business."

"Is business good?"

"Business is great. There's a lot of folks and goods that travel this trail. More every year—and they all stop here. They don't all spend money here, but just the stopping increases my prospects. And it's a big ole time here on Saturday nights. I get folks from Raton and Trinidad and ranch hands who come for the dancing and good times, just to get away up the country. The cantina does great. I rent my rooms. And my provisions store stays busy. I'm adding on more rooms this fall when the traffic slows down."

"Well, you sure are somethin', Annie. You've done a great job here."

She looked at him, smiling. "Thank you, Sammy."

They followed the trail its quarter mile, as it slowly rose along the granite face, then meandered in and out of the evergreen, and finally turned the corner of the granite, leading the last hundred feet to its end at a precipice. "Whoaa! Look at that," Sammy said, gawking at the wooden stairway that spanned a thirty-foot chasm, fifty feet deep with jagged rock below. The stairs rose across like a long ladder to the top of a great boulder standing alone. "That must have been quite a job building that across there," Sammy speculated, with just the thought of it bringing a more sober moment to his thinking. "How exactly did you do that?"

"We didn't build it," Annie replied as she started up the stairs. The Germans built it. We just maintain it with varnish and screws." Sammy followed her up the stairway, hearing the wood groan ever so slightly, but not for lack of strength. It felt solid enough to hold twenty at a time.

The top of the stairs fed them onto the beginning crown of the giant boulder. They walked up the remaining gentle grade of rock and stepped up onto the large wooden platform perched on the flattop far beyond the surrounding cliffs and mountainside with open air all around them. Sammy had the sensation of floating on a small island in the sky, the magnificent, panoramic view of the eastern plains far below, and the spine of the Rocky Mountain range disappearing into the twilight of the south. He slowly scanned it, all as his head turned from north to south. "What a grand sight that is. Sure enough a heart stopper."

"Pour us a drink and get it started again."

"I'll do it."

They sat down on a bench at the front of the platform, and he poured the tequila as she held the glasses. "This sure is fine, Annie. I appreciate all the hospitality. You've been so nice to me right from the start, I wasn't sure . . ."

"What? If I was a whore?"

He looked at her, embarrassed even in his current condition that she so aptly concluded his thinking, and he felt the fool.

She laughed. "No. I'm just a woman who likes men. But I'm very particular and infrequent about who I like and how much I like them. I liked you from the moment I saw you. That's unusual for me."

"It's lucky for me."

"I'm glad you think so. Are you married?"

"No."

"You have a girl?"

"Yeah."

"She's not here now . . . and she's not your wife. You're a long way from home."

"Yeah, it feels like a long way. A lot's happened.

She lifted the glass to her lips and drank half of it. Sammy followed her lead and drank his shot.

250

"Why are you up this way?"

Sammy paused for a moment. "It's a long story."

"It's a long evening."

He rolled a smoke and she poured two more. Then he began to tell her about the man in the bar that he'd killed and the trip to Denver to collect the reward. She knew instinctually that it was all true as she listened with rapt attention. It was so much more than she'd ever expected. Then he told her about the cave and the Indians and Emily and Claire and Margaret, and his saddle partner, Blaine. "If he sticks to what he last told me, he'll be passin' through here in a week or two."

"I'll keep an eye out for him," she replied. "You two are heroes for risking your lives and saving those women."

"We didn't have much choice in it . . . the way it unfolded."

"I get the feeling it wouldn't have mattered if you'd had a choice. You're the saving kind—all man."

Dusk turned to night as they talked about each other's lives and looked at the stars, each feeling the slow simmer of desire. "We should get back now," she finally said. "While we still can. I know my way, but it's dark and the drink is catching me."

They made their way slowly back down the stairs and down the path, Sammy singing an improvised trail song and Annie attempting to follow along, laughing.

"Goooodbye to the Jupiter Sky. . . . Adiooooos, my old amigo. Farewell, till the night comes again. . . . Then we'll ride, for the heavens my friend."

He was right next to her when she misstepped on the dark trail and began to stumble. He grabbed her by the waist and pulled her to him. She wrapped her arms around his shoulders, and they both knew the moment had unexpectedly arrived. They kissed deeply, the tension of desire suddenly unleashing in the heated meeting of their lips with their bodies pressed tightly together. They separated for a moment, then came together again in another sweltering kiss and embrace. After a long minute they came apart, continuing on till they reached the grounds of the Jupiter Sky. She took his hand and led him to her cabin. "You won't be signing the register tonight," she said.

The next morning, she heated water and drew a bath in the tub that snugly accommodated two, and they washed each other and wiled away the early hours in a blaze of passion.

Sammy finally rode north at noon, after a hearty breakfast and a long goodbye.

Chapter 49

Raton Pass emptied out onto the plains with the long Rocky Mountain range pressed up against his left flank and running due north, like a guiding arrow. He rode by the settlement of Trinidad, but did not stop, preferring to make time and camp ahead another thirty miles or so. Dobe was ready for the work, and they kept a steady pace through the afternoon, stopping just once so the horse could drink and crop some of the good grass that was present.

As the sun sank low in the sky over the western range and the sojourn of evening drew near, Sammy pulled up a mile west of the trail at the base of the foothills and made camp inside the edge of the trees near a creek. He cut some deadfall for a fire and began to fish in hopes of having something fresher than jerky and hardtack.

The creek ran full and deep, and the water slowed in places where the bank cut away in pockets. Sammy worked the banks of the creek for half an hour without luck. Then as the sun set and shade sprinted east across the plains, the fourteen-inch rainbow hit his line. "Hot damn!" he exclaimed, as he reeled the silvery thrasher up and secured it safely onshore.

He built a fire and rigged the fish on a spit, and then sat in the cool of daylight's last breath and smoked a cigarette while his prize sizzled. Jenny ran through his mind. And then he thought of Annie. He'd never met a woman like Annie before. She was assertive and tough and smart, and she had dealt with circumstances that demanded the rugged individual spirit of the west. And she was all woman. She had undone him like a tornado hitting a pile of hay. His mind ran back to Jenny with pangs of guilt that quickly faded in the cast of overwhelming events of the journey. He knew he loved her, but he also knew that the last six months of his life had changed him in ways he did not yet understand.

Sammy ate his supper, then built the fire up and laid out his bedroll near it. It had been a good day's ride, even with the late start and nursing a hangover. Now he was tired. Night came with stars visible up through the treetops while he lay stretched out smoking a last cigarette. He took a final drag and exhaled slowly then snubbed it out and drifted into deep sleep.

Somewhere in his dream he heard his horse whinny and snort, but even in the depth of his slumber he slowly realized the noise did not seem to fit. His mind untangled the oddity at a pace that spoke to how tired he was, how deeply he slept. His eyes opened before he realized he was awake. Then he heard the movement and his hand reached for the gun belt and rifle at his side. The firelight flickered against the black, dancing a pale yellow that lit the bottom canopy of close trees, but revealed nothing else. He listened hard. The sound of twigs crushing under foot cut the air, and Sammy pulled his pistol as he began to sit up. "You let go that pistol or I'll blow a hole in yer head!"

"Shoot 'm now Odie," came another voice from behind Sammy. The rifle barrel pointing at Sammy's face emerged into the light as the man stepped close. He was bearded and wore a greasy canvas coat, homespun trousers, and lace-up boots, and he had on a beaver-tail cap.

"You want me to shoot 'm?" came the voice from behind Sammy.

Sammy laid the pistol by his side and brought his hands to

chest height. "I don't know why you're drawin' down on me, but I haven't done anything and I'm not lookin' for trouble."

A perverted cackle of a laugh came from behind. "You hear that, Odie? He ain't lookin' fer trouble. You don't hafta look 'cause it's here," came the voice and stupid cackle again.

Sammy saw the man who'd been behind him come into view from the side. He had a cocked pistol trained on Sammy. He moved in close and used his foot to scoot away the guns at Sammy's side.

"Get up! Easy," Odie said.

Sammy stood up, carefully watching the two men holding guns on him.

"Whadaya wanna do with him, Odie?"

"Shut up and quit callin' me by my name, ya dumb bastard. Get a rope and tie 'm to that tree."

"Sorry, Odie."

"Move over there," Odie said, directing Sammy toward the nearest tree with his rifle barrel. "Now get yer back up against it and hold still."

The other man looped the rope around Sammy's chest once and tied it at the back of the tree, then looped it around Sammy and the tree a dozen more times before tying it off.

"Get his knife there and tie his wrists, Clip."

The other man looked over at Odie. "You just called me by my name."

"He knows mine. Might as well know yers, too. Yep, he's Clip and I'm Odie."

Clip finished tying Sammy and then stepped back to observe his work. "That'll hold 'm."

Odie put his rifle down and looked at Sammy's gear. "Fancy saddle here. Bring his horse into the light. See what we got," Odie said, then heaped more wood onto the fire that had little flame left, but a good bed of coals. It sprang to life, throwing more light around the campsite.

"What do you boys want?" Sammy asked, his blood rising as

Clip led Dobe into the firelight.

"Yer horse . . . saddle . . . guns. And we'll see what else you got. Got some money?" Odie asked. Sammy didn't answer. "We'll know soon enough," Odie declared.

Clip cackled away at that. "Looky here at this horseflesh. He's a good one," Clip said.

Odie looked the horse over. "Yeah, he could fetch a price. Or maybe keep 'm. Looks like a appaloosa."

Clip liked the idea of keeping him. "I'm the one ridin' a old mule. If we keep him, I want 'm."

"Heeaaaaw! Git Dobe!" Sammy screamed into the night, so loud and sudden that Odie and Clip jumped. The horse bolted, ripping the lead rope from Clip's hand. Clip drew his pistol and quickly pointed and fired as Dobe was disappearing into the dark. Sammy thought he saw Dobe's right hind-quarter flinch with the shot, but Dobe continued at a gallop off into the woods. "You son of a bitch!" Sammy yelled.

Odie strode over and backhanded Sammy with all he had, then punched him in the gut, causing Sammy's head to jerk forward as the air left him. "That might of cost you yer life, mister," Odie declared as Sammy sucked for air.

Sammy got his breath and his head came up. He was bleeding from the mouth and nose as he looked at Odie. "Well, ain't you just one big ball of tough. Why don't you untie me from this tree and we'll see whose life gives up first." Odie backhanded him again and Clip stepped in and threw a left hook to Sammy's ribs.

Sammy groaned with the body shot and worked hard to get a breath. Then he glared at both of them with contempt. "Looks like neither one of you shitbags will be ridin' my horse."

Clip drew his pistol and cocked it, pointing it at Sammy's face. "You just spoke yer last words," he said.

Sammy grimly smiled. "Here's a few more—fuck you, you gutless sack of shit."

Clip's eyes bulged as he shook with anger and backed up two steps. He pulled the trigger. The blast boomed and smoke shot forth and hung for a moment like a thick fog bank before it began to drift and break up in the light breeze.

"You missed," Sammy said.

Odie and Clip stepped in close and stared in disbelief at the bullet hole inches above Sammy's head, bored into the tree with splintered bark around it. "God damn!" Odie said in amazement. "Ain't he the saltiest dude you ever seen."

Clip re-cocked the pistol. "No!" Odie said as he put his hand over Clip's hand and pushed the pistol down. "That's too easy for this one. I got a better idea. We'll leave 'm tied to the tree. See how salty he is when the varmints start feedin' on 'm."

Clip broke into his cackle like he'd just heard the joke of his life. He squinted and looked at Sammy with delight. "Yeaahhh! Wait'll them coyotes and wolves come lookin' and them crows come peckin' on your eyeballs." Clip cackled some more. Sammy was quiet.

Odie reached for Sammy's pockets. "Let's see what he's got in here." He fished out the silver and gold coins Sammy had in a front pocket and looked at them. "There's nigh unto a hundred dollars here! We cut dead center!" Clip danced a little jig while Odie went through the rest of Sammy's pockets and found chewing tobacco and cigarette tobacco and paper and matches. "I'll have me a smoke now . . . and a chaw too."

"Got some more good stuff in these saddlebags?" Clip asked as he sat down by the fire and began to go through one of them. He pulled out a Colt Navy 36 and two knives. "Looky here Odie—another pistol and more knives. He's got three pistols and this Henry rifle and three knives . . . and a lotta shells."

"You fixin' on fightin a war, mister?" Odie asked. Sammy didn't answer.

Clip pulled out two tie cheesecloths that contained jerky and hardtack. He opened them and began to eat as he casually went through the rest of the bag. "Looky here," he said through a mouthful of jerky and cooked flour, "It's a little fishin' kit with hooks and such. And he's got hisself a fishin' pole rigged to this scabbard here . . . fancy one."

Odie sat down at the fire and put the money and other contents from Sammy's pockets on the ground in front of him. Then he grabbed the jerky and hardtack and began to eat.

Clip pulled out a brown paper bag and peered in it before pulling out a bit of the contents and examining it closely. "This looks like candy," he called out with the delight of a five-year-old. He put a piece in his mouth, right along with the unfinished jerky and hardtack.

"Lemme see that," Odie said, grabbing the bag. He dug out a few pieces, throwing them in with his mouthful and chewing contentedly, slurping and smacking.

Clip grabbed the other saddlebag and started in on it. He pulled out Sammy's extra shirt, pants, socks, and skivvies and a pair of gloves. Then his eyes lit up. "Oh yeah! Here's a little somethin' for us!" Clip pulled out the half-full pint bottle with a cork stopper. "We got us some 'shine!" He examined the label. "Looks like some homefire."

Odie was impatient. "Well, have a drink and pass it here."

Clip pulled the cork and smelled it. "It don't smell like corn or rye . . . or any other I smelled before. But it smells like alcohol. Say, what the hell is this?" Clip asked Sammy as he drew his pistol and aimed it at him, imagining he might get a fear-induced answer.

Sammy spoke slowly and sincerely. "My grandmother makes her moonshine with prunes. Keeps her happy and regular."

Clip looked bewildered for a moment then holstered his gun and took a sip.

"How is it?" Odie asked.

"I can taste them prunes . . . I think. It ain't much fer flavor, but it sure is fermented. He tipped the bottle to his lips and slugged back several ounces, then coughed from it. "Hoooo!"

"Give it here!" Odie demanded. Clip handed the bottle to Odie, who drank nearly all of it, but left the final ounce for Clip, and handed the bottle back. Odie took a deep breath as he felt the burn. "That *is* different ain't it? Kinda good—like pine tar liquor or somethin'."

Clip looked at the bottle again, then drank the rest and tossed it into the fire. Sammy watched closely as Odie rolled up several cigarettes then handed one to Clip. The two men lit up and began to smoke as they ate more jerky and candy and talked about their haul of booty.

Odie reached for the coins and divided them up in a way he was sure favored him, then gave the rest to Clip. "There's yer half." Clip didn't seem to notice any discrepancy and quickly pocketed his loot. "We might could find that horse in the morning. He'd bring a fast hundred," Odie said.

"If we find 'm, I want 'm," Clip said, resolutely.

"Then you gotta give something for 'm. You don't just get 'm."

"I'll give somethin'. We gotta find 'm 'fore I give it anyways."

"If you hit 'm with that shot he might bleed out or be no good. You gotta pay then anyways."

"Not if we don't find 'm. Then it's just like he run away and was gone . . . and that weren't my doin'."

"If yer shootin was anything like yer shootin at that feller, then that horse is just fine. So we oughta look for 'm."

"I hit 'm, I'm pretty sure."

"Maybe. But why'd you even shoot at 'm?"

"I didn't want 'm getting' away." Clip quite suddenly had a peculiar look on his face. "I don't feel right. I can't feel my body," he said slowly with a tapering slur. His expression became disoriented as his head began to roll around and his eyelids went to half-mast.

"What's wrong with you?" Odie asked Clip, who was no longer able to speak. His body looked like it was melting. His arms flopped limply to his sides, and his head teetered about with gurgling sounds coming from his deformed mouth. Then he simply folded backwards into the dirt and did not move.

"Clip! Clip!" Odie yelled. He looked over at Sammy. "What's

wrong with him? What was in that bottle?" Sammy didn't answer. Odie felt the wave rush over him like an ocean of warm honey permeating every pore. A look of drugged panic beset his face and he tried to get to his feet, wobbling badly as he did so. As he reached a standing position, the intensity of the drug's grip soared by the second. He sensed his final moment had come. Odie stumbled a few steps, then lost consciousness and toppled face first into the campfire.

Chapter 50

After the massive overdose of laudanum had brought an end to Clip and Odie, Sammy spent the rest of the night shimmying and squirming to try and free himself of the ropes. The loops around his chest circled down over his arms to where his wrists were tied in front of him. It seemed the upper loops had not relented at all, and his efforts had only left him tired and rope burned all over. Still, he made a little progress with the loops that ran down over his thighs because Clip had run out of rope just before he got to Sammy's knees, and tied off above them. By tiny movements up and down, pushing off the balls of his feet while flexing his knees up and down, one after the other, the rope began to gradually inch upward on his legs. Shortly before dawn, he stopped from exhaustion, and his head hung forward and down as he slept.

The gray of first light filtered through the trees, revealing the morbid scene in detail. Clip lay dead with his partially-open eyes fixed up toward the sky. Odie had hit the fire dead center with his chest and face. His jacket, shirt, and cap had burned completely, and his naked and charred upper torso lay smoldering, leaving the stench of burned flesh hanging heavy in the air. The horse and mule that Odie and Clip had arrived on stood tied to trees sever-

261

al hundred feet away.

Sammy thought about the stark circumstances. Two dead men lay fifteen feet in front of him and he was roped to a tree with bound hands and no perceptible means of escape. He was not near any trail, and it was unlikely anybody would happen by and see him, being a hundred feet inside the tree line and facing upslope.

Looking at Odie and Clip, Sammy wondered how they had managed to come upon him. Perhaps they had trailed him, seeing he was alone, and had planned to take him when he slept. He knew none of it mattered now.

Imagining a way to get loose strained his thinking. There was nothing viable that came to mind beyond somebody untying him or working his own way free. He'd already worked at it enough to understand the unlikely prospect of it. He prayed and thanked God for seeing him through his encounter with Clip and Odie, but he couldn't imagine that he had survived it to die tied to a tree. He wouldn't accept that, and he again began to shimmy and squirm and work his legs and twist his wrists.

After a while, he rested and tried whistling for Dobe. His lips were cut and swollen from Odie striking him, and he was unable to generate much volume. He whistled his weak fluted shrill into the woods, then listened. He whistled again and yelled, wishing he were tied to the other side of tree so he could see through to the east and onto the plains and perhaps spot his horse or any travelers. He listened again. All he could hear was the creek faintly running in the distance. He worked his body and wrists again, trying to note any discernable progress other than the fractional movement upward of the rope over his legs. Time dragged on. For long intervals he would work at moving, and then rest, and whistle, and yell, and listen.

The sun streamed high in the sky as morning gave way to the afternoon. Sammy kept up the routine of work and rest and calling out. His wrists bled from the rope cuts. His body was rubbed raw everywhere the rope looped around and where his back had rubbed on the tree. The more he worked at it, the worse the pain got. But the rope on his legs seemed to have come up several inches so that he could kick his feet out from the tree a foot or so. And he felt as if the rope on his torso had maybe loosened just a bit, but he wondered if it was just imagined. He urinated. His piss burned where it hit the ropes on his legs.

Late in the afternoon, he saw several buzzards begin their slow circling overhead. He knew it wouldn't be long before they came down. Other scavengers would soon catch scent and come seeking their portion.

With the twilight came the birds. Half a dozen landed one at a time, then walked cautiously around the campsite determining what was living and what was dead. Sammy grunted and barked demonically, kicking his feet at any bird that ventured his way. The birds settled on Clip and Odie, leaving Sammy alone, as if they knew his status at the tree meant a later opportunity.

When the darkness of night fell full, Sammy was beset by an insatiable thirst. His resolve at denying its torment had been whittled away as a fading refuge of defense. He was cold and exhausted and his pain abated to something tolerable only when he remained still. Doubt crept forth as he considered if he could ever work himself free. He began to make his peace, praying and asking God to bring him home quickly if his time on earth was to end. His shivering became uncontrollable, and he was consumed with enduring his pain and thirst. Somewhere he broke with it, and sleep came as the great deliverer of relief.

He dreamed the recurring dream he'd had as a boy in which he was deep in the dark woods. There was a cabin with a window, and it shone a soft yellow glow that drew his very soul forth with the sensation of consummate love and security. Although the dream had come many times, he had never entered the cabin, instead he just saw it and felt its power and allure as an infinite sanctuary. Now he saw it once again and felt the warmth. And he dreamed of his mother holding him as a young boy after he'd been hurt or had a nightmare, remembering the soothing sweetness of it when she told him everything would be all right. And in his dream the revelation came that these events were an extension of God's mercy and grace, and that one day he would enter the cabin in the dark woods and find that all along it had been a glimpse of heaven. And then he was awake again.

The night's blackness swallowed him, and the hair on the back of his neck stood up with goose bumps rising over his body. He could hear the pulling and ripping of flesh by strong teeth. The birds were gone, replaced by coyotes or wolves. He couldn't tell which, but either way would mean his end if they decided to turn their attention to him. His eyes adjusted slowly with the waxing slice of moon above, providing just enough light down through the trees to make out the shapes. It looked to be three of them. Coyotes he figured, as wolves were rare. Then as if on cue, they began a round of yipping with a few howls that confirmed their identity. The coyotes resumed their feeding with Sammy being fairly certain that Clip and Odie would provide more than enough to keep them at bay, for the time being.

He watched and listened to the frenzy, thinking that just a night before these men had been living beings, but now they were mere sustenance for the predators. He slowly began to work at the ropes again. The pain was not slow in returning, but he ignored it the best he could and continued. The ropes had loosened some. He was sure of it. Could he get them loose enough? He kept at it for an hour, confining his mind to anything that mitigated the pain his movement brought.

Somewhere during that time the coyotes left, with Sammy being completely unaware of their departure. He knew they'd be back. His pain and thirst were racking him again, and he eventually hung his head forward, hoping for sleep. It finally came as a prayer answered. There were no dreams this time, only a depth of refuge from consciousness and the hell it had become.

Sleep hung on him as a cloak until dawn, when it was peeled back by the scent, familiar and haunting like something lost that would always be beyond reach. It remained strong and invaded his peace like a cruel hoax of hope that would vanish with his awakening. Then, like the wind filling a sail, the reality awakened him as Dobe put his nose under Sammy's hanging head and nuzzled up against him, pushing Sammy's head up. Sammy's eyes opened and he smiled as his horse continued pushing his snout against Sammy's chest and shoulders.

"Man, oh man. It's good to see you." Sammy leaned his head forward and rubbed his face into Dobe's. "Yeah. That's some good lovin'. I need it." He caught a glimpse of the blood on Dobe's rear flank. "I see that dumb son of a bitch hit you," Sammy said, mad all over again that Clip had shot at his horse. "Well neither one of those geniuses could read, and that led to their demise, I'm happy to report."

Sammy looked over to Clip and Odie who had been moved about as the coyotes had fed on their soft bellies and intestines and thighs and buttocks. "Why don't you hang around and neither one of us will die here alone," he said to Dobe with a slight tone of resignation.

Through the morning mist, the figure on horseback appeared like an apparition in silent movement. Sammy watched and Dobe snorted as the figure weaved smoothly through the trees, heading right for them. It was an Indian. There was something familiar about him, but Sammy couldn't place it. He only knew it was not the surviving Indian from the cave. But it was someone he'd seen before. He wondered how that was possible, up here, so far from home. With his horse standing next to him, Sammy helplessly watched as the Indian rode the last hundred feet into the camp.

The Indian came to a stop and sat atop his horse looking at Sammy with expressionless eyes. He wore buckskin pants with short leather tassels down the side of each leg, and his vest looked to have been fashioned from beaver pelts. A bronze medallion in the shape of a quarter moon hung from his neck in the midst of several bead necklaces. Two red feathers stood up as a V from the back of his head where they were tucked into his leather headband. Sammy stared back at him, each man's gaze holding on each other for a long moment before the Indian swung a leg up and over the neck of his horse and dropped to the ground, landing silently like a cat.

The Indian walked slowly around the camp and stopped and squatted by Odie. He looked for a moment at the charred and unrecognizable face, then moved over to where Clip lay face down and mostly naked from his clothes being ripped off where the coyotes had fed. He rolled Clip over and stared at his lifeless eyes. Sammy detected the slightest expression of recognition on the Indian's face as he yipped loudly several times, like some victory call.

Sammy braced for his own ending as the Indian's attention turned back to him. He moved toward him now, but stopped as he came upon Dobe, looking at the blood on the horse's flank beneath the bullet's entry and exit wound. The recollection flooded Sammy's mind like the nightmare it had once been. It was the Indian from Sammy's dream those months back. The knife came easily from the sheath with a glint on the blade from the light above. Sammy's breath froze still in his chest as he prepared to die. The movement was swiftly elegant as the Indian stepped forward, his arm in a swinging arc that propelled the blade to its intended target. The tautness of the rope relaxed as the two cut ends fell away from each other. The Indian turned and walked to his horse, where he took one bounding spring and was remounted. A moment later he was fading into the landscape of the forest.

Sammy shimmied and pulled, and the rope came loose. He was free at last.

Finding his knife by the campfire, he squatted and clamped it between his knees with the blade up. Then he moved his tied wrists back and forth on the blade until the rope was severed and his hands were free. He grabbed his canteen and drank fully, then repacked his gear and collected his money back from what was left of Clip and Odie. After turning loose Clip and Odie's raggedy horse and mule, he took his change of clothes and headed for the creek.

The sun had cracked the horizon and shone brightly on the creek as Sammy stripped naked and threw his pants and skivvies away. He had pissed himself half a dozen times and shit once. He wanted no part of them ever again. The creek ran swift and cold as Sammy stepped into it. He went to his knees, then stretched out fully, submerging all of his body. The cold water stung his rope burns like a horde of wasps, but he welcomed the pain that came with living. He sat up and washed himself then lay out fully again for several minutes and let the water run over him. Minutes later, he stood naked drying in the morning sun as Dobe cropped good grass.

After dressing in fresh clothes, Sammy closely inspected Dobe's wound. The bullet had entered at the rear of the horse's right hind and exited several inches forward, having stayed close to the surface and tearing through muscle. It had not struck an artery, and the wounds were not bleeding at the moment, but the horse had a bad limp and certainly was not ready for any hard work.

Sammy found suitable plants and boiled the diced leaves along with charcoal and flour to make the poultice for Dobe. He gobbed it on and molded it thickly over the bullet holes. The remaining flour yielded a little frybread for himself. He was starving, and the coyotes and birds had eaten his jerky and hardtack. The frybread was good, but too little and quickly gone. A thought of fishing again was quickly thrown over by the compelling desire to get gone of the whole damn place.

Sammy strapped on his gunbelt, appreciating the weight of his 44s. He packed his rig and gear on Dobe and whistled for his horse to follow him as he walked out of the woods and headed north.

Chapter 51

In the late morning, Sammy crested a plains hill and saw the town of Walsenburg a few miles ahead. He reached it at noon and walked up the main street, leading Dobe by the reins. Strong wind blew dust clouds about, prompting several proprietors to close their windows and doors as he passed. A livery sat at the end of the street. Sammy tied Dobe at the hitching post in front then entered the barn and found a man cleaning a stall inside.

"Hello. Are you the man?" Sammy asked.

The man glanced at Sammy and kept working. "Yep. What can I do you for?"

"A stall for my horse. Feed and water 'm . . . and anything you might know about caring for bullet holes. He's got two on his right flank. Just one bullet—where it entered and came out. He's got a poultice on right now."

The man stopped and looked at Sammy's cut and swollen lips and his nose, puffy and slightly discolored with bruising that extended out under the eyes. He looked at the gashes on Sammy's wrists just below his cuff line. "I'm not an outlaw," Sammy said, noting the apprehension on the man's face. "A couple of men tried to rob me."

"Tried, eh?"

"That's right . . . tried."

The man seemed to roll that around for a moment. "Bring your horse in."

"All right," Sammy said, then collected Dobe, and walked him in.

The man took a good look at Dobe and his poultice. "This looks fresh. No need to change this till tomorrow. I can clean it then put some antiseptic on. Maybe bandage it and work his leg with some liniment . . . get it circulating."

"That sounds good. Can I leave him now?"

"Yep. It's fifty cents a day for the boarding and another two bits for the medical supplies and care."

Sammy gave him a silver dollar. "Is there anyplace to stay here? I didn't see anything comin' up the street."

"The hotel we had burned down New Year's Eve. They're going to rebuild it this summer. Try Beulah's just west a quarter mile. She don't post for it, but she's got an extra room or two, and whatever else you might fancy." The man cracked the slightest smile.

Sammy pulled his saddlebags and rifle off Dobe and hoisted the bags over his shoulder. "I saw the tracks and depot on the east end. Is there a train runnin'?"

"Yep. The Denver and Rio Grande. Just finished up a few months back. Runs all the way to Denver. And now they're laying track west to Alamosa."

"Yeah? That oughta be good for business."

"I suppose. Been a lot of prospectors through."

"You happen to know the schedule on that Denver train?"

"Runs north Tuesdays and Fridays. 9 a.m."

Sammy thought for a moment. "Is today Thursday?"

"Yep."

"Do they haul horses?"

"Yep."

"Much obliged, mister. I'll be back in the morning."

Sammy went to the mercantile and bought a pair of pants, a

shirt, some skivvies, a smoked ham, a can of peaches, and a jar of salve that advertised it was good for all skin ailments. He found a place on the side of a building that was mostly out of the wind and sat down and devoured the peaches and half of the ham. Then he headed for Beulah's.

There were no markings on the two-story frame building, but it was the only thing in sight, and the sign in the window read: Come On In. The front parlor had a small bar and two settees with faded pink tapestries behind them, one of which had stitched in large gold letters: Beulah's Sporting Palace. Underneath, in smaller letters it read: A Stiff Stump Needs A Good Hump.

A gal in her mid-twenties wearing a silk robe sat at the bar reading an old newspaper with a coffee cup in front of her. The bell on the door jingled when Sammy walked in. She looked up, a little surprised to see the cowboy with saddlebags and a rifle. "Hello, honey. You're early. You here for a little relief?"

Sammy looked around and managed a smile. "I'm not here for the sportin', ma'am. I'm lookin' for a room for the night."

"A room? That's all?

"Well, yeah."

"You sure look like you had a time of it. I can make you feel better."

"Maybe later. Do you have a room?"

"Wait here a minute." She left and came back a moment later with an older woman whom Sammy guessed to be the proprietor.

"Hello, baby. I'm Beulah. I understand you're looking for a room."

"Yes, ma'am."

"I usually have an empty one, but I've got a new girl and it's not available except for sporting customers—and they don't spend the whole night. If you want to sleep here tonight, it'll have to be with one of my girls for the whole night price."

"How much is that?"

"Four dollars. I'll throw in a bath and breakfast . . . and two free drinks. You can pick the girl."

"What time can I eat breakfast?"

"Seven a.m. I'll feed you good, baby."

"Okay," Sammy said and dug out the money. "I don't need to see the other girls, if that's alright with you."

"It sure is, honey. I'm Rita. You can come with me."

She led him upstairs to her room where he deposited his gear in a corner and then sat on the bed. "How 'bout it, honey? Would you like to have a go at it now?"

Sammy was pretty well shot. It had been a ten-mile hike to town that morning, and he hadn't slept much during his time tied to the tree. The feel of the bed made him woozy with exhaustion just sitting on it. "I'd like to have a go at this bed for an hour or so, if you don't mind."

Rita looked a bit deflated. "You paid for it, honey."

"Would you help me with something first?" Sammy asked as he began unbuttoning his shirt. His rope burns oozed slimy fluid that stuck to the fabric of his clothes.

"Yeah, honey. What do you want me to do?"

"My back needs some of this salve on it, and I can't reach it," he said as he gingerly pulled off his shirt. "Would you put some on?"

She gasped at the burns on his arms and chest, red and raw with puss. He turned his back to her and she stared at the middle of it, ripped raw from his back rubbing on the coarse tree bark as he'd worked to free himself. "Oh, honey. You're a mess! What happened to you?"

"Wrong place, wrong time. But more so for the two hombres who roped me up."

She looked at him, unsure of what he meant, but sure she wasn't going to ask and didn't want to know unless he volunteered the information. "Why don't you let me clean you up with a nice bath before we put on that salve. The tub is right downstairs and we always have hot water on. It's nice and private."

"Okay. A little later then. I've gotta close my eyes for a while right now."

Sammy pulled his shirt back on and kicked off his boots, stretching out on the bed with his eyes closed. "I'll be downstairs," she said and left the room. Sammy was asleep inside of a minute.

He slept for several hours, then had his bath. Rita gently washed his back with soap and applied the salve to it before he dressed. "Would you like me to get you anything, honey?" she asked. "I could cook you up something to eat. It wouldn't be any trouble. I was gonna make something for myself anyway."

Sammy gave her two dollars. "Yeah, I'd like that."

"You don't have to pay me."

"I want to. I appreciate your hospitality."

"Thanks, honey."

After they ate, Sammy rose from the table and began to head for the front door. "I'm gonna try out one of those rockers I saw on the front porch . . . have a smoke."

"You want some company?"

"Sure. Come on, girl."

"I'll be right there. I'm just going to clean up a minute."

The wind had died and sunset glowed deep red on the western clouds. He sat in one of the wooden rockers and smoked, content in the moment. Rita stepped outside and sat next to him. She asked if he would roll her a smoke. He rolled her several, and they went from small talk to more personal things and how they came to be in their particular circumstances. A few customers drifted in with the evening, each man nodding to Sammy and Rita as if they were entering the mercantile, and Sammy and Rita carried on throughout. They talked of remembrances of being kids, each being surprised at some of the same kinds of recollections of outings and hearing stories and folklore, and playing games with other kids, which they discovered had been rare for each of them. For Rita, it was the sweetest of diversions to have such a conversation with a man that didn't revolve around business and her line of work. Soon the evening was gone. And the next morning, so too was Sammy.

272

The livery operator had done a good job of cleaning and bandaging Dobe's wounds. Sammy felt no excessive heat on the area directly around the bandages, and was fairly certain that infection was not present. Nevertheless, the horse's limp had not improved when Sammy walked him down to the station.

The train left the Walsenburg depot at 9 a.m. sharp, rolling north into the clear, sunny day. Sammy relaxed in the nearly empty car and watched the countryside go by, excited at the prospect of reaching Denver later that day. With each of the half dozen stops along the one hundred and sixty mile route came more people. At 4 p.m., when the train arrived in Denver, every seat was taken and several men stood in the aisle at the front of the car. The novelty of the ride had long since gone, and Sammy was thankful to finally climb down the steps at the Denver Station.

Chapter 52

A three tier, crystal chandelier that held a hundred candles hung high above the center of the lobby of the Ducayne Hotel. There were several sitting areas arranged with French provincial chairs and settees, backed by walls with a wainscot of cherry wood below and peach-colored wallpaper above that had finely embossed stitching in the shapes of various lamps and carriages. The sitting areas flanked a main walkway that ran from the front doors through the lobby to the front desk like a runway for observation of style and gait of all who entered.

A group of visiting easterners occupied one of the sitting areas and looked like an advertisement of elegance and refinement as they waited for their coach to embark on an evening of fine dining and theatre. They stared appraisingly at the cowboy as he strode through the lobby with saddlebags over his shoulder, holding a rifle and wearing a gun belt with two pistols. His face was battered, and his appearance did not look consistent with the type of clientele for such a distinguished hotel. Sammy sensed them staring and tipped his hat to them, the gesture decidedly aloof and not lost on the easterners as a rebuke to their unmistakable highbrow judgment. Several of them looked away as if they'd been found out.

"Can I help you?" the clerk asked as Sammy stepped to the counter.

"Do you have a room available?"

The clerk's eyebrows hiked a bit. "Well, yes, but the rate is five dollars a night."

Sammy slapped a twenty-dollar gold piece on the counter. "Does this work for you?" he replied, wondering why Reuben had been insistent that he stay there. He remembered Reuben telling him he'd encounter some snobbery, but he also advised that the beds and service was the best in town, and some exposure to the elite crowd would be educational.

"Yes, sir," the clerk replied, aware of his miscalculation. "How many nights will you be staying with us, mister...?"

"Winds . . . Sammy Winds. I'm not certain of that yet, but at least until Monday."

"Very well, sir. If you will sign the register, please. Do you have a horse we can stable, sir?

"He's down a block at Talbot Livery."

"That's a very fine stable, but we have our own stables here if you would like to have your horse closer."

"Really? Well maybe I'll move him later."

"Just let me know and I'll arrange for a stall. Do you have anything else of immediate need, Mister Winds?"

"No, not at the moment."

"You'll find a list of available services in your room. There are water closets and bathing facilities at the end of each hall, and you'll find a bathrobe in your room. If you would like anything at all—room service, your bath prepared, anything at all—please pull the cord by your door and an assistant will report to your room."

"Where can I get a good steak?"

"The Olivet Garden Dining Room, right here in the hotel, serves a great steak. But if you prefer to dine out, Barrons Restaurant serves the best beef in the city, I've been told. They're open till 11 p.m. on Friday and Saturday nights. It's two blocks east and then north a block on Broadway."

"Much obliged. Oh, I almost forgot. Do you know where the Westerfeld Building is?"

The clerk seemed a bit surprised. "Why, yes. Go south to Speer Boulevard, then west about a quarter mile."

Sammy sat down on the bed then stretched out fully for a moment. It was the most comfortable thing he'd ever rested upon. "You sure weren't kiddin' about the beds, Reuben," Sammy said out loud as he lay there tempted to just drift off. He quickly got up and went to the window. The view revealed the avenue below, with its many brick and frame buildings and hard-packed dirt street thick with drawn coaches and wagons and singles on horseback. He had the urge to take a good look.

The cool of early evening drifted through the Denver streets as Sammy walked them and leisurely looked in storefronts. The array of goods and services was astounding to him. There were clothes of every kind for every occasion and appliances and tools he had never seen before. And there were saloons and eateries and bakeries and land offices and markets and jewelry and art shops and bookstores and cobbler shops and street vendors and lots of people. Denver did not look like Santa Fe or Albuquerque. There were not nearly as many Spanish or Mexicans, but instead many more Anglos whose dress varied from woolen suits and formal hats to cowhide trousers and leather vests. The women he saw were all escorted and wore dresses with petticoats underneath and fancy hats, some boasting plumes of ornamental feathers of lavish color.

He watched a two-man crew working with a wagon and ladder as they moved down the street lighting lampposts. They knew their business. Sammy was impressed with the speed of their operation and wondered how many crews there were and how long it took to light the downtown area. It seemed an enormous city. The biggest he'd ever been in.

He walked up one block and down another like a tourist. He

was taking it all in when he happened upon Speer Boulevard. Sammy turned to the west and walked a little faster with a destination in mind. Several blocks down, he came upon it.

The Westerfeld building rose from the street six stories high in red brick. Its huge, arched entrance was faced with moss rock, above which sculptured large bronze letters read: WESTERFELD. Sammy climbed the dozen steps to the entrance and peered in one of the framed ten-foot glass doors. A uniformed guard sat behind a reception desk in the lobby, reading a magazine in the light of two brightly burning desk lamps. Sammy pressed on the door and was surprised to find it began to open. The large wall clock behind the security guard's desk read 8:30. The guard's eyes came up as Sammy entered.

"Hello," Sammy said as he walked across the lobby toward the desk. "You folks work some long hours. I sure didn't expect to find anybody here now."

"Yes. . . . Why are you here?"

"I'm in town to see Mister Westerfeld," Sammy said as he came to a stop in front of the desk.

"Do you have an appointment?"

"Well, of a sort."

"What does that mean?"

"It means he's been expecting my arrival. I've traveled up from New Mexico Territory, and it wasn't a certainty when I'd arrive."

"Does he know you?"

"He knows *of* me."

The guard rose from his chair and rested his hands on his gunbelt. "State your business."

Sammy took a step back. "My name is Sammy Winds, and I'm here to collect a reward that Mister Westerfeld posted. I killed the man who murdered one of his engineers."

The guard cocked his head just a bit and took on a slight squint of the eyes as he seemingly examined Sammy more closely. "Sure, yeah. We all heard about that. You're the fella? Sammy Winds, you say?"

"Yeah."

"Do you have any papers that can prove that?"

"No, not on me. They're back at my hotel room. I didn't plan on doin' this tonight. I got into town late this afternoon. I was just out takin' a walk and happened by. Can I make an appointment for tomorrow or Monday and come back?"

"I suppose you could, but Mister Westerfeld won't be here. He'll be out of town for several weeks."

Sammy's head fell back then came forward. "Well ain't that just a damn dandy! It's been a time just gettin' here." Sammy took a deep breath and shook his head in disbelief.

The guard pushed a button on the desk and a moment later a man in a suit came from a doorway. "Wait here," the guard said to Sammy as he walked to meet the man. The guard spoke to the man in whispered tones as the man listened and looked at Sammy. "Come with me please," the man said to Sammy.

"All right," Sammy replied, and followed the man. They left the lobby and went down a hallway and around a corner. Two other men stood in front of a contraption that Sammy didn't recognize. "What are we doing?" Sammy asked.

"We're going to see Mister Westerfeld," the man replied.

"He's here? Now? I thought he was out of town."

"He leaves tomorrow."

One of the men slid open the gate to what looked like a closet. "What's this thing?" Sammy asked.

The man smiled. "It's a lift. It will take us up to the floor where Mister Westerfeld is."

"How about stairs? Don't you have stairs?"

"Yeah, we have stairs. This is faster. It's Mister Westerfeld's private lift."

Sammy looked a little anxious. "Relax, kid . . . nothing to worry about, unless you're not who you say you are."

Sammy stepped into the lift with the man, and one of the other men closed the gate behind them. The man who closed the gate pulled down hard on a lever on the wall and the lift began to rise

278

quite rapidly. Sammy felt his stomach drop and instinctively put his hands out to the side to steady himself. The lift went to the top floor.

Chapter 53

The gates opened and Sammy and the man exited. Sammy turned around and took another look at the lift. "Ropes, pulleys, and weights, huh? Is that how it works?"

"Smart kid. Yeah, I think that's it—except it has steel cables, not ropes."

Sammy followed the man down a hallway that had doors along both sides. They came to a large foyer where two more men in suits sat in chairs on either side of massive oak doors. A woman sat at a desk to the side of the foyer. "Hello, Faye," the man said to her.

"Hello, Burton. What brings you up?"

"I've got somebody here the boss wants to meet."

She looked Sammy over, curious about who he was. "He's in with Roy and Louie. It's been a while. You can knock and see. He might like an excuse to run them out."

"Okay, Faye. Thanks."

Burton nodded to the two men sitting in chairs, then knocked temperately on the door. "Come in," a voice boomed from the other side. Burton eased in and closed the door behind him. A few moments later Roy and Louie and Burton exited the office with Burton leaving the door slightly ajar.

"Go on in, kid. He's waiting,"

Sammy entered and closed the door behind him. It looked to be forty feet across the room to where Mister Westerfeld was rising from behind his desk. But Sammy's attention was caught by a full mount of a nine-foot grizzly bear that was just to his left, standing in an attack position with its arms high and its mouth open in a snarl, revealing its giant teeth. Sammy took a quick step to his right. "Lord Almighty! That's the biggest bear I've ever seen."

Barclay Westerfeld began talking as he walked from behind his desk. "He looked just like that before he fell dead not more than ten feet in front of me. I thought he was going to take me. Charged from about three hundred feet. I hit him twice with a 50 caliber, but he kept coming. I unloaded six from a 44 as he stood up close, and one of them took him through the heart. Harrowing it was."

"I would imagine." Sammy looked at Westerfeld and judged him to be in his early sixties. His hair was brown and gray, and his manicured beard was nearly white. He looked very fit and wore a gray cotton shirt with black wool trousers and beautifully tooled black western boots.

"Mister Winds, is it?"

"Yes, sir. Sammy Winds."

"I'm Barclay Westerfeld. It's a great pleasure to finally meet you."

"Thank you, sir. I'm honored."

The two men shook hands. Barclay Westerfeld began walking back to his desk. "Come and sit down," he said to Sammy. "It's really quite fortunate you showed up tonight. I'm leaving tomorrow for three weeks, and I'm not usually here at this time of night."

"I'm glad of it, sir. I don't know that I could have stayed on and waited."

"You wouldn't have had to. I left instructions with an assistant if you showed during my absence. No, I say it's quite fortunate for me because I so wanted to meet you personally...shake your hand, and thank you."

Thank you, sir. I appreciate it. Mister Westerfeld, I don't have the paperwork with me verifying who I am."

"Yes, I understand that. I wouldn't have put much stock in that anyway. Anybody could have walked in here with some phony paperwork. One man tried it. No, I prefer instead to ask you several questions. What's the name of the head cook at your ranch?"

Sammy was more than surprised. "Her name is Jacqueline, sir."

"Does she have assistants?"

"Yes, sir. That would be Lucilla and Raquel."

Barclay Westerfeld looked down at the paper on his desk. "Tell me about the cat you had when you were a boy."

"I never had a cat. I had a dog."

"What was his name and what happened to him."

"His name was Angus and he died from a snakebite."

"Well, that's quite enough with the questions."

Barclay stood up and leaned across the desk to shake Sammy's hand once more. "Thank you for killing that son of a bitch who murdered my friend, Henry Salmon. Henry and I knew each other for fifty years—met when we were kids. He worked for me for the last twenty and refused any special treatment. Just wanted a job in my railroad business. He was a great employee and a damn fine man. Good and decent in every way. Anyone who ever knew Henry knew that. He left a large legacy behind—lots of family. His wife, Milly, is a wonderful woman. Henry would have told you he was lucky to have her. He was."

"Yes, sir."

"Would you like a drink? Whiskey?

"Only if you're having one, sir."

"I am." Barclay poured them each a very hearty portion, then held his glass up. "To Henry Salmon, may he rest easy."

"Amen."

After they drank, Sammy's curiosity came forth. "Mister Westerfeld, how did you get that information you asked me about?"

"I have my sources. In this case it was your employers. Although we've never met, I know very well of Homer and Reuben Taylor. Their reputation and success is well known in the west. I wrote to them."

"They didn't say anything about it."

"I asked them not to." Barclay looked closely at Sammy's face and noticed the rope burns on his wrists. "Are those marks from your scrap with the Apaches?"

"You know about that?"

"As I said, I have sources. But it's no secret now. The story is all over Santa Fe. If you save three women from Apaches, word gets around. You found them in a cave?"

"Yes, sir."

"And how many Apaches were there?"

"Well, eight in all. We had one tied up already, and then had a showdown with seven more."

"You killed seven Apaches?"

"Blaine and I shot five of them, and the women killed two others. One got away."

"That's damn heroic," Barclay said and poured them both another drink.

"We just did what we had to. We were lucky."

"Modest too, I see. Where's your partner, Blaine?"

"Well, he's probably still healing up down in Santa Fe. He took a bullet in the leg and it got infected. He said he'd head up here when he could travel. He may be on the way now."

"Where are you staying?"

"At the Ducayne Hotel."

"You picked the right place. Stay there as long as you want . . . and your friend Blaine, too, if he shows up. It's on me. I'll have an assistant make the arrangements."

"You don't need to do that, sir."

"I know it. But I made you come all the way up here to collect the reward. So please accept it as a small part of my appreciation."

"Yes, sir."

Barclay reached into his desk and pulled out several cards. "I made the arrangements for the reward long before I heard about you saving those women. After hearing about that, it only made me happier to give it to you. You've certainly earned it. These are the business cards for the bank presidents of the Western Bank of Denver, the Rio Grande Bank of Santa Fe, and the Cimarron Bank of Albuquerque. I own these banks. There is an account in your name at each with twenty thousand at Cimarron, twenty thousand at Rio Grande, and ten thousand here at Western of Denver. These presidents know you'll be in to activate your accounts and have specific information about how to verify that you are Sammy Winds. They will ask you some questions as I have— some of it well beyond what I have asked you here. Then you may do with your money whatever you like. No one else knows of this information or these methods, and I advise that you keep it to yourself." Barclay handed him the business cards.

Sammy was thunderstruck. "Mr Westerfeld, I was told the reward was ten thousand dollars."

"Well, son, I upped it. It was certainly worth it to me. If you're still in town when I return, we'll have dinner together." Barclay held up his glass. "Congratulations."

"Thank you, sir."

They drank the whiskey down and then Sammy knew it was time to go. He repeated his thanks and said his farewell. A few minutes later, Sammy was back outside in the cool of the Colorado night. It was all too surreal with people walking by and carriages rolling up and down the street in the bustle of life under the sky above. He could hardly imagine what had just happened and all that had happened along the way. He thought about the money and was astounded. But he was most happy just to be alive, realizing that the measure of his life was not something he would ever find on deposit at any bank.

Sammy rolled a smoke and lit it, then began to walk. A block later it occurred to him how hungry he was, and he remembered the steak. "The best beef in the city," the hotel desk clerk had said. He headed for Barron's Restaurant. It was open late.

About the Author

 Harvey Goodman grew up in Los Angeles and attended the University of Colorado where he studied history and developed a love for western literature and the great outdoors. He visited and worked in some of the west's remotest locations during his years running an oilfield vessel-buildings outfit. Mr. Goodman went on to teach history and coach football, eventually becoming a high school principal, and superintendent of schools. He excelled as an athlete, being named the MVP of the University of Colorado football team his senior season, and was drafted by the St. Louis Football Cardinals. Mr. Goodman played in thirty-two NFL games, including the 1976 season with the Denver Broncos. He and his wife, Gabrielle, have three sons. Mr. Goodman lives in Westcliffe, Colorado.

CPSIA information can be obtained at www.ICGtesting.com
Printed in the USA
LVOW081025230712

291171LV00001B/13/P